A Shameful War

A novel set in

The English Civil War

Bovey Heath and Devon in

1646

By

Jim Marshall

Contents

Dedication

To my wife, Janet who, despite all evidence to the contrary, still believes in me after 53 years.

About the Author

Jim lives in South Devon. He is an avid history student –with a specialization in the English Civil Wars of 1641-1651

He lives in a village only 6 miles from Bovey Tracey, where one of the 'battles' took place on the 9th January 1646

With the mystical and ancient area of Dartmoor only a few miles distant, it has been the setting for many novels of times past and present – and this is no exception. It is Jim's favourite place!

Chapter 1

The remains of a game pie sat on the large granite stone that poked above the rushing current of the river Bovey. It had sat there for the last hour, stubbornly refusing to yield its position to any of the small stones that the young man lobbed at it. Either the pie was now a limpet, or he was a very poor shot indeed.

Yesterday, they had quietly celebrated the Christ's Mass – a long morning service in the church dedicated to Peter and Paul, and after the murder of Becket nearly five hundred years before, to Thomas. It gave the church the unique distinction of three dedications. That had been followed by an afternoon of quiet family gatherings and the happy prospect of the next day to come – the feast of St. Stephen.

"For the love of heaven – give it up, Gil. That pie has magical properties and will stay there until the day of judgement!" So said his companion. He turned to look at her – always a source of quiet joy.

Ella fourteen years old and nearing fifteen. A mass of shiny, chestnut waves surrounded a face that was nearly always smiling. Deep, large, brown eyes atop a pert nose and a mouth that he had started kissing at least three years ago.

The two had known one another since birth – hardly surprising as they were neighbours. Her father, Abel Smith, was a man whose strength and muscles had been a wonder to him all his young life. The blacksmith's workshop and home were next to Gil's father's bakery. Abel's wife, Faith, had been a second mother to him, as his had been to Ella. From the tender age of six or seven, it had been taken as written in stone that Ella and he would marry – and so they would when he reached his sixteenth year, now only three months away.

"I give up!" he grunted, rising to his feet and holding out a hand to Ella to help her – not that she needed it. Far from it. Ella had always been faster up any tree that he could manage!

"Back to our feast dinner!" she laughed, gathering her skirts in one hand and setting off at the pace of a hare. He could have overtaken her with ease, hampered as she was with skirts. But, as they crossed the grassy open space between the river and the lane through the village, he fell in beside her and took her hand so that they arrived at the lane together.

The winter had been cold and wet before Christ's Mass, but now the sun shone from low in the sky and warmed them as they slowed to a more dignified walk. Turning left, they proceeded over the bridge that spanned the fast-flowing river and started the climb into the village of Bovey. Straight on at the crossroads, and they would have climbed up onto the moor to Hay Tor and beyond. Turn left, and the way was clear to Newton Abbot; whilst a right turn would have taken them to Moretonhampstead and the small stannary town of Chagford.

Still holding hands, they soon came to the start of the houses along both sides of the lane. First, on the right came the house of his uncle James Ramsay, his father's younger brother. The lower window had its shutters closed – shutters that, on other days, would be lowered to display his apothecary's wares. He and his wife, Gil's aunt Avril, would be at his house already, awaiting the start of the feast dinner.

For some reason that nobody had ever been able to explain, there came a gap of three house widths before the next dwelling. The space was occupied by a small herd of goats that belonged to a farm to the south of the village – one that took up a goodly portion of the area known locally as Bovey Heath. Not one of the goats looked up as they passed; not one rectangular eye peered at this trespass on their grazing.

Having passed more homes to both left and right, they arrived at Ella's home on the right – the open smithy empty and silent, the fire cold and the tools arranged on hooks in perfect order. And then they were at Gil's own home – the village bakery where his father rose at three every morning to prepare the daily bread for all of the village; where his mother toiled at his side – kneading, proving and shaping loaves, where Gil rose at dawn to help in the final

3

preparations and then to load the cart for the two-hour round of deliveries.

The bakery took up all the ground floor, with the vast bread oven in a separate, stone-built erection well away from the house itself – fire being a constant threat and one to be feared above nearly all else. Above the bakery was the main hall of the house – a long room where they sat and talked, ate meals, played games and entertained guests. Three rooms led off the hall; one large room for his mother and father, one smaller one for him and another small one for his sister Mary – just turned her twelfth birthday.

As Ella and Gil arrived in the long room, they were met by a festive sight. Longboards supported on trestles were covered in cloths of many colours. Scrubbed wooden platters were set in places along either side; benches ranged along the sides, and small branches of greenery festooned the walls.

"Oh, you two at last grace us with your presence," his mother greeted them with hugs. In her thirty-first year, she looked like she always did – immaculate and as pretty as a picture. Unlike his father, nearer forty as makes no difference, and had a face like an ill-formed potato. He made up for this with a shock of unruly ginger hair and a laugh as loud as the trumpets of heaven. Gil inherited the hair but neither the looks nor the unquenchable merriment. He said that Gil was far too serious for any son of his! Little Mary –

as flaxen-haired as her mother, was their own little angel. Petite, quiet and serene. Her thirst for knowledge put the rest of the family to shame.

"You been looking after our lass?" Boomed Abel Smith. His massive frame was almost too much for the stitching of his shirt. One expected that they would give way at any moment. Ella's brother Simon, although still only eleven years of age, seemed destined to be another to test the skills of any seamstress. He gave Gil and his sister a cheeky grin. Ella's mother, as elfin as her husband was huge, simply laughed and hugged the two in her turn.

"Indeed, I have, sir," Gil replied. "I guard her every moment I am with her. No harm shall befall her whilst I have breath to defend her!"

"Not precisely what I meant!" Abel gave vent to a plaster-cracking guffaw.

Uncle James Ramsay and Aunt Avril made up the full dozen who would partake of the feast dinner. Uncle, junior to Gil's father by three years, was known as the most learned of all the village. His pills and potions were trusted far and wide, due in no small measure to Aunt Avril's compendious knowledge of plants and their medicinal properties.

They all sat down, six at each side of the table. Father, being the head of this house, said a grace – to which they all added 'amen'. And then they started on the feast – a soup of every imaginable vegetable with the best white bread. The talk started, as it did at most tables at most meals in most villages, with the state of the current unrest.

"Where are the king and his forces now?" Gil's mother asked the inevitable question. Every eye turned to Uncle James – like they always did, regarding him as the fount of all knowledge. He laid down his spoon and wiped his mouth on a napkin.

"Last reports had Prince Charles somewhere to the north – possibly Okehampton. Exeter will fall to parliament – that seems inevitable. It also means that Fairfax will probe further west."

"Then the parliamentarians will be heading this way," Gil's father grunted. "What of this fellow Cromwell – everyone seems to believe that Fairfax will use him and the new model army to spearhead the advance."

"Such intelligence will surely please Hubert Green and that shrew wife of his!" James laughed.

Hubert and Mercy Green owned the village bookshop – and were fanatical puritans.

"Master Green berated Gil and me last week," Ella remarked. "Just because we were walking hand in hand and laughing together. Said we were blatant sinners and destined for the flames of hell by our show of shameful wickedness!"

"Don't suppose I helped matters by calling him a sour-faced slug!" Gil admitted.

"Why have we got a Scottish king?" Mary interrupted, deep in thought as usual. "Why don't we have an English one?"

"James – time for a history lesson!" her mother poked her brother-in-law in the ribs.

"King Charles would demand that he's as English as you or I," Uncle James responded. "Yes – his father, the first James, was Scottish, and his queen was from Denmark. But – James' great-great-great uncle was no other than the eighth Henry.

"I must write all that down," Mary decided. She would, too – adding yet another couple of pages to her book of knowledge. She would be a very learned woman!

Back they went to roasted capons and delicious sauces. How anyone managed to produce all this whilst at the same time helping to produce bread for the village was a mystery to Gil. Naturally, chatter went on, mainly concerning the conflict between the king and parliament. Ella proved once again that she was not just a pretty face!

"But where is the king? Some say he's with his son down here somewhere; others say that he's taken the queen to Scotland, but some say he's gone to France until all the troubles are over!"

"I would say that they're all probably wrong," Uncle James said in his quiet way. "My bet is that he's in Oxford – where he knows he's amongst his staunchest supporters.

Prince Charles is probably down here somewhere, although it's said he's leaving some of his troops under Lord Wentworth and the rest under Lord Hopton. Where they all are is anyone's guess."

"Where's Prince Rupert?" Ella was relentless at times.

"Oh, him – our blessed Duke of Cumberland!" James grunted. "Even though he's a cousin to the king, he was dismissed after he lost Bristol last year. He was sent packing. Parliament seems to be winning everywhere we look!"

Gil glanced down towards Mary, who was frowning in concentration. Her notes would be supplemented that very afternoon if he was any judge!

"I'm as strong for the king as any man," Gil's father put down his cup and looked at them all. "But he's ill-advised on every matter. But one thing worries me – his queen! She would have him return to Rome – and drag all of us with her. And that I will never do!"

"Nor I!" his wife put her hand over his.

Abel Smith, soon to be Gil's father-in-law, went one further and stood up. "Damnation to the thought!" he growled. "We, like you all, stand firm for the king and for the English Church. I raise my cup to them both!"

Suiting action to words, he drained his cup and put it firmly down on the board; every one of them, young Simon included, followed suit. Not for any of them the flummery of Romish practises!

Things seemed to have passed from the fun of the feast dinner to matters of serious import. Gil decided that the mood was too good an opportunity to let pass. he gave Ella's hand a squeeze and rose to his feet.

"Father, mother – with your permission, I must beg your attention."

Ella looked up at him and nodded. Everyone else looked at him, knowing full well what he was about to say. They gave him quiet and their attention.

Chapter 2

First, he turned to Abel Smith.

"Sir, I have some time past told you of my wish, and both you and your good wife have honoured me with your blessing. Mother, father – your blessing was given a long time past readily. Ella and I grew up together and played our games together as little children. I have loved Ella for as long as I can remember. I now ask you to accept my formal declaration of intent to marry as soon as my sixteenth year has begun. Ella, will you accept me as your betrothed?"

Ella stood beside him, took his hand and gave him that loveliest smile.

"Willingly and with all my heart," she replied.

Pandemonium broke out at that point – albeit that everyone had been expecting this for months past. Cups were raised, toasts were drunk, and Gil's back slapped, causing him to stagger back as Abel's hand – a hand the size of a shovel – landed between his shoulder blades. Everyone seemed to think this was the time to hug and kiss everyone else. Gil's family, Ella's family, Uncle James and Aunt Avril – they would all become one large family – one of ten in number.

As they all resumed their places – to start on a plum pudding – Uncle James then added to the joyful spirit with an announcement of his own.

"Brother John, Evelyn – we have discussed this for a while now, and it seems appropriate that I inform everyone else of our intention. As you know, my dear Avril and I have never been blessed with a child of our own – much to our great sorrow. But we have both seen the application for study of your own daughter Mary – how she is far advanced in literacy and knowledge. We would dearly like to have her join our business – as our apprentice. We know that you have to assist your mother every morning with the bread, so you could come and join us after dinner to learn the business of an apothecary. So, what say you, Mary?"

Gil's little sister sat as if a bolt of lightning had struck her atop her blonde head of curls.

"Come, Mary – we have never known you struck dumb for words!" her mother laughed.

"But girls cannot be apprentices!" she managed.

"And who says they may not?" her father demanded. "Are you saying that girls have no place in work of this kind?"

"Oh, no – I should be struck dead sooner than say such a thing!" she replied forcefully. "But does the law allow this?"

"What have you been doing for the last four years?" her mother asked.

"Why – learning from you how a house is run and how to make and bake bread," came the answer.

"And so, in everything but title, you have been my apprentice!" mother laughed.

"The most important thing is this," father added. "Do you want to learn the apothecary business?"

"Oh yes, father – it would be my fondest wish."

"Then you go to your uncle and aunt with our blessing!"

Mary, never backward in demonstrating her emotions, rushed to both her parents and to her uncle and aunt. Each received a hug and a kiss.

"And now, young Gil, we come to the business of you providing a safe home for our daughter," Abel boomed. "How far have your plans proceeded?"

"I have spoken to Master Barton, and he has promised to raise the matter with Lord Vickery. I hope to have my plans ready to present to his lordship when he returns from London."

The area occupied by the goats, plus a sizeable plot to its rear, was what he had in mind. The farm to its south had no real need for this land – the farmer had never used it for anything else except additional grazing. He had raised no objection when Gil had tentatively proposed fencing it off for a smallholding of his own – rented, of course, from his lordship. On it, he and Ella would grow their own crops – vegetables such as carrots, cabbage, leeks, onions and these still-new potatoes. It would be hard work to start with, but

Father and Abel had promised to assist in building their own modest house.

"I will still be on hand to deliver the bread every morning," Gil added. There was no way he would simply abandon his parents, forcing them to employ someone else for this necessary task.

"And you're happy to become a farmer's wife?" Faith asked his intention.

"Mother, I would be happy to be Gil's wife no matter what role we play."

"Huh!" snorted Simon, her little brother. "Ella up to her waist in mud and cabbages! That will be a sight!"

"Any more from you, and we'll use you as our scarecrow!" Ella retorted.

Having exhausted all three courses of the feast dinner, they sat back, digesting and supping at cups of ale. Gil would have been happy to remain there with Ella at his side for the rest of that day – but it was not to be. There came the sound of knocking at the main door. Father gave a grunt of annoyance and went down the narrow stairs to see who was disturbing the peace. He came back up with a familiar figure following in his wake.

"And the season's greetings to one and all," he announced with his usual beaming grin.

William Garlick had been, for many years, an officer in the king's service – a service that he never fully divulged to anyone. Now in his sixth decade, he was a widow, rotund, as bald as a pebble, and the churchwarden. They made him loudly welcome.

"I think it's time for some honey mead," John announced, producing a large stone bottle. Master Garlick inserted himself between Evelyn and Mary and was presented with a cup of his own. When the mead had been passed around, John proposed a toast.

"Here's to us all. May the good Lord grant us health and happiness and a new year full of promise and peace."

"Amen to that – and frustration to the king's enemies!" Garlick added. No doubt where his sympathies lay!

"Talking of which, have you any news of where the armies are situated?" Uncle James enquired – never doubting that the old soldier would be better informed than anyone else in the village. Apart from Lord Vickery, of course.

"Just rumour added to rumour," the old man growled. "Blasted Fairfax – may he rot in hades – is slowly securing everywhere to the west of Exeter. That I do know, he's reported to be assigning this new chap Cromwell to probe south and west. Where Hopton and Wentworth are is a complete mystery. Still – nobody will want to climb onto the moor. Nothing there to fight over! So, as we are at its eastern foot, we should be passed by."

"What of the stannaries?" Abel prompted. "Their tin revenues would be a prize worth their effort!"

"Chagford and Ashburton are nearest – so they could be at risk. Tavistock is a lot further for them to travel, and they are staunchly for the crown!"

"But we are on the road to Ashburton!" Evelyn said, somewhat nervously.

"But we are not Ashburton. We are just on the way there."

"Let us bring Master Garlick better news, shall we?" father announced, loth to let anything dampen the feast. "Gil and Ella have announced their betrothal and wish to be married soon after his sixteenth anniversary."

"Oh – that is good news, indeed," old Garlick beamed at the two. He raised his cup and drank a toast. "So, you need me to arrange the banns and the wedding, I suppose?"

"Indeed, Master Garlick – that would be a great kindness," Evelyn said, topping up his cup with more honey mead.

"Reverend Forbes will be returned from his other duties in a week from now. I shall take great pleasure in arranging things for you." Reverend James Forbes, along with his duties as vicar, was also personal chaplain to Prince Charles – wherever on earth *he* was.

The rest of the afternoon passed without any more talk of the troubles between the king and parliament – much to everyone's relief. However, it was too large a worry for it to last the whole day. Mother and Mary busied themselves lighting lamps as the short winter day drew to an early close. The distant church struck seven before anyone was ready to eat a modest supper.

Mary, her insatiable appetite for information, was the inevitable one to pick up the threads of the country's problems.

Putting down her spoon by the side of her empty bowl, she again turned to Uncle James for more things to note in her journal.

"Why are the parliamentarians really fighting the king? Do they want Prince Charles instead?"

"No – that's probably the last thing on their minds," Uncle snorted. "What they are fighting for is for a proper role of parliament in the governing of the kingdom. We have our members of that parliament – supposedly there to represent the interests of their constituencies – and the king rules without them. He hasn't called a parliament for at least two years now. What we have is what everyone calls The Rump."

"That ignores one very salient fact," Master Garlick broke in. "The king is God's anointed sovereign. He needs no other authority whatsoever."

"Indeed, that is so," admitted James. "However, it would do no harm to call a parliament for its advice. There are sane and sensible heads there. Surely it would do no harm to call on their thoughts?"

"I hardly think Sir John Northcote would give the king impartial advice," Garlick growled. "His sympathies are all with parliament. To hear him, one would believe he would do away with a king altogether!"

Sir John was a member of parliament for that large constituency. Not that he, or any of his fellow members, represented anyone other than the landowners!

"The main problem for the king is that he is surrounded by ineffective commanders," James continued. "Look at Lord Wentworth and Prince Rupert – parading around in their finery. Lord Hopton might be effective, given proper authority. But the king seems to favour only his own kith and kin!"

"Unfortunately, that is true," Garlick admitted. "I got to know Hopton and have the greatest regard for his abilities. But he is of less than noble stock."

"The greatest fear I have is that there just might be some truth in the rumour that the queen is doing her best to drag the king – and thus, the country – back into the folds of Rome! Is that not one of parliament's main concerns as well?"

"Yes – but that again overlooks one very vital point," Garlick responded. "The king, at his coronation, became not only God's anointed sovereign but also a defender of the English Church. How could he even contemplate setting aside that solemn vow?"

"Yes – but that doesn't stop many people from being afraid of the mere possibility!" James retorted.

"And fear is a rumour that spreads and multiplies with the telling," Aunt Avril spoke up. "A small stone falls out of the wall of the church – and by the time word reaches the furthermost house in the village, a huge, granite boulder has rolled down from the moor and has crushed five people to death!"

That remark, as had been intended, broke the solemnity of the evening and had them all laughing – despite it being so very near the truth.

Chapter 3

"Where the bloody hell are we going now?"

Kit Warden, never one to mind his tongue, grumbled the question to the man riding beside him. Luke Farmer, never one to waste breath on unnecessary words, simply shrugged. No, so the man riding two ranks in front, Sergeant Michael Brown turned in his saddle and favoured Warden with a glower of disapproval.

"For your information, Warden, we are riding to meet up with the remainder of the regiment – all twenty of us. There – does that meet with your approval?"

"Yes, sergeant. Sorry, sergeant," mumbled a very unapologetic Warden. His question had not been answered at all – no clue as to *where* this meet-up was planned to take place.

The small detachment was part of the remains of a cavalry regiment. They had narrowly avoided the rout of their royalist comrades in Exeter, the rump of the regiment now trailing dejectedly westwards towards some as yet unspecified site where it was hoped they could regroup.

Two days into the new year, and they had very slowly made their unobserved way through woodland, following tracks that led them just west of south. At that precise moment, they were in the narrowing end of Whiteway Wood, about two miles to the north of the small township of

Chudleigh. Very soon, they would emerge from the tip of the wood and have to cross Bramble Brook.

Brown, who had been raised in the little village of Trusham, now only a mile or so to their west, knew every hill, valley, wood and stream for miles around. Glimpsing the end of the trees about a hundred yards to his front, he halted the column and had them dismount. Being a prudent sergeant, he immediately detailed two of his men to walk back up the track for a quarter of a mile to hide as sentries.

"Well, Warden – you seem to be all mouth this day. Gather five panniers and get yourself down to the brook down yonder and fill them with good, clean water. Off you go!"

Because of his intimate knowledge of the area through which they had travelled, he had no difficulty in obtaining bread and cheese as they went. He seemed to know everyone. More importantly, he knew of their loyalties and approached only those he knew were committed to the king. Despite the cold of winter, those acquaintances had been only too willing to share their meagre provisions. How the rest of the regiment – what remained of it – under Sir Stephen Long, he had no idea.

Despite his inability to hold his tongue – or to refrain from near insubordination – Warden was an excellent woodsman. His abilities enabled him to get to and from the little brook totally unseen. He arrived back between the trees, staggering under the weight of panniers filled with crystal-clear water.

"We stay here under cover until nightfall," Brown announced when the meagre meal was over. "Now let us satisfy Warden's curiosity. Under cover of night, we leave the wood, cross the brook and make our way through Coombshead Brake to cross the River Teign. Going to get wet and very cold! We then hide in the small wood by Higher Crockham. I'll take two of you whilst you make camp there and walk the small distance to Teign Village – where I know I can get more provisions. We will stay in that wood all tomorrow."

Having relieved his two sentries, he rolled himself into his blanket and found a soft spot in which he immediately fell asleep.

"But I still don't know where the bloody hell we're going!" Warden growled to his mate.

"Yes, you do. Higher Crockham. Sergeant just told you!" That was quite a speech from Farmer.

"Yes – I know that!" Warden grumbled on. "But where after that? We've got to regroup eventually – or we'll be doomed to wander Devon for all eternity. And what use is that to me, you, the regiment, and the king?"

The farmer took a deep breath – one long enough to make what was for him the speech of a lifetime.

"Soldiers like us don't ask questions. We do what others tell us. We don't get explanations. We go where we're told, get shot at, die, or live on to do more of what we're told. Now, shut up and get some sleep!"

Warden was so taken aback at this rare loquacity that he found himself unable to form yet another grumble. He, like his sergeant, rolled into his blanket and went to sleep.

Just south of the hamlet of Tottiford, another royalist cavalry trooper was raising the same questions of his fellows. Only about two miles to the west of Brown's little detachment, the rump of the regiment under Sir Stephen Long was camped in what was locally known as Great Copse. Poorly named as it was quite a small copse.

Unlike Warden, Farmer and the other seventeen soldiers under Brown, Sir Stephen knew *exactly* where he was heading. He was to rendezvous with another four regiments in two days at a place named Bovey Heath. Sergeant Brown was similarly privy to that information – and kept it to himself.

Long's complement was down to eighty-three after the debacle at Exeter. He had ordered Brown's detachment to stay outside the small city, ostensibly to guard the supply route. Long now knew that he had only just over one hundred left, not a significant number to add to the other regiments he was supposed to join. What his commander, Lord Wentworth, would say about that was best left unimagined for the moment.

Sergeants Hooper and Franks were not privy to the destination or the time of the rendezvous. Troopers Buskin and Ford were as vociferous as Warden had been.

"Bloody gadding about the countryside – that's all we're fit for!" Ford made sure his words reached only his mate's ears.

"Not really gadding, are we?" Buskin replied equally softly. "Creeping about like mice in the skirting. Traipsing along after fancy-pants!" Thus was his description of his commander. It was not that far from the truth.

Stephen Long was the eldest son of a major landowner to the south of Guildford in Surrey. He was used to fine dining, the best wines, and games of cards with his equally pampered friends – not to sneaking about the Devon countryside and dodging the bullets from this damnable New Model Army that the parliamentarians had come up with.

Unlike the men under his command, he failed to see the effectiveness of this enemy and failed utterly to recognise its efficiency and organisation. He simply regarded it as unsporting! They, to his mind, didn't fight fair. The fact that the parliamentarians were making idiots of the royalist troops never entered his thinking. He would have much preferred a gentlemanly duel between picked opponents. Sneaking through woods and along river valleys was, to his mind, utterly demeaning.

Not to his sergeants, who were seasoned soldiers and knew full well that their opponents were to be greatly respected. Not that they would have joined them -they were totally committed to their king. But neither Hooper nor Franks were blind to the shortcomings of their leaders. The only one they had any respect for, military-wise, was Lord Hopton. But he wasn't their commander. Their regiment, what was left of it, came under Lord Wentworth. Their opinion of Prince Rupert, now in disgrace overseas, was unprintable.

"Surely, we must make a stand somewhere," Hooper grunted. "All this sneaking about is all very well – keeps us all alive. But that's all there is to be said for it. Unless we form a proper army again, we might as well start waving white flags and give England to the likes of Fairfax."

"With the king supposed to be in Oxford, it's up to Prince Charles to bring that about – and he's hardly experienced enough to bring order out of this chaos!" Franks muttered. "Hopton is the best hope, but I'm buggered if I know where he is!"

"Me neither!" nodded Hooper. "Wentworth is cut from the same cloth as Long – all chivalry and gentlemanly conduct. Neither has proved himself able to command a retreat, never mind a set battle!"

"Okehampton, Tavistock and Plymouth – that's where we should be!" Franks had thought this through many times in the past few days. "Put the moor between them and us – make them come north of the moor, or south. No way even Fairfax would go across it, not in winter. Then, when we know which way they're coming, we gather in force and take them on in a proper battle."

"But you're thinking like a soldier – and we don't have one of them leading us!" Hooper growled. Then, like good soldiers, they ate a meagre ration and went to sleep.

Half a mile to the east of Long's position, three soldiers sat in a hollow between oak trees in Netton Cleave Wood. The Beadon Brook tumbled among rocks close by. They had discarded their pot helmets and buff coats days before and were dressed in normal clothes – greens and browns. Only the short muskets and short swords, secreted under their thick woollen cloaks, would have told of their real identity.

They had been specially picked for their mission. All three were in their third decade; all were woodsmen; all were expert trackers; all were detailed by their commander to follow Long's regiment, find out what they were up to, and report back.

Richard Lovelace, Hugh Ratcliffe and Samuel Garvey huddled together in the hollow to get some respite from the cold wind. Being woodsmen with years of experience between them, they didn't lack food. Pigeons were plentiful at any time of year.

Lovelace, the patrol leader, had already sent back the fourth member of his patrol – to appraise his captain of their whereabouts and those of the small royalist regiment that they had been following for two days past.

"Not the hardest task we've been given, is it?" Ratcliffe grinned at his two comrades. "That oaf might just as well leave a paper trail behind him. Never a backmarker to watch their rear – and not a sign of any pickets to safeguard their position."

"And that's going to be their downfall," Lovelace nodded, still watching for any signs of movement. "Look at the idiots they've been given to lead them – fancy playboys. Rank and privilege seem to be the only qualifications needed! I must say that I expected better from Prince Rupert. He's a far better soldier than he displayed at Bristol!"

"Like you said, his captains were mere playboys. Nobody can command with captains like that!" Garvey added his thoughts.

"Looks like they're settled for the rest of the day," Lovelace decided. So – let's set watch – two on and four off – like as usual."

The three drew lots, and Garvey took the first two hours. The other two simply rolled up into their blankets and went to sleep. The fourth member, known affectionately as Haddock (from his round, fishy eyes), returned silently two hours after darkness had fallen. Now they could do two on and six off!

Chapter 4

Twelfth Night – the 5th of January – dawned bright and sunny. So far, it had been a kind winter; no snow worth mentioning. Even atop the granite tors, there was but a slight dusting. Down in the Bovey valley, all was serene – albeit with a slight breeze lowering the temperature.

Gil wheeled the empty barrow back into the small shed behind the bakery, the day's deliveries all done. He went indoors for a second breakfast of warm, crusty bread and a couple of eggs. His mother was sitting at the long table, finishing her own meal as Gil emptied his small satchel of coins. His father bustled in and made the remark that had Gil wincing – the same remark that his father made every single day as he returned with the takings.

"Oho! Money, money, money!"

"Yes, father," Gil replied, sneaking a glance at his mother, who was successfully smothering a large smile.

"And now you must get into your best clothes to go and see the steward," his father added. "I'll not come with you – it's your plan, and you must present it as your own. Nervous?"

"No, not really," Gil answered. "The plan is sound. You have looked at it, as has Master Smith and Uncle James. You all agree it is sound and workable."

"Then speak up boldly and be your own man."

"Yes, father. I will."

"And may God bless your endeavour," his mother added.

Getting to the manor house involved a walk down the village street, over the bridge and across the junction of the lanes. On the right of the track that led directly up onto the moor was the entrance to Parke – the estate of Lord Vickery. His steward, Luke Barton, had a house not far from the entrance. Gil paused before the door, looked down to see that his shoes shone, and then knocked.

A young maid answered the door and gave Gil a cheeky grin.

"Master Steward is expecting you," she said, making sure that Gil noticed her dimples.

Gil said nothing but followed the maid into a passage and through a door on the left. This was where the steward had his office. It was certainly a functional room rather than a salon in a dwelling. The walls were covered in lists and a map of the vast Parke estate. The steward, a man in his forties, was sat behind a desk that was littered with papers, ink bottles and a heap of quill pens. Luke Barton looked up as Gil entered, gave him a broad smile of welcome and indicated a chair facing him over his desk.

"Good morning, Master Barton," Gil gave the semblance of a bow of his head before sitting to face the steward.

"And God's blessing on you," the steward replied. "Now – straight to business, shall we? I spoke to Lord Vickery about your proposal, and he said that he was happy to leave the matter in my hands. And now I suppose you want to know my determination?"

"Er, yes, please, Master Barton." Gil was starting to get a trifle nervous. If the answer was a flat 'no', he was utterly at a loss what he and Ella could then do to start their life together.

"Be not afraid, young Gil," Barton laughed, his black beard and moustache effectively hiding his mouth, which was set in a wide grin. "You come from a well-respected family – as indeed does your betrothed. Your uncle is a pillar of the village and also highly thought of. The land that you want for your enterprise can certainly be yours. And now, tell me exactly to what use you will put this parcel of land."

Gil was at least well prepared for this. He fished out a rolled paper and passed it over the desk.

"On that paper, sir, I have listed the vegetables we wish to grow. I have also entered against each the weight per annum that we plan to produce – in three different figures. The first is for a poor year, the second for a fair year, and the third for a very good year. I know full well that only a fool would make a proposal based on the very best figures. Had I done so, I doubt full well that you would fail to laugh aloud. I have taken my uncle's advice and made my proposal based on two-thirds the way up from poor to fair."

"Then his advice, and your acceptance of it, is sound indeed!"

"We would hope to achieve this in our second year. Between the three families, we have already collected many bags of seeds, ready for when we have prepared the soil for the first planting. We have also kept back enough money to tide us over until we can start to market our produce."

"Good – so far," Barton grunted in approval. "And now – what happens when the local farmers realise that there is another source of supply – one that will encroach on their livelihoods?"

"Surely there is room for one more grower, sir? Every year my mother makes moans that there is an insufficient supply of good, fresh vegetables. And in winter, as we are now, supplies are already short. A further source of supply would surely be welcomed by all the goodwives for miles around!"

"In advance of your visit here today, I made enquiries of his lordship's kitchen. What you say is what I heard from the cook herself. Indeed, supplies are running low. My own household is already feeling the results of last year's harvest. And we are only a short way into this winter! So, yes – I agree with your conclusions."

Gil breathed just that little bit easier. Was all this to prove possible?

"When do you wish to make a start?"

"Oh, sir – as soon as is possible! Ella and I are to be married after my sixteenth birthday. It would be a great blessing if we were allowed access to the land – for two purposes. The first being the building of our modest house; the second being the earliest possible start on preparing the ground."

"I have heard a rumour that your father, Master Smith, and your own uncle have agreed to help in the building. Also, Master Smith is well placed to produce the tools that you will need."

"That is so, sir. Ella and I are to be given every assistance in starting our life together. In this, we daily offer thanks to God."

"And now we come to the matter of the rent for the land. How have you accounted for this in your plan?"

"We have jointly arrived at a figure that we think reasonable, sir."

"And will I believe it to be reasonable?"

"We have calculated the acreage and applied the normal figure, sir."

"Let me tell you what I have calculated. Seven shillings per quarter, payable in advance on the quarter day."

Gil very carefully masked his reaction to that statement. It was exactly six pennies more than they had determined.

"Then, sir – I am happy to accept that figure."

"Excellent! Now – when do you wish to start this new enterprise?"

"Immediately, sir – should that be possible. There is much to do."

"Next quarter is on Lady Day – and that's probably about the time you and your Ella are to be wed. The last one, the day of Christ's Mass, has just passed."

The steward used a chequered board.

"That was eleven days ago, leaving seventy-nine days until Lady Day. If we draw up the agreement for signature tomorrow, are you able to come with six shillings for the remainder of this quarter? That will allow you to get your boundary marked out immediately."

"Yes, indeed, sir. I shall certainly be here, ready to proceed."

"Come here again tomorrow at ten of the clock. The agreement and deed will be ready for our signatures. The estate bailiff will then accompany you to the plot and will supervise and agree the boundary. I wish you a good day."

"And I wish you the very best day, sir!"

Gil stood, repeated his small nod, and almost skipped out of the room. Outside, he couldn't help doing a skip and a small crow of sheer glee. His walk home was the best he had ever experienced.

A small gathering greeted him as he arrived at the smithy. Ella was standing there, almost shredding a small handkerchief in her anxiety. One look at Gil's face, and she ran to him and threw her arms around him.

"It's all agreed – and at seven shillings the quarter," Gil shouted for the world to hear. He was engulfed by two families.

"I have to go again tomorrow with six shillings for the remains of this quarter. Then the bailiff and I will draw up the boundary – and it's all ours!"

"Honey mead and cake!" announced Faith Smith, leading everyone through the smithy and into the parlour behind.

Chapter 5

"Movement!"

Haddock's urgent whisper got Lovelace, Ratcliffe and Garvey alert and crawling to peer through the low cover towards the Great Copse.

"Lots of movement," agreed Lovelace. "Looks like they're on the move. Right – let's give them a head start and see which direction they're going."

Whoever was in charge of the royalist cavalry was bedecked in lace and a hat with waving feathers. He sat atop a black horse, followed by an ensign holding the regimental colour aloft. The troop that followed seemed to be in fairly good order, riding out two abreast. The four watchers counted almost eighty – so the same number that they had been following. The line of march looked to the four to be almost due south.

"Heading for Bovey?" Lovelace wondered aloud.

"That's my guess as well," Garvey nodded. He was a local from south Devon. "Going that way, they're going to hit Furzeleigh before they get to Bovey."

"I'll stay here watching. The rest of you get ready to move. Garvey – which way's best?"

"If they're really heading for Bovey, then we keep to the east towards Bottom. That way, we'll keep them in sight and under cover ourselves."

"How far to Bovey?"

"No more than three miles. We'll have to do four – maybe a bit more if we're to keep to the east of them."

The last of the cavalry column was well past their line of sight when Lovelace led the four just inside the wood, also heading a little east of due south.

"Don't need to see them to follow where they're going," Haddock muttered. "They're hardly going quietly!"

"More like a herd of bloody elephants!" agreed Lovelace. "Still – we have to keep well out of their sight. Still no back markers. Bloody stupid"

Garvey was soon proved wrong. The column veered off more to the west, allowing Lovelace and his men to proceed down the track to Furzeleigh themselves. That track offered little in the way of cover until, after just over a mile, more wooded areas appeared to their right. When these woods eventually ended south of Furzeleigh, they stopped and heard the jingling of harnesses, plus the laughing and joking of the royalist troops to their west.

"Maybe wrong about Bovey," Garvey admitted. "If they stay on that track, they'll end up in Newton. They're passing just to the west of Bovey at this rate."

"Isn't that where Lord Vickery has his estate – they must be crossing his demesne now?" Lovelace pondered. "Wonder whether that's where they're going? After all,

Vickery has declared for the king – when he is not declaring for Parliament!"

However, the troop carried on down the road towards Newton, leaving Lovelace in a bit of a quandary. He had somehow to get past Bovey but could not dare go to its west. He had no choice but to confer with Garvey again. His local knowledge again came to the rescue. He led them at a fast walk to the south-east, crossing a couple of lanes and the road that joined Bovey to Chudleigh Knighton. Once across that road, and still unobserved, he led the group to a grassy area just before the meandering River Bovey. Hidden in the long grass, they were able to see across the river to an area of heathland that was just south of Bovey village itself.

"Well – that's where they were heading," Lovelace breathed, looking at the heath area where not only the troop they had been following were milling about but also what looked like two more troops already there. They watched silently as a large camp was struck.

"Looks like where they might be regrouping," Ratcliffe observed quietly. "What do we do now?"

"Watch, wait, and see how many more get here – if any," Lovelace decided. "If by tomorrow evening, they're still here, we get word back about numbers, position and anything else we can think of. Sam – anywhere near here, you know of where you can get us some food? Someone safe?"

"Yes – simple. There's a small farm just over yonder. Don't know who works it, but it doesn't matter. With all that rabble on the heath, who do you think's going to get the blame for food going missing?" he gave a sly grin, slithered away and gave thanks for the fact that the ground was firm beneath his belly. Can't last, he thought. Winter will bite us in the arse sooner or later!

Just over an hour later, he slithered back to his three colleagues. From a small sack, he produced the remains of a cooked chicken, two loaves of bread, and a large chunk of cheese.

"More arrivals," Haddock, who was on watch, whispered. Across the river, another group of royalist cavalry trotted onto the heath. Yet another led by what Lovelace referred to as a bedecked popinjay.

"That's about three hundred of the buggers," Haddock breathed.

"Near as dammit," agreed Lovelace. "Here's what we do. We stay where we are and observe. Ratty – you have the best hand at writing. We need a full report to go back with whoever reports."

"Using what?" Ratcliffe grunted. "I have neither paper, pen, nor ink!"

Lovelace gave it some thought, then turned again to Garvey.

"Could you sneak into yonder church and borrow a hymn sheet and a stick of charcoal?"

"You mean to steal from a church?" Garvey didn't quite like the sound of that.

"Unless you've a better idea where to get the means to pen a report!" Lovelace retorted.

"There be a bookshop in that village. That I remember from when I was there back in the summer of last year. If I leave it until nightfall, I can surely 'borrow' what we need from there."

"Place will be swarming with king's men!" Haddock snorted.

"And you think any of that lot will see me?" Garvey grinned.

----------------- OOOOOOOOO -----------------

"Can't say I like the look of this place," Lord Wentworth said. His small mouth beneath his clipped moustache turned down in disapproval.

"We'll be gone within the week, my lord," Sir Steven Long said, trying to lighten the mood of depression. They all had been on the move for well over a fortnight, fleeing in some disorder after the disastrous times about Exeter.

He, his commander and two other regimental commanders were standing at the northern tip of the mass of troops. To their left, the river churned restlessly along it's curving way to Newton and beyond.

"Still – there's a goodly tavern to wile away our time. Have your sergeants been told where to picket the horses?"

The three commanders all nodded. Between the encampment and the river was a large grassy area. Men were already driving stakes into the ground to mark out the boundary. Others were trailing thin ropes between the small posts. Horses were standing, grazing contentedly, some going to the shallow bank of the river to drink.

Even the grumpy Wentworth could see that all was properly in hand. He gave a nod of satisfaction and went to his palatial tent. Laying his vastly plumed hat on a folding chair, he lay down on his camp bed, waved his servant away, and dropped off to sleep.

----------------- OOOOOOOO -----------------

Sergeant Brown and his small detachment had used the previous night to head south, crossing the river Teign and the Dunsford road bypassed the little village of Chudleigh Knighton and were hidden in a small wood at Ventiford, just south of the point where the river Bovey joined the Teign.

They were about a mile south-east of the heath where the main body of their colleagues were camped.

Even from that distance, in the late afternoon, they could hear the noise from the encampment.

"Why aren't we with them, sergeant?" Warden wanted to know.

"Because we're here!" came the terse reply.

Farmer joined in. "Much better if we were with our mates," he groused.

"Listen – and listen well," Brown snapped. "They may well be there in a large huddle. But I've a nasty suspicion that they're being tracked. This new army of parliament may be on the wrong side, but they're nobody's fools. If I were their commander, I'd want to know where my enemy was, how many they were, and where they were going. It stands to reason that they're being tracked. If we stay just a little away, we might just be able to spot the trackers and put a stop to their game. That's why we're here and not there. Now – shut up, watch, and keep your clacking tongues silent in your otherwise empty heads!"

And so, as evening turned into early night, the twenty men took turns to watch and listen. It turned cold just after midnight, so their watches shivered and cursed – silently.

Chapter 6

The village of Bovey had changed dramatically during that day. People went about their business in silence and as quickly as they could. It was very noticeable that Goodwives went either in groups or with male escorts. This apprehension had nothing to do with their loyalty to the king – most of them were staunchly loyal – but with their fear of massed troops in general. They had yet to encounter any parliamentarian troops, but royalist troops had a poor reputation because of their general indiscipline and lack of proper order and command. So, the inhabitants were wary and stayed indoors as much as possible.

Gil had finished his bread deliveries well before the arrival of the first of the cavalry troops. He was horrified to see them milling about just to the south of the very plot of ground that he hoped to start renting that very morning. He hurried back to the bakery, calling at the smithy on the way.

"A big troop of the king's cavalry have just arrived at the north end of the heath," he announced.

Abel immediately ordered his wife and Ella into the house with strict instructions to stay there out of sight. Gil's father was about to say the same to Evelyn and young Mary when his wife gave him a scathing look.

"Mary – yes, by all means, let us keep her safe. But if you believe for one moment that I'm going to cower away like some frightened rabbit, then you've got another think coming! Far more to the point – what does this all do to Gil's plans?"

"I'd better run to the steward and see what he thinks," Gil replied.

By the time he had trotted down the main street towards the bridge, he had passed a couple of officers in their plumed hats, swords and high boots. Peering down at the plot as he had passed, he was relieved to see that there had as yet been no encroachment on his future plot. The journey to the steward's office took him no more than fifteen minutes. He arrived, knocked, and was shown immediately into the office. Not only was the steward there, but also the estate bailiff. Peter Cove was a thin, wiry man with seemingly boundless energy.

"I thought I might have an early visit from you," the steward grunted. "I know all about our visitors. The wonder is that they've not already been here to announce their presence. After all, his lordship is *thought* to be loyal to the king. But I suppose you are wondering what this does to your marking out and the agreement."

"Well, yes, sir. Can we go ahead with the marking out, given that the soldiers are already very close to the plot?"

"It would be sensible to delay that matter. Do not worry; it will happen in due course. I, for one, cannot believe they will be here for very long. As far as anyone is aware, they will be off to Tavistock – where it would be far more sensible to regroup and set up a proper defence. They would have the moor on one side, and the river Tavy on another. Making a stand here makes no sense at all."

"If that is what you think best, sir," Gil could not hide his bitter disappointment.

"Cheer up, lad," the bailiff riffled Gil's hair. "They will certainly be gone within a few days, and then you will be able to start your own little empire with that lovely young maid."

If Gil found the action a trifle demeaning, he made sure not to show it. He gave the tall bailiff a rueful grin and ran back home. As he passed over the bridge and glanced again towards the heath, he was a bit alarmed to see that the numbers had doubled. He reported back to his family, only to find a sergeant and two troopers standing in the shop doorway.

They were armed with swords – the sergeant also had a carbine slung across his back. They were on the point of leaving, so Gil shuffled out of their way, then burst into the shop to find his mother and father exchanging worried looks.

"They've ordered a hundred loaves to be delivered this very afternoon," his father reported.

"Then I'd better help you as the marking out has been put back until the soldiers have gone," Gil stated.

And so, with young Mary also helping, they set to mixing, kneading, proving and eventually baking a hundred loaves. Evelyn regarded their now very depleted stock of flour.

"We will need to get a good supply back, or our normal customers are going to go without," she observed.

"Gil – run to Wat Groves and ask if we can have the loan of his cart this very afternoon," his father said. "You and I will have to visit the mill."

Wat Groves lived up past the church. He owned a large cart and a horse with which he undertook carting jobs for anyone and everyone. Gill raced off, dusting flour out of his hair as he went. He was back a half hour later.

"Mistress Groves says that Wat will be back in about two hours – and he will come with us and help load the cart."

"Well, one problem solved. The next is a bit more pressing. How are we going to get paid for the bread we deliver? I'm not at all sure that those soldiers will be ready to empty a purse!"

As it turned out, his fears were unjustified. He and Gil wheeled the heavily laden barrow down the main street and onto the heathland, following a beaten track to the start of the by-then-enlarged encampment. They were met by a harassed old officer who counted the loaves as three soldiers emptied the cart.

"One hundred loaves as ordered," he grunted. He then handed a purse of coins to John Ramsay and stumped off after his soldiers into a large tent that was obviously set up as the stores. John and Gil said not a word and went back to the shop as quickly as they could. John emptied the purse on the counter and counted the coins.

"Well – I never thought that would happen," he gasped. "One hundred loaves paid for in full. Wonders will never cease!"

"May the good Lord be thanked!" Evelyn whispered, gathering the coins and taking them into the back room, where she stowed them away in their strong box.

Wat turned up soon afterwards so that John and Gil could clamber aboard for the short journey down to the mill that stood by the side of the bridge. They were back again at the bakery an hour later, with the flour store bulging with supplies. The whole family heaved a sigh of relief and sat down to a very late meal.

By nightfall, the village was buzzing with the news that around four hundred troops were now gathered on the heath – or billeted in the town. Lord Wentworth and his officers had taken up residence in the tavern and were making merry, playing cards and generally behaving as if this was simply the most natural thing in the world. Bovey village went to bed that night apprehensive but reassured that at least the soldiers were 'on their side'. All except one house. Hubert and Mercy Green, above their book shop, knelt at either side of their bed and prayed for deliverance from these agents of Satan, as they referred to anyone loyal to the king. Having offered up their prayers, they climbed into the bed and composed themselves for sleep.

The next day saw little change. Many people thronged to the church, thinking that a few more prayers would not come amiss. The Ramsay family, however, were busy making bread for the village and then turning to fulfil another order for bread for the soldiery – one hundred and fifty loaves that time. Once again, exhausted by their efforts, they were at least thankful for the money which had been paid punctually and in full.

------------------- OOOOOOOOO ------------------

As darkness fell that night, two sets of people were about their business. Brown and two men set off and crept about the woods, searching for any sign of the enemy watchers. Garvey had successfully managed to 'win' paper and a stick of charcoal from the bookshop. Lovelace had dictated a report to Ratcliffe, who wrote it all carefully down. Haddock was again instructed to take this to where their captain would be waiting. Haddock was back before first light. Brown and his two men were again back with the small troop. Neither group had seen hide nor hair of the others.

As morning dawned on the eighth day of January, the parliamentary captain was reporting to his commander. Cromwell listened in silence, read the paper, and then sat back with what was for him, a rare smile of satisfaction. He gathered his captains and started issuing orders.

On Bovey Heath, sergeants roused their soldiers and got the day started. Their officers, asleep in comfortable beds, slept on.

Bovey village roused itself, yawned, stretched, and started their endless chores. In the bookshop, Hubert and Mercy Green remained true to their prayerful promise and kept the shop closed. Instead of sorting their stock, they spent the morning on their knees praying for deliverance from the invasion of the king's vile followers. They also prayed hard for the downfall of not only the king but for the destruction of all churches and 'romish' practises. They ate bread and cheese and drank water.

That evening saw another gathering, this time in the back room of the smithy. Abel and Faith dispensed ale and honey mead. James and Avril had brought a large cake as they knew that John and Evelyn had baked more than enough for one day.

"Has anyone an idea when these soldiers will move on?" James asked.

"Don't know if there's any truth in it, but I managed to speak to one of the sergeants in the tavern this afternoon,"

Abel offered. "He said that they would be here for only two more days – then they would make their way to Tavistock – where Lord Hopton hopes to regroup."

"At least we have been spared any trouble," Faith said, falling into the old ways of crossing herself before stopping with a guilty look. Troops of any creed or colour were renowned for theft, pillage, and rape whenever they were billeted near civilian life.

"That is in itself a wonder," Evelyn remarked. "The officers seem to have scant regard for their duties. They seem to spend all their time wining and dining and gaming. It's just as well that the sergeants seem to have good control of the soldiers – or this could be a nightmare for us all."

"The sergeant I was speaking to was less than complimentary when I mentioned those same officers. His opinion was that Lord Wentworth was as suited to be archbishop as he was to lead a small army. And then he begged me not to repeat that to anyone. But I can see his frustration. Soldiers need to be professionally led, not ignored, as this lot seems to be. They are only concerned with their own lives of fun and laughter. War is *not* a laughing matter!"

"Then let us hope and pray that they are soon gone," Gil said fervently. "I know this may sound selfish as it's interfering with our plans, but they need to be under Lord

Hopton's control as soon as possible. Everyone says he is an able commander. Perhaps *he* can turn the tide for the king."

"Sure as anything, Wentworth cannot!" Abel Smith scowled.

Chapter 7

The first thing that John and Evelyn noticed as they arose was that the temperature had fallen overnight. At three in the morning, it was a typical winter night – dark, silent, and cold. Their routine was second nature and needed neither speech nor gesture as they hurried into warm clothing and went down to the bakery. John immediately went to the large oven and set about rekindling the embers left from the previous evening. Evelyn, having lit the two lamps, started pouring large scoops of flour into the trough, which had been cleaned and left to dry thoroughly overnight. She added salt and yeast, then mixed it all together with a large wooden paddle.

Unlike a lot of bread troughs, theirs was set at a far more convenient height. No bending double and slowly ruining their backs. Abel had constructed an iron frame on which the large trough stood. When John was satisfied that the fire in the oven was going properly, he joined his wife with pails of water. This he added to the trough in separate puddles along its length. Then, with him at one end and Evelyn at the other, they started mixing the dough with their bare hands until it was ready to start kneading.

They were both so experienced that they both knew when the dough was ready. It was lifted into four smaller troughs, covered with cloths and set by the side of the warming oven to start proving. And then they started all over again on the second batch.

At one side of the bakery was a long, wooden table, always kept scrubbed clean and fresh. When the first four batches rose, they were emptied onto the table and cut and shaped into many small loaves and again left in the now warm room to prove yet again. By five in the morning, baking could start, and the two could then relax with a mug of warmed ale. Soon, the tantalising aroma of baking bread permeated the entire house, waking Gil and Mary as it nearly always did.

And then the second routine began. The loaves were set to cool on a separate table that had a stone top. By then, Gil had yawned his way downstairs with Mary close behind him. Mary fetched butter as more loaves from the second batch were loaded into the oven. And then there was nothing to do until all the loaves were baked and cooling. The family of four broke open two of the loaves, spread butter on them and broke their fast – all in near silence.

When Gil had left at nearly six o'clock with his cart, Evelyn and John set to cleaning the trough and the tables whilst Mary started putting baked loaves ready for the early customers in the shop itself. Later that morning, Evelyn would make pastries for sale, plus some pasties for anyone not fancying cooking a midday meal.

Gil returned just after seven with the latest news.

"The encampment is very quiet," he reported.

"Hardly surprising, seeing the drunken state of some of them yester evening!" Evelyn replied. "I doubt many of them will be in any state to emerge until noon, even then!"

"One thing I did notice," Gil added thoughtfully. "I didn't see any soldiers at all posted as sentries. I couldn't dare stop and look, but it seemed very strange."

"Yes, it is very strange – considering the beating they received in Exeter not so long ago. One would think they'd learned a hard lesson from that!" John remarked. "No sentries at all?"

"Not that I could see," Gil said. "No movement at all anywhere. I suppose there *could* have been a few dotted around the trees, but nobody at all moving about the encampment – not even a soul with the hundreds of horses that are picketed down towards the river."

---------------- OOOOOOOOO ------------------

That observation was being confirmed by two more sets of eyes. Sergeant Brown was deeply concerned as he viewed the encampment from a distance. He still refused to make a move to join the main body of troops. He had no orders to do so. On the other hand, he had no orders *not* to do so. His reluctance to move came from a deeply held feeling that all was not well. Despite the aura of calm and peace that overlaid the encampment, he just knew that something was amiss – and he was determined to find out what it was. And then he would move.

At a slightly nearer vantage point, Lovelace viewed the encampment with a far greater degree of satisfaction. He now knew that the main body of parliamentary forces was already mounting up for a stealthy approach using the line of march that he had noted in his report. The peace and stillness of that encampment made him chuckle very quietly to himself.

The Ramsay family had just settled down to their midday meal when there came the tinkle of the bell from the shop. Mary jumped up and went to see the customer. She was back again after only a minute with a visitor. The tall frame of the bailiff stood in the doorway and offered his apologies.

"I'm sorry to interrupt your meal," Peter Cove said in his deceptively deep and quiet voice. "But I've been asked by the steward to make enquiries about the village. Has there been any order for bread from the king's men?"

"No, bailiff – not today so far," Evelyn replied. "But they can make the demand any time of the day."

"Any reason for the enquiry, bailiff?" John asked, setting down his mug of ale.

"Well – as far as anyone of us can tell, they will be making a move tomorrow. There is much talk about a gathering towards Tavistock. If they are moving on the morrow, then I would have expected them to make a very large order for supplies today."

"Well, as I say, nothing so far," Evelyn reiterated.

Gil put down his spoon into an empty bowl. "Bailiff – one question if I may. The goats that were on the plot – where are they now?"

"Oh – farmer Atkins moved them some days past. Said they'd cropped the area almost to the roots. One thing about your plot, young Gil – it's well-manured!"

The bell tinkled again, and Mary made as if to rise. It was unnecessary as their neighbour Abel came through, ducking to pass under the lintel.

"Ah, bailiff – saw you coming in here. I've been out the back of my workshop all morning – making tidy the mess that I've allowed to gather there. Only just noticed that the encampment is stirring. Lots of men standing around and yawning – doing precious little in the way of preparing to move out!"

"Any sign of any order to it? Any of the officers present?"

"No – one sergeant was starting to bellow at a fellow who had dropped his pike in the mud – oh, and a few milling about among the horses. But no sense of order, really?"

Yet another tinkle heralded the arrival of a further visitor. Dick Allen, the rotund and jovial owner of the larger of the two taverns, also apologised for the intrusion.

"Oho, bailiff – saw you come here. I've just had word that I'm to render my account. It would seem that Lord Wentworth is planning to move out by tomorrow afternoon. A young ensign came with the news. He is to return later for the account. I've no doubt that there will be some haggling over that tally!"

"Then I can return to Parke and relay the news. Gil - perhaps, in another two days, we can finish settling your plot and get the papers signed."

"That will be a happy day for me, sir," Gil replied as the tall bailiff departed. Abel eyed the pot of stew. Evelyn simply laughed, filled a bowl and pushed it towards him with a spoon. Abel grinned his pleasure and sat on the end of the bench. Dick Allen also left to go back to his busy tavern.

"I would like Ella to be with me when we mark out the plot – if that would be agreeable to you, sir," Gil tentatively said to the massive smith. "She is to be my partner in life and needs to be my partner in business also."

"That's a very worthy thought, young Gil," the smith rumbled. "I shall make sure she is there by your side when it all takes place."

"I also intend to ask Aunt Avril to be there. When the plot is measured out, she will know more than anyone what will grow best, and where, and when."

"One thing also," Abel added. "We need to attend to the site of your house. Not any old place will do. It must be drained and firm before we settle on the materials for its construction."

-------------------- OOOOOOOOO ------------------

Sergeant Brown was itching with worry as he sat and shivered. Still, he hesitated in ordering his small troop to go and join the main body on the heath. Warden and Farmer were certainly not silent in their questioning of the wisdom of their inaction.

"We should be there with the regiment," Warden muttered to his mate for the umpteenth time.

"What's holding the sergeant back, really?" Farmer muttered back. "If it was anyone else, I'd say it was fear. But he's never shown any fear of fighting. The trouble is, he thinks too much. Us soldiers aren't supposed to think!"

Although the two were at some distance from their sergeant, it was as if their words had carried clearly to his ears. Sergeant Brown slithered back and left another to keep watch. He joined the small detachment.

"I know what you buggers have been muttering for the last couple of days. Why aren't we with the regiment instead of skulking in this wood? Well, I'll tell you – and if any one of you laughs, I'll fetch the flat of my sword to him! There's something very wrong. It's all too peaceful and quiet. There they all are - five regiments in an encampment acting for all the world as if nothing has happened – or is likely to happen. Remember this well – Fairfax took Exeter, and we all managed to escape. We made one useless attempt to regain the city but were again soundly beaten. So, here we all are. Far to the west and probably going further still. Does any man here think that a general like Fairfax is not after us? Somewhere to our east or north – there he will be – or if not him, then this Cromwell. The one thing they can't allow is for all of us king's men to gather in large numbers – no matter where. I chose this place so that we can watch behind us for any approaching enemy. But that's not to say they'll come this way. That's why we're here, and that's why we're staying here until our lot move out. Then we join them."

------------------- OOOOOOOO ------------------

By the time the sun was setting, there had still been no order for bread. Then, as John lit the first of the lamps, he saw to the fire in the oven, making sure that it would leave enough glowing embers for the morning.

Slowly, the village settled down. Shops closed doors; shutters were fastened; dogs returned to their homes; cats started their prowling. The only place where life went on its raucous way was the large tavern. In the main hall of the tavern, sergeants and senior troopers supped ale and made jokes. In the upstairs room, Wentworth and his fellow officers settled down to cards and wine. Piles of coins were set in front of the players. In the main encampment, troopers scraped the last of the food from their bowls, and most of them stretched out on their bedrolls, heaping cloaks on top to ward off the cold wind. Down towards the river, the mass of horses chomped the last of the grass and hay – before the frost got at it.

The last glimpse that Lovelace and his three comrades had was one that gave them quiet satisfaction. Hardly a royalist trooper was in evidence; none guarded the encampment; none guarded the horses.

------------------- OOOOOOOOO ------------------

Just over three miles from the encampment, a large body of troops made their quiet way around the small hamlet of

Sandygate. After a mile, going south-west, they crossed the River Teign, then headed due west to meet the road that ran south from Bovey to Newton Abbot. Turning up this road, they kept to the grassy areas to deaden all sound until they reached a small track that went west towards Liverton. Here, they separated into three. One went onwards towards Liverton, then headed north into woodland. A short time later, this group halted. They were less than a half mile to the west of the encampment.

The second group headed north-east for the short journey to their destination – through more woods to a point on the River Bovey just south of where the horses were picketed.

The third group simply carried on for another short trip to the south-west tip of the encampment.

By nine o'clock, all were in position, and not a sound of alarm had been raised anywhere. General Cromwell, leading the third group, let his features settle into a grim smile – the second one he had permitted himself that week.

Chapter 8

That evening, the Randal family, together with James and Avril, were at the Smith's house. Although the front doors of the smithy were closed shut, the door between it and the main room of the house was open, allowing the residual heat from the furnace to help warm the place. Most blacksmiths' workshops were situated away from the dwelling – the fear of fire was always present. However, Abel had constructed his own premises in such a way that his furnace was enclosed on all sides by thick stone; the fumes were taken aloft through a long brick chimney – long enough that any spark emanating from the fire would be well out by the time it reached the cold air.

"Are we sure that the king's men will be gone tomorrow?" Evelyn asked. "I know this does not sound like it should – I am as staunch a supporter of our king as anyone. But the extra work is hard, and the threat of violence makes me tremble."

"Old Will Garlick is as certain as he can be," Abel rumbled. "And we have the need for accounts to be rendered."

"And then you two can get on with planning your new lives together," Avril smiled at her nephew and his intended bride. Gil and Ella were, as usual, sitting in a corner, holding hands. It was common knowledge throughout the village that they were soon to be wed – most had anticipated that for some years past. What puzzled a goodly few – notably Gil's male contemporaries – was that it was also common knowledge that he had not bedded his betrothed. After all, Ella was a very pretty girl, and Gil was a strong, fairly good-looking lad. What they didn't know was that the two had a pact that they would keep themselves chaste until the day of their wedding. Both, being normal and healthy young people, had found it hard to keep to this pact, but keep to it they had.

By eight o'clock that evening, all had gone to their own homes in the fond hope of a peaceful night. Some of the drunken rowdiness had kept half the village awake until the small hours during the previous nights – and with most having to be up with the dawn, this was starting to get very wearing – especially on John and Evelyn, who had to be up hours before anyone else.

Apart from the occasional shout of laughter from the tavern, all was reasonably quiet for a change. Wentworth and most of his officers were in the upstairs room playing cards – as usual. In the main downstairs hall of the tavern, sergeants and a few senior soldiers quaffed ale and relayed the latest bawdy jokes.

Sergeant Brown continued to watch. His men, anxious to join their mates, tried to sleep in the bitter cold and waited to see what the morrow would bring.

Lovelace and his three simply watched. Of all the people either in the encampment or any that might be watching, they were the only ones who had any idea what was about to happen. All four watched with mounting anticipation.

------------------ OOOOOOOOO ------------------

It was just after nine o'clock when the large village of Bovey awoke to the fact that this was not just another night – this one was going to be one they would relate to their grandchildren.

Suddenly, all was thunderous noise, shouting, shooting and utter confusion. Confusion throughout the encampment, confusion in the tavern; pandemonium amongst the horses corralled down by the river.

Each of Cromwell's groups knew exactly its purpose – and all three set about it with an order, precision and ruthless efficiency.

Wentworth and his officers, startled out of their wits by the sudden onslaught, peered out of the tavern windows to see roundhead cavalry in great numbers outside. They immediately knew that escape through the front of the tavern was impossible. Only the rear of the tavern offered them any possible means of escape.

In sheer desperation, they gathered armfuls of coins and threw them out into the roadway, hoping to distract enough of the parliamentarians. By the greatest good fortune, this worked. Wentworth, his five regimental commanders, plus some junior officers, were able to scramble to comparative safety out of the back, past the buttery and the cookhouse, and up the hill towards a wooded area.

In the encampment, chaos reigned. Soldiers roused brutally from their sleep, suddenly became aware of hooves thundering past tents – sometimes over them. A few started to offer some resistance - but were ruthlessly cut down. With no one of sufficient stature to instil some discipline, the majority simply took to their heels, grabbing whatever came to hand. Their way eastwards to the horses was cut off by a solid line of mounted soldiers. Their only recourse was to take to their heels and run across the road that led towards Newton and disappear into the woods and fields towards Liverton. The road itself was an impossibility as more mounted soldiers were there to make sure that didn't happen. Just a few decided to take the road up towards the moor. They were to regret that decision!

By midnight, the so-called battle of Bovey Heath was over. Not so much a battle as a rout! The village inhabitants stayed firmly locked in their houses with not a light showing anywhere.

Cromwell set up his headquarters just by the bridge over the river at the western end of the road through the village. One by one, his troop commanders came in to report.

The first to do so brought with him a couple of very junior officers who had been the last to attempt the escape from the tavern. The pair, neither above the age of twenty, looked terrified as they stood before the general. Cromwell looked them up and down, gave a sniff and motioned for them to be taken away and kept under guard.

"Surely, the king had better than these," he remarked. "I assume Wentworth and his senior officers have made off?"

"No sign of them. We believe they ran out of the back of the tavern and made their escape."

"Good!" Cromwell snorted. "My hope is that his lordship is granted another command. This one caused us no problem whatsoever!"

The second one to report came with two sergeants and a large soldier who was carrying an armful of captured colours.

"I think, General, you will be especially pleased to see this one we have captured," said the officer, pointing to a standard in red, white and gold.

"By merciful heavens – we have the king's own colour," Cromwell said, an exultant expression. "Find me the soldier who captured it, and I'll show you a new sergeant!"

By three in the morning, it became apparent that the rout was complete. Over four hundred horses had been captured, the five colours, and over fifty royalist soldiers. The rest had escaped and were scattered miles away to the west. Seven of Cromwell's soldiers had been killed and eight more injured. Less than a score of royalist troops had lost their lives.

At first light the next morning, Lovelace led his three men into the village and made for their captain. He led them straight to his commander. The four of them stood before Cromwell as he took in their dishevelled appearance.

"My apologies, sir, for appearing before you in this state," Lovelace muttered, a bit shamefaced.

"I want to hear no apologies!" Cromwell replied. "None is necessary. Your intelligence helped this about, and I know that to do so, required you to spend days without support. You have served superbly well. Be assured that your efforts will be used again. And now get to your rest; you have deserved it."

Sergeant Brown surveyed the area from his cover. His feelings, like those of his men, were mixed. Horrified at the ease with which the king's men had been routed, ashamed that they had been put to flight without seemingly any attempt at resistance.

"And what the bloody hell are we supposed to do now?" Farmer put into words what they were all thinking.

"The very first thing we have to do is to remain concealed. I, for one, don't relish the thought of becoming prisoner."

"No sense going either north or east," Warden groused. "West is the only option – that's where safety lies."

"I agree," Brown nodded. "But – where to the west – and how to get there. Who knows this part of the country best?"

"I suppose that's me, sergeant," Farmer acknowledged.

"Well?"

"First of all – where do we head for?" Farmer asked.

"Tavistock seems the best choice."

"Well then – three ways to get there. The worst way would be the longest. Up to Moretonhampstead, past Chagford, then west to Okehampton, then down the west side of the moor."

"How far would that be?"

"Probably forty or so miles, sergeant. But it would mean sticking to known roads and paths – and that bloody lot came from the north!"

"So, that's not the best way. What's next?"

"Oh – that's simple – across the moor, up to Hay Tor, down into Widecombe, then across to Postbridge and on to Merrivale. That would lead us down to the Tavy and into Tavistock. That's about twenty-five miles. But we'd be crossing the moor in the dead of winter – and that's not something to be done lightly!"

"And I suppose the other way is south of the moor?"

"Yes, sergeant. From here to Ashburton; then through Buckfastleigh and on to Ivybridge and Sparkwell. We'd have to skirt the southwest tip of the moor before turning north to Tavistock. But that's the way that all our mob will go – you may bet on it. It's also the way these bastards will go in pursuit of them!"

"Yes, that's true. No other way is possible?"

"Oh, anyway is *possible*! We could go south to Newton, then west to Ipplepen and Totnes. We'd then have to get up to Ivybridge and follow the southern route again. That's one hell of a long way around, though!"

Brown moved a short way from his men to think this through. They were in urgent need of supplies – their food was almost finished. Across the moor was certainly the shortest way, but in winter, the most hazardous. However, the small villages up there were very isolated and, therefore, unlikely to prove a threat to them. He dismissed the northern route out of hand. It was far too exposed. Following the probable route of the escaping horde of king's men could end up being suicidal, with the parliamentarian army in almost certain pursuit. So, the moor it would have to be. He slithered back.

"Here's what we do," he announced quietly. "We move north of Bovey under cover of the woods. Then we strike west and aim for the road up to the moor. But we can't move until nightfall – those bastards down there will be on full alert. Farmer – if we manage to get started up that road, how long to get to Widecombe – and how likely are we to receive help and food?"

Farmer thought long and hard. He certainly didn't want to raise false hopes, or he just might get lynched when they didn't work out.

"If we get to the road safely – say, a mile up and out of sight – then about ten miles. We should be there by daybreak. But the hills are very steep, and it's going to be bloody cold!"

"Right then. We're safe enough here. Get as much sleep as you can today and be ready to move out as soon as the daylight has gone."

------------------- OOOOOOOOO -------------------

John and Evelyn had woken as usual and had produced their normal batch of loaves. Gil and Mary had loaded the cart, which Gil set off with on his usual route. He was very surprised that the new batch of soldiers didn't make a grab for the bread – until he realised that there was something very different about this lot. They seemed more upright and disciplined – none of the banter and filthy language of the royalists who had been put to flight. His round ended an hour later, and he trudged back with a bulging purse to find an officer standing in the bakery.

This man spoke firmly and politely – asking for a large amount of bread to be baked as soon as possible.

"Have no fear for your purse," he said. "You will be paid in full – as will the butcher when he fulfils our order for meat. Thank you."

Evelyn, who had been prepared to spit on the floor after he had left, was left standing with her mouth open in amazement.

"He said 'thank-you', she gasped. "I was not expecting that!"

"It's like I've been seeing through the village," Gil reported, emptying the coins he had collected. "They are all well-mannered and disciplined – not one attempted to snatch a loaf from my cart!"

"But I still want the buggers gone!" John grated.

Cromwell had sent a messenger to ask the bailiff to attend him as soon as he could. Peter Cove arrived on horseback as soon as he had broken his fast. He was waved to a camp chair and looked at the craggy face of this new commander.

"Bailiff – you will have no doubt noticed a slight change in conditions. Now, I have no doubt that your sympathies are not with me and my army. But we will be here for today at least. Let it be known that if there is no hostility shown to us, we will show no hostility in return. That is not our aim. Our aim is solely to get the king to bend to our very reasonable demands – and then the country can return to peace."

"I will convey that message to all in the village, general. I will make sure that your stay here is ignored – as far as that is possible."

"Ignored? Yes – that's probably for the best. Please do not let me find any villager sheltering king's men – that will be something that I could not allow!"

"I will convey that message also."

The bailiff stood, nodded to the general and went out. Leaving his horse, he walked the length of the village, stopping at every shop and dwelling, relaying the double message. Only then did he return to the Parke estate to appraise the steward what was happening.

71

"Then let us pray for two things," the steward said. "That the king's men get safely away to regroup and fight on; that the general's troops, however well behaved, bugger off as soon as may be!"

"Amen to that!" the bailiff nodded.

Chapter 9

"Don't suppose we're good enough to speak to you now, are we?" Haddock said, pulling at his forelock and bowing.

"Don't be so bloody daft," replied *Sergeant* Lovelace, giving Haddock a clout around his head. "We're still the same team as always. I suppose we're going to be sent west soon – find out where the king's men are gathering. After all, we're damned good at it!"

The four were sitting on bundles of old, smelly straw that they had discovered in a broken-down shed at the southern end of the old royalist encampment. Unlike those previous occupants, they had found a use for the ruin, kicking the old planks apart and fashioning them into a small, temporary shelter. Throughout the force, they had been feted and given cheers when it had been made known that it was through their efforts that the king's men had been so effectively trounced.

One old officer was not so entranced with the victory – the general's master of horse, wondering just what he was supposed to do with an additional four hundred and three animals. He had had to beg an additional ten soldiers to help his usual small team – making him very unpopular with all the other junior officers.

Some others were equally a bit miserable – seven groups of three soldiers had been immediately detailed to set up sentry posts at various distances from the heath. It was bitterly cold, and they shivered and grumbled – but they did their jobs properly and kept a careful lookout just in case some royalists decided to avenge their dismal showing earlier.

Down by the bridge, by the side of the mill, Cromwell sat in his rather spartan tent and looked at his two senior commanders who were sitting in camp chairs and drinking weak ale.

"Tomorrow morning, we set out for Ashburton," they were told. "It is less than ten miles distant. We need to ensure that it is free of the king's army. It's an important town – being one of the 74tannaries' that yield much income to the royal coffers."

"As are Tavistock and Chagford, sir."

"Tavistock is the likeliest rallying point for them now that we're in effective control of the east of the moor."

"Is it safe for us to leave the area north of the moor?"

"That may indeed come later," Cromwell replied, gazing at a map spread over his knees. "The moor in winter is no place for man nor beast! It's cold enough here to its south. Our obvious line of march is through Ashburton, on to Ivybridge, and then up to Tavistock. Our mission is to drive them as far west as possible. Then, with a line of defence from north to south, they will be effectively trapped at or to the west of the Tamar. Whatever happens, we must deny them escape eastwards again."

"Latest intelligence has the king still garrisoned in Oxford, sir. It is not yet known where Lord Hopton or Prince Charles are."

Cromwell gave a grunt. "Young Charles is proving as ineffective as his cousin Rupert was! Hopton is altogether another matter. If he is able somehow to extricate Wentworth's rabble from their westward flight, we could be facing a more serious threat. Hence the need to block that possibility."

"Sir – what about their possible route north up the western side of the moor. Lydford would be within easy reach from Tavistock – and then they might double back to Okehampton and Crediton."

"Yes, that possibility *had* occurred to me. However, we cannot be in two or more places at once. No – we proceed west to Tavistock with all speed. If we then spread north towards Lydford, we may well be able to deny them that opportunity – and force them further west."

"We proceed with the whole force, sir?"

"Yes – but with one small exception. That very resourceful group of trackers. I want them to take a shorter route – over the moor. When we get to Ashburton, depending upon what we find, then I will divert them. It is just conceivable that some of Wentworth's men took that route.

If so, I want to know so that we can divert enough men to deal with them. After all, most of them will be on foot!"

------------------- OOOOOOOOO ------------------

By two o'clock that afternoon, John, Evelyn, Gil and Mary had produced the required number of loaves. The same young officer, with ten men, had collected the bread and had paid the agreed amount.

John looked at the pile of coins in the strong box. "This has been a very profitable few days for us – but it would be very nice for us to be able to get some proper rest!"

Gil, at last, released from bakery duties, slipped next door to have a word with Ella.

"If, as is expected, we are free of armies tomorrow, it might be possible for us to meet with the bailiff and set out our boundaries."

Abel, who had been hovering nearby at his roaring furnace, dipped his head in a trough of water to cool himself down.

"The stone for the lower walls must needs be collected. Is old Wat briefed that his oxen and cart will be needed for the task?"

"I saw him the other day and agreed a price for carting the loads," Gil nodded.

Abel and Faith had long since planned for the cost of erecting the small house. It was to form the major part of Ella's dowry. It would consist of one large room on the ground floor, with two smaller rooms above. One for the married couple and one for the expected child's nursery. A smaller shed behind the tiled cottage would be erected as the kitchen. By its side would be an even smaller privy.

One special benefit of living so close to the granite moor was the ready availability of mountains of stone. Given the proximity of large areas of woodland, timber was also not a problem. But cutting the timber would need the permission of the lord of the manor. Bailiff Cove had said that he would sort that out as and when the need arose.

Sitting on a bench together in the hot smithy, Gil and Ella allowed their thoughts to imagine a life together in their new house. Gil with mounting excitement at the prospect, Ella with similar excitement, coupled with some anxiety on the role of a wife – especially the part that involved the wedding night. She knew that, initially, she would suffer pain. But her mother had told her repeatedly that it would bring the two of them closer together. She would never regret what she had gone through!

-------------------- OOOOOOOOO -------------------

Cold and miserable, Sergeant Brown and his small troop watched the enemy army feed themselves and start to relax in their new surroundings. They couldn't wait for the light to fade so that they would be able, at long last, to get on the move and get some heat into their limbs. Farmer had explained in some detail what he believed to be their safest route around the village – a route that would enable them to reach the road that led up past Hay Tor and onwards to Widecombe.

The dead had been buried – both parliamentarian and royalist. The surgeon had tended wounds – the injured bandaged, moaning and cold, were huddled together and trying to sleep.

Cromwell and his officers briefed troop commanders, who, in turn, briefed sergeants for the next-days march.

The Ramseys, and Smiths, along with the remainder of the families in the village, settled down to their supper.

In the tavern, Dick Allen and his wife were their usual harried selves – serving jugs of ale to soldiers. Their daughter Glory was well used to helping out and swatting away hands that tried to pat her backside, even encircle her waist. She regarded it as no more than what was expected of men in their cups. However, one soldier was incensed at her refusal to give him a kiss.

"What? Not good enough for a tavern slut, am I?" he snarled. The man was quite drunk.

Dick, well used to this, made his way to his daughter's side.

"Perhaps you would do well to step out and refresh yourself with some clear air," he suggested.

"This slut will oblige me first!" the soldier slurred, his face twisted into a snarl.

"No – my daughter most certainly will not!" Dick retorted, looking at the soldier's companions for support. They mostly looked down at their cups of ale. One of them spoke up.

"Hal – leave it alone! Go and do as bid, or you will get us all into trouble."

The drunk ignored that and made a grab for Glory – but was stopped in his tracks by a bellow from the doorway. He turned to see his sergeant standing with hands on hips.

"You – outside this minute! Call yourself a disciplined soldier? You are a disgrace and shall be flogged. Now leave immediately!"

The man slunk out, knowing full well that his punishment would hurt. It was not the first time he had been flogged. The sergeant spoke up again before turning to follow the drunk outside.

"Please excuse the behaviour of that wretched man."

He gave a stiff nod of his head towards Dick, then went out, leaving behind a group of soldiers who then got on with their drinking and storytelling – but quietly. Dick looked at Glory – who would have dealt very adequately with the drunk anyway. She gave her father a wink before going on around the tables, filling mugs.

------------------- OOOOOOOOO ------------------

In the biting cold, just after ten o'clock that night, Sergeant Brown led his small force back northwards the way they had come. He had decided to give the village a very wide berth, going halfway towards the small village of Hennock before turning west. He assigned Warden and Farmer to bring up the rear – leaving a gap of some hundred yards between them and the rearmost soldier.

Brown had gone no more than a mile before he was challenged. He had almost blundered straight into one of the sentry posts. Without a second's thought, he led a charge at the three soldiers who had been manning a junction where two tracks intersected. The three were no match for the eighteen who pelted towards them. They were simply knocked out of the way and went sprawling into bushes – one of them knocked senseless. However, the remaining two were still alert enough to deter Warden and Farmer, who had hidden when they heard the skirmish in front of them.

Brown led his now shortened force at a headlong rush, turning left onto the track that led to Drakeford and thence westwards up onto the moor.

The two sentries tended their comrade and saw that he would not be with them for some time. One stayed put whilst the other ran as fast as he could to his sergeant, who was stationed with another post near the church.

Fifteen minutes later, the sergeant and ten soldiers arrived.

Warden and Farmer, hidden behind dense bushes, heard the sergeant quite clearly as he ordered his men to form a long line and watch out for any more royalist troops trying to escape. They shared a look. Very carefully, they crept backwards until they were at some distance from the extended sentry line.

"We could get around, but our chances of meeting up with the rest are remote," Warden muttered.

"Why would we even bother?" Farmer grunted. "This has been a complete mess from the day we gave up at Exeter. I say we get back to the village and hide up and wait until the army leaves. I've had enough of this!"

"What? Desert, you mean?"

"Yes – why not? No good's ever going to come out of this shambles. I can be home again in five day's walking."

"But I can't!" Warden retorted. "All right for you, being local. My home's a hundred miles away."

"Still best if we hide up for a bit," Farmer repeated.

Warden could see no other alternative, so they very slowly and carefully made their way back to the eastern outskirts of the village, where they found shelter in a disused barn that leaked like a sieve, allowing the bitter wind to whistle through the holes and cracks.

Still, thought Farmer, better than wandering the Devon countryside on a fool's errand.

Chapter 10

Despite a chilling wind, the next day was at least dry. Gil finished his delivery round and was free to witness, along with the rest of the village, the departure of Cromwell's large force. They clattered across the village, making for Ashburton – a journey that would take them less than two hours.

As the last ranks clattered over the bridge, a small contingent of twenty or so peeled off and made for the side of the mill, where the commander had pitched his headquarters. It seemed the village had not seen the last of the occupying force after all. Sergeant Franks, along with troopers Buskin and Ford and seventeen others, settled themselves into their quarters – tents deliberately left by the departing guard.

Seeing the massed villagers, Franks wandered over to them.

"As you can see, we are left here for a purpose that you may well know. We will be searching for any remainder of the king's men who may be lurking in your village. We will also be patrolling regularly until such time as we are called to rejoin our army."

"It is no crime to shelter king's men!" James Ramsey shouted out. A chorus of voices added their agreement to that statement. Franks held up a hand for silence.

"As you say, 'tis no crime. But we will still search and, if we find, we will apprehend."

"And if we resist you?"

"Be sure to arm yourselves well. We wish you no harm, but I urge you all to see that we are trained soldiers – we will deal with any resistance in force!"

"But you will still steal from us and mistreat our women!" came a voice from somewhere in the middle of the assembled village.

Franks again had to quell the angry outpourings.

"Should any of these soldiers act in any such manner, believe me, that he will be punished – and severely so. There was an incident yestereve in the tavern. That soldier will wear the stripes upon his back for weeks to come."

"That much is certainly true," Dick spoke up. "My Glory was subject to vile behaviour. His sergeant dealt with him exactly as has just been said."

"My soldiers will start a search throughout the village. Offer them no resistance, though you may resent it, and no harm will come to anyone."

And with that valedictory remark, Franks marched back to his little camp and detailed two patrols of three men in each. One group to search the houses and buildings on the left, and the other to do the same on the right.

The inhabitants were uneasy – it was all very well to say that no harm would come to them. But what if some royalists had hidden away unbeknown to the householder? Would they start a fight? It was not a happy village that went about its day's work.

Warden and Farmer, by now starving hungry, peered out between the broken slats of their broken-down barn. During the night, Farmer had at least managed to fill a large canteen with water from a little brook that meandered down the hillside to join the river. Cold – indeed, shivering continually – they peered out and wondered where they would next be able to find a meal. The wind, unusually from the east, had at least spared them the agony of smelling the aroma of baking bread around daybreak. All they could do was gather as much of the old mouldy straw and huddle down to preserve whatever warmth they could manage.

-------------------- OOOOOOOOO ------------------

By two o'clock that afternoon, Brown had led his tired and dispirited force down into the valley in which nestled the village of Widecombe. Making doubly sure that there were no parliament soldiers in residence, he decided to march boldly into the village and ask for food and drink.

Nobody there had as yet heard of the humiliating rout of the king's men in Bovey – so they were greeted with dismay as they told of their defeat and escape. However, they were fed and given shelter, promising that they would be gone the next day. They hoped to reach as far as Merivale.

"You will have to have the devil's own luck," the parish priest said. He was joined by a host of agreement. The moor was a treacherous place in the winter.

"Be warned by us who know it well," one grizzled old chap said, removing his toothless mouth from his pot of ale. "If the mist come down, find a hollow and stay still until it passes. Wander on through the mist, and you will get lost – or fall down a pixie hole and never be seen again!"

"Either that, or you will just disappear into any one of the hundred bottomless bogs!" said his companion. "Walk only when you can see the firm ground!"

With such dire imprecations making the soldiers thoroughly alarmed, they settled down to see out the day and the night. One large barn, massed with warm, dry straw, was their bedroom – and they were thankful for it.

------------------- OOOOOOOOO -------------------

Earlier that day, the parliamentary column had arrived at Ashburton. The place was as busy as usual – shops open, mining bosses bringing their tin for assay, goodwives

86

bustling about with their purchases – but not a royalist soldier in sight.

"It would seem that they've abandoned one of their prime locations, sir," one of the senior officers said to the commander.

"Find me a reeve," came the order.

It was hardly surprising to any of the columns that, as soon as they had massed in the main square and the roads leading from it, that the local inhabitants had found urgent business elsewhere. Within fifteen minutes of their mass arrival, the place was almost deserted.

A junior officer approached Cromwell accompanied by a portly man in his middle years.

"This man claims to be the reeve, sir."

Cromwell looked down from his saddle.

"Then tell me, reeve – have the king's men been through here today? And, if they have, where are they now?"

"As to where they are now, I have no idea. And neither would anyone here have any idea. As to their passage through Ashburton, I can tell you that many groups came through. Some in large groups of fifty or more, some in much smaller groups. They stopped neither for speech nor for refreshment. They all simply hurried on their way."

"And mostly on foot, I daresay," one of Cromwell's regimental commanders laughed.

"Indeed so. Very few were mounted."

"Did you catch sight of Lord Wentworth?"

"I would not know the gentleman, sir. Some officers, by their dress, were mounted and were the earliest to canter through the town."

"So, master reeve – were I to order a search of the town, I would find no king's men being offered succour?"

The reeve stiffened and considered his reply carefully.

"I cannot answer for every man and woman in the town. But, to the best of my knowledge, all His Majesty's men entered the town and were anxious to pass through it as quickly as they may."

"Then, master reeve, I will detain you no longer."

The man needed no second bidding and almost ran back whence he had come. Cromwell turned to his commanders.

"And what, gentlemen, do we learn from all this?" he barked.

"That they have an urgent need to get to Tavistock?" one of them ventured.

"That we have already guessed! What else?"

"That they are poorly led. If the senior officers came through first, who is then left to see to the proper order of their retreat?" came another voice.

"Precisely! They *were* poorly led by an incompetent buffoon – and they are *still* poorly led, in effect, not led at all! What we are pursuing, gentlemen is various groups of frightened and dispirited people. We have seen Ilsington, and now Ashburton abandoned. I want one of you to take your men south to Totnes – to see whether the same applies there. I suspect you will find it in the same condition. You will make all speed and meet up with us again at Ivybridge. The rest of us will proceed as we are. When we inevitably meet up with these groups, we will deal with them appropriately if they offer any resistance. If they do not, we recommend – forcefully – that they abandon their useless flight and return to their homes. Now – someone please fetch that tracker and his men."

It took a while for the four to be located. Being independently-minded like all trackers, they had found a small inn and were refreshing themselves with ale.

"Sergeant – you will use your skills again for me. I want you to divert to the north – towards Poundsgate and Dartmeet. I need to know if any of the rabbles have decided to use the moor to affect their escape. They would be ill-advised as the moor is no place to wander in this weather. Find two of the fastest horsemen and take them with you. Should you discover any using that route, send word immediately."

"Yes, sir. Um – you called me sergeant, sir?"

"Yes, I did. Do you not want the promotion?"

"On yes, sir – and I thank you most sincerely."

"Then be off with you and try to bypass any more taverns on your way!"

Half an hour later, Ashburton was again a thriving small town – with not a soldier in sight – of either loyalty.

------------------- OOOOOOOOO ------------------

That night, Farmer again made use of his skills. He crept along a hedgerow until he came to the rear of the bakery. Following his sensitive hearing, he made for the sound of scratching, knowing that rats – or some similar animals – were grubbing amongst discarded foodstuffs. He slowly and silently approached the back of the wooden structure and found what he had been looking for – loaves discarded as either underweight or misshapen and, therefore, not fit for sale.

His senses had not let him down. At least a dozen rats were burrowing into a small mound of loaves. That suited him fine. He selected four from the very top of the small pile, leaving the rodents to gorge themselves on those they could more readily access.

Ten very quiet minutes later, he was back in the broken-down barn and sharing his find with Warden. He also had some other news for his mate.

"There's a small patrol left in the village – heard two of them nattering as they walked past the front of the bakery. Don't know how long they're going to be here, but we'll have to be a mite careful."

"Depends on how long we want to stay here. I thought you were all for going home!"

"Yes – that I am," Farmer whispered back. "But we're going to need provisions before we start out – and a good night's sleep!"

"At least we're warm here. But you said 'we'. "I thought you intended going to your home."

"That is my intention. But you will come with me – we've been mates for far too long for me to abandon you to wander the countryside alone. Same goes for me, if truth be told. I would welcome your company on the way."

"That offer is one I accept readily!" Warden was relieved as he had thought the two would go their separate ways. One man alone was an easy target; two could watch out for one another.

The two of them again burrowed deep into the old straw and fell into a rather uneasy sleep, knowing that a patrol was still in the village – presumably on the lookout for royalist stragglers.

------------------- OOOOOOOOO -------------------

Gil had again just finished his deliveries the next morning – a morning that was again bitterly cold but with bright sunshine. He upended his small cart behind the bakery, took a flying kick at the few rats that were shuffling around the by-now tiny pile of discarded bread, and was about to go in for his second breakfast when he was hailed by a youthful voice.

"Hoi! Gil! Master Bailiff says to meet him at the plot at eleven of the clock!"

Gil looked around to see the small figure of Hob, the Bailiff's young servant. Hob was just nine years old and was used as the Bailiff's messenger. Invariably finding life hilarious, the young lad was always seen scampering around the village on some errand or other.

"Hungry?" Gil asked, somewhat needlessly. Hob was always hungry.

The little lad scampered after Gil into the bakery and gave John and Evelyn a huge grin. Mary, two years Hob's senior, gave him a look of disdain. Not abashed in the slightest, Hob accepted a slice of a new loaf that had been spread with butter and honey.

"Thanks, mistress. I was starving!"

"No, you damned well weren't!" John gave him a clump around his tousled head. "Master Bailiff feeds you enough for five grown men already!"

"Bailiff wants me at eleven at the plot," Gil explained. He wolfed down his food and went next door to appraise Ella that things were at long last getting underway. Abel, hearing what was said above the din of his hammer on anvil, stopped what he was doing and fetched a dozen short poles for the corner of the smithy, plus a wooden mallet. He had been prepared for this moment.

Wrapped in their warmest cloaks and hoods, the three made their way down the street to the empty plot. There they waited until a few minutes later; Peter Cove arrived on his horse. An hour later, the plot was marked out with the short poles. Gil and Ella ran twine between the little posts and stood in the middle of what was to be their own miniature farm.

"I cannot believe this is all really happening!" Gil said, looking around in awe.

"This will be our home soon. It's exciting, isn't it?" Ella whispered, equally awestruck.

Gil looked furtively towards the street where Abel and Cove were chatting, their backs turned. Gil took Ella by the shoulders and gave her a soft kiss -which she returned with equal vigour.

Abel bade goodbye to the Bailiff and turned to survey the area he and John had already decided on as the best site for the new house.

"We'll get that stone in here on Saturday – as long as Wat remembers we need his cart," he announced. Saturday would be two days hence.

"You know that tumble-down barn in the field opposite the church?" Gil said. "Well – we all know that ownership has never been decided. I thought I might go and see whether I can rescue some timbers. Some might still be serviceable."

"That's a good thought," Abel nodded. "Let me and your father know what you find."

Avril arrived just as Abel was about to return to the smithy. Work still needed to be done, and fees for repairs were earned.

Gil greeted his aunt. He, Avril and Ella then started walking down the large plot to see what would best grow, where, and in what quantity. They were still at it when Mary came down to say that dinner was ages ago and was now cold.

That afternoon, Gil walked alone up to the church and clambered over a low wooden fence into the field. It had been left fallow for the past ten or more years, as nobody had ever claimed ownership – a very rare occurrence. He approached the old barn and started walking around it, tapping the main support timbers to test their soundness. Five, he reckoned, were sound enough to use. He then walked around to the gaping entrance and peered inside.

Two grubby faces looked back at him. It took Gil only a second to realise who they were.

"King's men?" he asked softly.

He received one nod and one scowl.

"Bovey is for the king – well, with two exceptions," he replied equally softly. "None here will betray you. Our lord is with the king – or so we believe. And our vicar is chaplain to Prince Charles. You are among friends."

The two faces stayed where they were – but looked relieved at the news.

"Come to the bakery after nightfall. Come silently, and we will see you fed and kept safe. Do you know your way there?"

"He does," Warden poked a grimy finger towards his mate. "We thank you, and we will endeavour to bring no harm to you."

Gil left them, being careful to stay casual as he retraced his way home.

His parents greeted the news with a calm acceptance. Mary, on the other hand, was excited at the prospect of meeting two of the king's soldiers, imagining tall, stern men who she could hero-worship. She was to be a tad disappointed.

Chapter 11

It was unfortunate that the stars shone brightly that night – shone brightly from a black sky that was cloud-free. It was also bitterly cold, the cold almost made worse by a three-quarter moon that shone like a beacon, throwing long, impenetrable shadows. These shadows, as far as he was able, were used by Farmer as he led a shivering Warden from one to the next, careful to make no sound.

Arrived at the rear of the bakery, he paused as on the previous night to observe the colony of rats braving the bitter cold to scavenge amongst the discarded loaves. From force of habit, he swung a boot at the nearest rat. He missed and could have sworn that the rat looked up at him with a disdainful sneer.

On their short journey from the old barn, they had neither seen nor heard the patrol. They wondered if, in fact, the patrol, which would undoubtedly have been sent out, had not found some warm spot in which to sit out their period of duty – and who could have blamed them; it was bitter.

Farmer crept to the rear door of the bakery and gave a series of quiet knocks. It was opened almost immediately, and Farmer and Warden were ushered inside – into a darkened room. It proved to be the flour store. Gil, who had admitted them, immediately closed and barred the door. It was of very stout construction and fitted closely into the door jamb – keeping rats and other vermin from entering and spoiling the means of the bakery's livelihood. He made for an inside door, around which a faint light showed.

Passing through into the main living room, the two soldiers blinked at the light that shone from two lanterns. Then they became aware of the other three people in the room – all sitting around the table.

Gil was the first to break the silence.

"My mother and father and my sister Mary," he said, waving his arm around.

"And you be king's men," John said. "How did you come to be hiding in that barn and not escaping with all the others?"

"We were part of a small unit that was separate from the main army," Warden started his explanation. "We were by ourselves in a small wood that overlooked the heath. We saw all that happened and knew we had to make our own escape. Our sergeant led us to the north, hoping to pass around the village before turning towards the west. But we were spotted by a watch post. We two were at the back of the unit and became separated. Having no other course open to us, we crept back and hid."

Farmer, who had slightly more social grace than his mate, thought it time to effect introductions.

"This be Kit Warden, and I'm Luke Farmer," he said. "And we are truly grateful for your hospitality."

"Aye, that we are," his mate added.

"Then you must both be cold and hungry," Evelyn stated, pointing at two vacant stools. "Sit you down and eat."

She fetched a large loaf of bread, a platter of butter and a large wedge of cheese, putting these before the two men. Gil had already filled two mugs with warmed ale. Mary just sat and gaped at the two soldiers – very far indeed from the vision she had conjured up. Her two 'heroes' were dirty, dishevelled and shaking with cold – one even had a dripping nose. Then, aware that she was staring, she composed herself and looked down at the table – a disappointed young lady. However, they were the king's men and had to be sheltered.

The impromptu meal over, John returned to the business in hand.

"You will be safe enough here," he said. "We shall bring down two spare palliasses, and you can sleep beneath this table. We also have spare blankets for you. We must all now get to our beds, for our day starts all too early. You will be warm enough in here."

"We have an idea to keep you safe from discovery," Gil added. "My father, the master smith next door, and I will start building my new, small house when the work of the bakery is over tomorrow. We will say that you are distant cousins, arrived from Dawlish, come to help us in the building."

"Believe me, we will play our part willingly. You have offered us safety and food, so the least we can do is to give our help in the building."

"Then let us all get what sleep me may!" Evelyn rose and made for the stairs that led to the bedrooms above.

A half-hour later, the bakery was in darkness, its normal nightly noises added to by the snores coming from beneath the long, scrubbed table.

The first light of dawn brought little in the way of relief from the cold. Sheltered in the valley, Widecombe was distinctly warmer than the surrounding hills of the moor – that was made unpleasantly clear to the men that Sergeant Brown led southwards through Dunstone towards Ponsworthy and Dartmeet. As they climbed higher, the wind picked up and penetrated even the thick coats of the soldiers, making them shrivel in on themselves. At the crest of a hill, Brown made for the shelter of a stand of stunted trees and called a halt. They had travelled only one mile of the five that would see them in another valley – where the West and East Dart Rivers met.

It was far too soon for them to start eating the provisions that the people of Widecombe had provided. They simply sat in huddles and shivered.

"With this wind, no fear of a mist descending on us," Brown muttered to the soldier next to him.

"Maybe so, sergeant – but 'tis bloody cold. How far more to Tavistock?"

"I reckon about another twenty miles – and we must climb much higher before we get there. But our next stop is right by the Dart – and that's bound to be in a valley."

A short while later, Brown called them to their feet and again started off, leading them even further south towards the hamlet of Ponsworthy. The day slowly warmed as they marched; the wind dropped, and the skies clouded over. The men, unused to the weather on the moor, were grateful for small mercies. They ceased to shiver and marched onwards with a better purpose. Had they been able to read the signs, they would have realised that winter clouds and warmer weather was *not* a combination to be devoutly wished for – it could be, and often was, the precursor of wet mist!

------------------- OOOOOOOO -------------------

Newly promoted Sergeant Lovelace set off earlier that morning, following a northwest route from Ashburton. His first goal was Poundsgate – a small village high up on the moor. A few miles into the first leg of that journey saw them pass the settlement known as Hawksmoor. The track led them slowly towards a bridge that spanned the Dart, then through the densely wooded area known as Holne Brake, climbing up and then down again to re-cross the Dart. At a place called Spitchwick, they halted and started on their provisions – bread, cheese and a flask of ale.

"From here on, we go undercover," Lovelace decided. "So far, we've had the entire area to ourselves. Any king's men would easily have gone through here either yesterday or some hours ago. Now, we have to start searching. Ratty – you take the first lead. Garvey – you next, and then Haddock. We keep off the track but never lose sight of it."

All four of them were expert trackers – well used to wooded areas – and this was a home from home to them. Proceeding as the sergeant had ordered would halve their rate of progress – maybe even worse than halving it if the woods closed in even tighter than where they were. That was a penalty they all knew was worth paying.

Up to that point, the two horsemen attached to the group had stayed in their saddles, rather enjoying the slow walking pace as they had trailed behind the four trackers. Now, they would have to walk quietly behind – some way behind – and lead their mounts. They tied bits of sacking around the bridle rings and any other metalwork that could possibly make sounds and thus give away their presence.

Ratcliffe, dusting breadcrumbs from his clothes, set off through the wood, keeping parallel to the track but some twenty yards from it. Anyone on that track would have had to have the eyes of a fox to see them. And then they started to climb – steeply, as it turned out until they ran out of trees.

Garvey, who was then in the lead, raised a hand and stopped the silent group. They all joined him and gazed through the last of the trees at what lay before them.

The track, away to their right, wound upwards through open moorland, sometimes below the level of the surrounding moor, sometimes level with it. Lovelace immediately became aware of the drop in the wind. Inside the trees, they had been sheltered from it and comparatively warm as a consequence.

"Don't like the look of that lot!" Haddock muttered, pointing to the sky to their west. Thick, dark clouds were massing. He, of all the soldiers on the moor that morning, could read the signs.

"Why?" Lovelace grunted.

"Winter, wind dropped, getting warmer, and western gathering clouds. That means either cold rain or mist – perhaps both – and *that's* not good for man nor beast up here!"

Lovelace considered what he had just heard.

"By my reckoning, we've got another couple of miles – maybe three – to the hamlet of Poundsgate. How soon will that weather be upon us?"

"Reckon an hour, maybe a mite less," Haddock (whose name was actually Hook) muttered.

"Then we've no alternative. We can't be caught out here. We march as good soldiers on that track, and to hell with being spotted. We are going to need shelter – and there's none to be had here!"

One hour later, as the first drops of freezing rain fell on them, they arrived at the little village and found shelter in the first barn they found. The horses were possibly the happiest amongst the group – they were undercover and had found an old bundle of hay in a far corner. The six men huddled, shivered, and did what all good soldiers do – they grumbled.

------------------- OOOOOOOOO -------------------

Warden and Farmer had spent a peaceful night in the long parlour but had been woken when John and Evelyn had begun their work. Dozing fitfully as the dough was made, set to rise, and then baked, they had wondered at the fortitude of a couple who did this every working day of their lives.

Long before daybreak, the aroma of freshly baked bread proved too much, and they stirred at last. Knowing that they could not allow anyone else in the village to be aware of their presence, they stayed where they were – until Gil, readying the delivery cart, bent down and gave them a cheery 'good morning' and handed them a warm loaf.

As there was a closed door between the parlour and the bakery and shop, they were allowed to sit with the family as another breakfast was served – the usual bread, cheese and weak ale. John then told them of the plan that he and Gil had devised.

"As soon as we are finished here, Gil is going to fetch the wagon and horse from old Wat. He'll drive it around the back, and you two will get in the wagon and cover yourselves with old blankets. Gil and I will drive over to the place where we're going to load the first of the stones that we are going to use for the foundations of his house. You can then come back with us so that everyone can see you. We will tell everyone that you are distant relatives of Evelyn from Dawlish – and she did come from there. You are here to help us with the heavy work with the lower courses of the house."

That seemed to Kit and Luke a very well-devised plan. Luke certainly had a west country accent, so they would fit in without too much comment. Each time the shop doorbell sounded, Mary, hopped down and went to serve the customer. Then, she came back with a massive man who greeted everyone with a grin, dumped a sack on the floor, sat down and started to make inroads into a fresh loaf.

"This is Abel Smith – he lives and works next door. His daughter Ella is Gil's betrothed."

Abel reached down and opened the sack. "Brought you some clothes more fitting to the story. Can't have you coming back here dressed as soldiers, can we?"

There were two sets of old breeches, worn tunics and padded jackets against the cold weather. Their royalist clothes would be bundled up and well hidden in an old sack that Gil would throw over the back hedge – as if discarded by fleeing soldiers.

"Who, apart from your good selves, know that we are here?" Kit asked.

"Why – not another soul. Just us four here, Master Smith and his family. Nobody else," Gil answered.

Everyone apart from the two escapees left the room to let the soldiers change into their new apparel. Their uniform clothes were bundled into the sack which Gil collected and, making sure he was unobserved, tossed over the blackthorn hedge into the field behind the bakery. And then he went to Wat's home to collect the horse and wagon.

The wagon was large – with four wheels, sloped sides and a tailboard that lowered on hinges. The horse was a massively strong beast with huge hooves covered by long, muddy brown hairs. Gil thanked old Wat and climbed up onto the diving board, grasped the reins and drove slowly back to the bakery, turning into the back and stopping as close to the rear door as possible.

John, wearing the warmest coat he could find, ushered Kit and Luke into the body of the large wagon, threw them a large old blanket with which to conceal themselves, and then closed the tailboard before climbing up beside his son.

The wagon made its slow way up towards the church and beyond to load the first of what would be many consignments of stone.

Chapter 12

Brown and his men had carefully gone around the small hamlet of Ponsworthy and were slowly heading towards the point where the two rivers joined together to form the Dart. They had just as good a view of the approaching bank of dark clouds as did Lovelace, further to the south of them.

To Brown, who was leading, it seemed as if a cloud was slowly approaching ground level. He remembered only too well the warning he had received back in Widecombe. Was this the dreaded Dartmoor mist, he wondered?

Suddenly, he could see no further ahead than a hundred yards. He called a halt immediately and searched around for somewhere they could sit it out. To his right was a hollow bordered on three sides by large granite boulders. He made for it, shrugged off his pack and laid down his musket.

"We go no further until this all passes," he announced.

Most of the soldiers were only too happy to stop and rest. They had been alternately climbing, then descending. All but three of them shrugged off their packs and settled down for what they expected would be a long rest.

Three remained standing and started to protest.

"But we can still see ahead, sergeant," one of them objected. "Surely we'll still be able to see far enough to stay safe."

"Don't you ever listen to what's said?" Brown looked the chap in the eye. "Those local people told us to sit it out – and they know this moor a lot better than we do."

"Lot of old folklore, if you ask me," another of the three muttered. "They believe in demons and pixies – and think the moor is looked over by some giant or other. A load of bollocks, if you ask me!"

"I did not ask you," Brown grated. "I'm the sergeant, and I say we stay here!"

The three looked at one another, went to the entrance to the hollow and peered out westward.

"That mist is still away in front of us. We will be bound to see the ground at our feet. I'm going on! You two coming with me?"

"You step outside this hollow, and you betray your oath to the king!" Brown shouted.

"I, for one, didn't make my oath to you!" the man replied. "I'm off!"

He marched out and was followed by his two mates. Brown could either order the remainder of his men to arrest them, or he could let them go. He made a quick decision.

"Herrick, Porter, Andrews," he bellowed at their retreating backs. "If by any chance you get to Tavistock, I'll have you flogged for desertion!"

"We ain't deserting, sergeant. We're going on to where we were ordered to be!"

They had gone no more than twenty yards when their figures became blurred by the incoming mist. In another ten seconds, they had disappeared completely.

"Wonder if we'll ever see them again," one of the remaining thirteen laughed.

"Any more of you lot want to wander off into the mist?" Brown demanded.

"Not bloody likely!" the same man answered. "This is damp, and it's going to get very cold – but I'm staying put!"

Brown looked at his remaining baker's dozen men. He knew he would far rather get to their destination with the majority of his unit than have the remainder of the journey hampered by dissension and unrest. He shrugged and sat down on his pack.

------------------- OOOOOOOOO -------------------

The afternoon sun shone brightly from a clear sky as Gil drove the large wagon back into Bovey. John, his father sat beside him, and Warden and Farmer, dressed in workaday clothes, sat atop the pile of stone. This did not escape the notice of Sergeant Franks.

One of his men on earlier patrol had reported the departure of the wagon with just two people aboard. He was himself wandering up the road with the intention of going as far as the church. The wagon, its wheels making squeaks as they turned on the axles, grew louder as it approached. His eye alighted on four people, so he stood in the middle of the road and held up his hand. Gil pulled the reins back a bit and brought the wagon to a halt.

"Who might you be, and what's all that stone for?" he was asked.

"I'm John Ramsey, and this is my son Gil – and this stone is for the new house we're building for Gil and his betrothed," John called down. "Why? Is there some new law that forbids us to collect building material?"

Franks ignored the question, which re rightly supposed to be frivolous.

"That wagon left with just two. It returns with four. I ask again – who are *all* of you?"

"Well, that's simply answered," John replied with a shrug. "The two on the back are Kit and Luke – relatives of my wife. They're come to help in the building."

"And where did they magically appear – for they were not on that wagon when it left here!"

"No – they would not have been," John agreed with a grin. "They are come from Dawlish way – where my wife comes from originally. We sent a message over a week ago to tell of Gil's marriage, and to tell of the house we're building for him. We were very glad when these two said they would come to help as they had no work. We were expecting them yesterday but met them on the road."

It all sounded plausible, but Franks was a born sceptic.

"Show me where this house is to be built!" he ordered.

"That again is easy," John laughed. "Follow us, and we'll show you the plot – it's already marked out, and others are expecting us."

Franks stood aside as Gil got the wagon lumbering on. The sergeant walked by the side of the load down the main street of the village. The wagon stopped at the long gap on the left where people were waiting.

"And who may these people be?" Franks asked.

"First – my wife, Evelyn. Then there is Abel, the smithy and his wife, Faith. The young maid is Ella, their daughter and Gil's betrothed."

Franks saw an opportunity. He pointed at Evelyn.

"Mistress Ramsay – you tell me who these two me may be." He waved at the two on the back of the wagon.

"Why – they be Kit and Luke – come from Dawlish to help us. Work be scarce down that way, so they said they would be pleased to come and share the work."

The two in question played their part magnificently. They jumped down and went to embrace their 'relative', calling her by her name.

Franks watched this reunion for a moment and then made up his mind.

"Hmm," he said. "Then I wish you all luck with your task. Good day!" He marched onwards, down to the mill. If he had bothered to look back, he would have seen the group at the plot breathe a sigh of relief before starting to unload the stone into a large pile.

Gil, with just Kit and Luke, turned the wagon around and went off to get a second load.

------------------ OOOOOOOO ------------------

Wilf Andrews was barely eighteen years old. As he stumbled along in the wake of his two colleagues, he wondered why he had been persuaded to go along with Herrick's scheme. Not for one minute did he doubt that the older man was doing this out of a sense of honour – obeying the demand to get to Tavistock as soon as maybe. He had failed to understand the reasoning of his very experienced sergeant – that delaying was a good idea.

Herrick had had the good sense to insist that they march in single file so that they could at least see the man in front.

No gaps, he had warned. Porter was two steps behind Herrick, and young Andrews a further two steps behind Porter.

Herrick had immediately made for the same path they had left – there had been just enough visibility to ensure that he reached it safely. He turned to his right and stepped out with a will. When they had gone no more than a hundred paces, he was aware that Porter behind him had been talking.

"What?" he turned his head.

"Just said that I thought there were supposed to be tin miners all over this moor – and we have seen nothing of them," Porter repeated.

"Maybe there's no tin where we've been," Herrick grunted in reply. "Maybe they've all given up; maybe there's no tin left here. I don't know!"

Herrick knew that Brown had halted them no more than a mile to the west of Ponsworthy. He, being a well-trained soldier, had been counting his paces, starting again at one every time he reached a hundred. So far, he had counted up to nine hundred. He was convinced that they had gone no more than a further half mile. And then, dimly about two yards ahead of him, he saw that the track divided.

One way went almost back on him to his left. That, he reckoned, went south and east – not the way he needed. The other went at a slight angle off to his right – a bit north of west – and by far the better choice. What he failed to see was a third option, one that led straight onwards. Without any hesitation, he led the way along the one that led slightly right, reckoning that it would soon bear around to the west again. He started counting again.

Had there been good visibility, he would have seen high tors to both his left and right. Instead of going west, he was now going almost due north. He stopped again after reaching what he firmly believed was another half mile.

"Be truthful," Porter growled. "We're bloody lost, aren't we!"

Unable to get any sense of bearing, Herrick knew that to be true. However, he would never admit that.

"Course not!" he replied firmly. "We keep on this way, and we'll start dropping down into the valley where the Dart flows."

Setting off yet again, he gave up counting. He concentrated solely on the faint track in front of his feet. The mist had got no worse, but visibility allowed him no more than two or three paces ahead. Sometime later, he was aware that the track was, at long last, bearing left. With a sigh of relief, he kept on for another hour until Porter, whose senses were the sharpest, called out to him.

"I smell smoke," he announced. "Must be someone living hereabouts – somewhere downwind of us."

Herrick stopped dead in his tracks. He had memorised this route from peering over his sergeant's shoulder at the map. The next habitation should be at Dartmeet – and they had certainly not gone down into a deep river valley. He was a trifle perplexed.

"Go on, admit it," Porter snarled at him. "You've got us completely lost!"

"Must have taken a wrong turning back where the tracks divided," he admitted.

"And that means we are north, south, east or west of where we should be?"

"I don't know," Herrick was forced to admit. "This bloody mist makes a fool out on you."

"And that's precisely what those folk back in Widecombe told us," Andrews spoke up. "So, what do we do?"

"Find shelter, that's what," Porter urged. "Look – we are king's men, so people hereabouts will give us succour."

"You hope!" Herrick muttered. Aloud, he continued, "Let's carry on and find the fire that's making this smoke."

"All you've got to do is to follow that bloody great nose of yours!" Porter grinned.

About a hundred paces more, and Herrick almost walked straight into what he thought was a wall of granite. It turned out to be a rough dwelling. He shuffled sideways to discover a crude door. Drawing his dagger in one hand, he knocked.

The clouds arrived in Bovey just before nightfall. By then, Abel, John and Gil had sunk the main foundation stones into the rough rectangle for the new cottage – aided in no small measure by the strength of young Simon.

Abel straightened his back and looked with satisfaction at what they had achieved on their first day.

"Next, we need the corner posts and the posts for the doorway."

"Tomorrow after dinner, I can start getting them from that old barn," Gil replied if someone is able to help me."

Simon said that he could do that if his father didn't need him in the smithy.

"Nay – shan't need you. You go with Gil and do what you may. We need six at least. We will sink them down about two feet into the corners, so they need to be at least nine feet in length."

"Those posts I saw are longer than that," Gil said. "We can only carry one at a time between us."

"So – you get them here, and on the next day, we will need Edgar to saw them to length – and to nail up the crosspieces."

Edgar was the town's main carpenter – he had said he was willing to lend a hand as and when needed.

As the workforce departed for their supper and early bed, Gil and Ella stood in the middle of what was to be their cottage.

"It's a mite small," Gil observed.

"Small it may be, but it's to be our home," Ella replied, sliding her arm around Gil's waist.

"Aye – that it will be. We'll have the fireplace down the east end so that our smoke goes away with the west wind."

"And we will sit before it and make our plans."

"Your birthday is the next week," Gil reminded her. "I must needs buy you something special."

"Nay, Gil – have Edgar make us our own settle in which we can sit together. That is what I would like most of all."

"I shall do better than that – I shall make it for you."

"And will it hold together?" Ella asked mischievously.

"If it does not, we shall have to sit on the floor!" Gil replied. "Then we shall have some extra firewood."

They ambled off together to get their supper.

Down in the field behind the bakery, one of Franks' soldiers on patrol came across an old sack. He kicked it and found it yielding. He opened the neck and found two sets of uniform clothes. He bundled it under his arm and went to the mill to report his find.

-------------------- OOOOOOOO -------------------

No more than a mile and a half apart, two sergeants sat and pondered their next moves. Brown, in his granite-enclosed hollow, determined that he would not budge one foot until he could see at least a hundred yards ahead. Lovelace, in his barn, came to the exact same conclusion.

Brown's route lay westwards, some two and a half miles to Dartmeet. Lovelace's route was longer to the same destination. First, he would have to travel north, then northwest, and finally west. A journey of a bit over four miles.

Strange to relate, their journeys would take them both past the junction in the tracks where Herrick had gone wrong. Neither was aware of the fact. Neither was aware of the presence of the other, although Lovelace had a suspicion that some of the king's men had *probably* tried to escape over the moor.

Both groups settled down to sleep the hours of darkness away, both hoping that the rising of the sun would break through the mist.

Chapter 13

The Ramsey's were settling down to their second breakfast. As was normal, they had to attend to the shop every few minutes as people came to buy their daily bread – those who had not received a regular delivery. Mary was very used to having her breakfast either standing up or going to and fro to answer the bell.

The table had been cleared, and the family, augmented by the two 'relatives', were at last starting to relax when the bell went yet again. Mary gave a groan and went to answer it. She returned with Sergeant Franks.

"I believe this to be one of your sacks," he said by way of greeting, holding it out for inspection. He was, as the saying goes, flying a kite. His suspicions had been aroused by two things – the arrival of the two from Dawlish and the sack of royalist garb found in the field behind the bakery.

If he had hoped for a look of guilt or alarm on any of the six faces, he was disappointed. He had made the mistake of holding the sack in full view as he entered. Kit and Luke deliberately got up and wandered out of the back door before he even opened his mouth. They started moving logs around and making 'busy' noises.

Mary was behind Franks and so was able to follow her parent's lead. Gil took out his small knife and began cleaning his fingernails. Evelyn managed a blank look. John rose and went to take the sack. He looked at it closely.

"Could be one of ours, I suppose," he said. "But I cannot see any traces of flour in it – so if it indeed is one of ours, someone else has been using it since. Why is this so important?"

"It was found in the field behind your bakery."

"Gil," John said, looking at his son. "Have you been throwing away empty sacks?"

"No, father – they are too useful to be discarded."

"It was not empty when it was found by one of my men," Franks added. "Inside it was two royalist uniforms. On the same day, two men mysteriously arrive from Dawlish. You can see why I have to make enquiries."

Evelyn looked at the sergeant with what she hoped was an amused expression.

"You believe that Luke and Kit be two king's men? That they threw away their uniforms and now pretend to be from my family? I had never heard such a tale! Kit wouldn't know one end of a musket from 'tother!" she ended this with a laugh and looked at John. Both John and Gil joined in the laughter. Mary, after a second, joined in.

"What's the merriment?" Luke asked, poking his head back through the doorway.

"This sergeant thinks you be two of the king's men from the Heath."

"King's men? What, us two? Kit jumps like a startled rabbit every time there's thunder!"

"Where in Dawlish do you live?" Franks would not give up quite yet.

"Nowhere in Dawlish," Luke answered, joining his mate. His local knowledge came to the fore. "'Tis up on headland near to Holcombe. That's two miles at least from Dawlish itself."

Franks knew that there was no way that he could have that checked out before the next day had ended – and he couldn't spare any of his men to do the checking. He satisfied himself with a grunt, turned on his heel, and marched out. Mary ran into the shop and peered out through the side of the window. She ran back in.

"He's gone," she announced. "Going back down to the mill."

"Then we must be very careful to make sure the tale of Dawlish is the only one we speak of – apart from Abel and his family – and they know the truth of it already!" John remarked. "Remember everyone – Luke and Kit are from the Dawlish area!"

Simon called for Gil soon afterwards, and the two set out with a hammer and pick to start dismantling the old barn. By dinner, they had managed to bring back two of the large timbers. They planned to fetch another four at least before nightfall.

Abel arrived at the plot later in the afternoon with another pick and a shovel. He started to dig deep holes for the corner timbers. Things were progressing.

--------------------- OOOOOOOOOO ---------------------

That same morning, three groups of soldiers gazed out at the early light – and they could see for some distance.

In the tiny settlement that went by the name of Babeny, Herrick looked back into the small cott where they had spent an uncomfortable night. The old man who lived there had existed all alone for the past three years – his wife had died of a bloody flux, and their only daughter had married years before and had gone to live in Okehampton. He managed to survive on his small herd of goats – from which he got milk and then cheese – and from a patch of ground where he raised onions and cabbages. He bartered some of his milk and vegetables with another cottager who baked her own bread – and brewed what she fondly believed to be ale.

There was no food for the three renegades – but they had been told of a further cottage where they might be in luck. The old chap was happy to shelter the king's men but was also happy to send them on their way with directions.

"Get thee down this path to the south. Tain't far to the river. Ye will find stepping stones so that ye may cross. Then stay right by the river, and it will take ye to the Big Meet."

It took some moments for Herrick to realise that the old chap meant Dartmeet.

"So, this river is not the Dart, then?"

"Lord bless ye, no. 'Tis the East Dart. Down at Big Meet is where it be joining the West Dart. God speed ye."

Having taken their leave, they set out along the path that led down to the river.

"So much for your river valley!" Porter grunted. "River Dart indeed! We are nowhere near it!"

"One thing I forgot to ask the old man," Andrews muttered. "Where are the tin miners? We don't want to run into any of them. I hear they are a fierce lot and don't like strangers."

"We're armed with muskets and swords!" Herrick replied. "Think we can't see off some miners?"

They crossed the small river on the stones and then started walking along its meandering bank. The old man said they would be at the Big Meet in less than two hours.

--------------------- OOOOOOOOOO --------------------

For the past three days, Sir Stephen Long had been bored – bored almost to distraction. The stannary town of Tavistock had ceased to be a pleasure and had become a place he was only too anxious to escape. This had nothing whatsoever to do with the town itself; Tavistock was a very pleasant town. It had all to do with the fact that Long could see no purpose in remaining there. As soon as he and his fellow officers had arrived, following their headlong flight along the road south of the moor from Bovey, his commander Lord Wentworth had been summarily dismissed as being grossly incompetent.

During the days that followed, remnants of the king's men had arrived in dribs and drabs – tired, hungry, dispirited, and in some cases, verging on the mutinous at the way they had simply been abandoned by their officers.

Troopers Buskin and Ford, from Long's regiment, were particularly vociferous in their condemnation of this neglect. Sergeant Franks had been left behind at the order of the commander of the company. Sergeant Hooper, on the other hand, had joined the headlong flight and had unsuccessfully been trying to instil some order and discipline on the way. He had been less than successful.

Sitting and shivering under a tree on the bank of the River Tavy just outside Tavistock, Buskin was again airing his grievances. He had an audience of about fifty dispirited, ragged, and very hungry soldiers.

"How far have we had to walk?" he shouted. "Over twenty miles, that's how far! And those bloody pansies rode all the way and covered the ground in less than a day! And now that we're here, what do we get? Nothing! That's what we get! There they are in a tavern, quaffing wine and scoffing meat. We have to make do with old bread and hard cheese – and hardly a drop of ale either!"

"That's enough of that!" Hooper called out from behind the group. "You're a soldier – or at least – you're *supposed* to be one."

"Yes, sergeant. I am a soldier – and so are we all, sitting here doing bugger all! Soldiers fight – they don't run away like we had to."

That raised a chorus of agreement from the men packed along the bank.

"And what's for us now, eh lads?" Buskin went on. "Over the Tamar into Cornwall? Up the moor to Lydford and beyond? Down the Tavy to Plymouth? Up on the moor where we can dance around they bloody big stones? One thing's sure, though – we will have to walk there!"

"And they fancy buggers will ride in comfort!" Ford added his voice.

"Yes – not for them a march on sore feet! They made sure they had their horses, whilst we had ours taken without so much as a fight. We are shamed! Shamed! That's what we are!" Buskin was red in the face.

Hooper was in a bit of a quandary. He totally agreed with what his loud-mouthed soldier had said. On the other hand, he was sworn to command them – to keep order and discipline. If Franks had been here with him, the two of them would have attempted to silence what was slowly turning into another shambles. But Franks was not with him. He would be a lone voice. Useless going to his captain – he was playing cards with the other officers, almost as if nothing bad had happened. He said nothing, deciding to wait to see whether or not this got any worse. It was a bad decision.

Ford, not wanting to play second fiddle to his more outspoken mate, then decided to turn things up a notch. He just did it and never for one moment took any heed of the possible consequences.

"Well, my mates," he said loudly to get their attention. "Not for me any more of this! I say we start to fend for ourselves – down to the coast where we can find shelter and food. Who's with me?"

Buskin simply had to add his voice. The alternative would be that he surrendered leadership to Ford, who had always been in his shadow. He was joined by about twenty others. Ford stood up, prepared to start doing what he had said – walking off. Buskin and the other twenty or so stood as well.

"Hold fast!" Hooper bellowed, realising that his previous hesitation had been a gross error. "You are in mutiny against the king!"

"And where is the king?" Buskin bellowed back. "Somewhere safe, warm, and well fed. Not here with us poor sods!"

"I order you to stop where you are. Buskin, Ford, I am placing you under arrest. You others, do your duty and restrain them!"

Nobody made any such move. Buskin, asserting his position, led Ford and the others who were standing back east along the Tavy. Hooper watched in disbelief as twenty-two soldiers simply marched off. The other thirty-one sat where they were in silence. One of them looked at Hooper.

"Best say nothing, eh, sergeant? After all, nobody has counted us; no officer has even been to see us. We never saw anything amiss, did we, lads?"

Hooper was in yet another quandary. If he did as suggested, he knew full well that not one of the officers would notice – or even care if he did notice. But to do nothing was tantamount to approving a mutiny. He didn't like it one little bit. He turned on his heel and marched off. He needed somewhere quiet where he could sit and examine his conscience.

By nightfall, he had done absolutely nothing. Where Buskin and the others were, he had no idea.

Two hours after deserting, Buskin led his small group into Plymstock – where they were, at last, able to steal some food and commandeer a large barn for shelter and sleep. Buskin had some notion of going as far as Kingsbridge and Salcombe, where he thought it possible to get a ship to take them somewhere else. He had no idea then where that 'somewhere else' might be.

-------------------- OOOOOOOOOO --------------------

By that same nightfall, Brown had led his diminished troop down into the Dart Valley and had set up camp in a small wood very close to the meeting of the two rivers. They had again been fed some meagre rations by a small community at a nearby clearing that the inhabitants called Badger's Hole.

Herrick, Porter, and Andrews were not far away – about a mile to the north, sheltering between large boulders.

Lovelace, with his three trackers and two messengers, was also close by. They were on the opposite side of the combined river, silently watching the woods on the other bank. They had counted the king's soldiers, having almost stumbled across them two hours previously.

"They're settled for the night," Brown whispered. "We get back under cover and out of sight and sound. Then you two get going at first light. Make for Ivybridge and report.

Say that we're tracking that group, and by my reckoning, they're making for the high moor to get down via Merrivale."

The two messengers were only too happy with that order. They had not enjoyed being on foot, leading their horses. Back in the saddle, they could cover the distance in a few hours.

Tavistock went to sleep. The remnants of three regiments settled down in the cold and suffered. Their officers fell asleep at their card tables. Hooper stayed awake and wrestled with his thoughts. Buskin and his group huddled under old straw and slept.

Chapter 14

The late January weather decided to add further misery to a very dispirited West Country – in the form of driving sleet. It tore across moor and valley, bringing life almost to a standstill. Back in the town of Bovey, work on the house came to a standstill, even though the roof had been erected and newly slated. The eaves, protruding a good foot beyond the walls, directed the fall into the gulley dug around the house. The inside was bare, the ladder-like staircase still to be built. Access to the upper floor under the roof was still via a ladder. Doors and windows were in place, thanks to iron hinges and catches manufactured by Simon – who had learned that craft from his father.

On the day before work had ceased, Gil and Ella had stood in the middle of the main room, inevitably holding hands and contemplating their future together.

"It will be a fine place to raise our children," Ella said, looking at the new fireplace and its stone chimney.

"If the good Lord sees fit to bless us with such," Gil answered.

"I see three children," Ella was daydreaming. "A girl of six years, a boy of four, and another girl of two. They are sitting before that fire, holding out chestnuts on sticks. I am in the kitchen preparing a good broth, and you are coming in after a day's labour."

"And there is laughter in this house," Gil got caught up in the vision. "Laughter and storytelling before bedtime. The children are well and strong – and learning their letters."

"When are you two going to lend a hand with the lime wash?" came a disgruntled voice from the doorway. They turned to see young Mary, her apron covered in white dots and a large brush in one hand.

Gil and Ella looked guiltily at one another and shared a knowing grin. Yes – lime wash needed to be applied.

Brown and his men had climbed up to the high moor. On the last day before the weather turned, they had seen to their north the highest points of the moor – Wilhays and Yes Tor. They sheltered for the night in a small wood. Not half a mile distant, Lovelace and his small squad watched, having slowly and carefully tracked the king's men for two days. The two messengers had left two days previously but had not as yet returned.

Herrick, Porter, and Andrews had spotted Brown's group the day before but had deliberately held back, not sure of their welcome.

And then, just after a weak sun had awoken all of them, black clouds massed to the west, and an hour later, all were huddled miserably under whatever sparse cover they could find as the sleet came at them, numbing faces and hands, soaking through clothes and rendering every one of them utterly wretched.

Far to the south, Buskin and his entourage remained in relatively clear weather. They had reached the small town of Kingsbridge, where most of them had gone their separate ways. Buskin, Ford, and only two others remained. Luck had been with the four of them as they found that the bridge over the end of the estuary south of the town had collapsed. In return for food and rough lodging, they had volunteered to help in its repair. Flat-bottomed barges were poled out with stones that were slowly and painstakingly positioned under the direction of an experienced mason from the town.

Unknown to Brown, the king's men in Tavistock had been ordered north with all speed. They were headed to Torrington to reinforce the king's army under Lord Hopton.

Cromwell's force had also received orders. They withdrew east along the southern slopes of the moor. They were to meet up with General Fairfax at South Molton – at the north-east corner of the moor.

Lovelace was to be disappointed that his message, having been delivered, had been ignored. Cromwell's force had urgent business elsewhere. The two mounted messengers were ordered to stay with the main body. Lovelace was, in effect, on his own and uninformed.

132

The miserable weather lasted all that day and well into the night, only releasing its stranglehold in the early hours of the following morning. Brown, summoning all his remaining energy, forced himself to do a tour of his men. The first two he came to were in no better state than he was – shivering uncontrollably. The next one he came to was still and as cold as marble. Of the remainder, three more had perished that night, and the rest were in very bad shape. Brown knew that he had to get them moving. To stay where they would mean that none would survive.

The remaining soldiers were roused to their feet. Four bodies were moved under a tree. There was no way they could be buried – the ground was as hard as iron. All they could do for them was to cover them with fallen branches.

"Unless we move from here, we will die here," Brown said through chattering teeth. "We are near the start of the hill down off the moor. There is a settlement down there called Peter Tavy – not more than five miles distant. There, we will get food and shelter."

Whether they would find either of these was just a guess on Brown's part. But without hope of both, he knew that his men would have no heart in trying. He led off at a fast pace – a pace that soon dwindled to a slow march. They were all too weak to keep up that pace for very long.

However, within a mile, they started downhill, and as they did so, the skies slowly cleared to reveal the valley into which they were headed – and a group of small houses from which smoke was arising from chimneys. It was all they could have wished for. Their pace quickened at the sight, and Brown gave up a brief prayer of thanks.

--------------------- OOOOOOOOOO ---------------------

Herrick and his two friends were in no better shape. In fact, Porter was shivering uncontrollably and muttering to himself in what the other two thought to be delirium.

"Poor bugger's had it, I reckon," Herrick muttered to Andrews.

Andrews, in slightly better shape, than the other two, made no reply. He crouched down by the stricken man and started to chafe hands with his own, which were in almost the same state.

"Come on, mate," he urged. "Keep awake, or you will die here."

Porter, if he had been able to hear and comprehend what had been said to him, would not have paid any attention. All he wanted to do was sleep and sleep and sleep. So, he did. Ten minutes later, Andrews found no response at all and sat back on his heels. Tears, which almost froze immediately, sprung from his eyes.

"He's gone," he said to Herrick.

"Just as well – he would have held us up in that pitiful state," came the unfeeling reply.

Andrews regarded Herrick with a look of utter loathing. How, he wondered, could anyone be so heartless and selfish? He slowly summoned his remaining strength and stood up, pulling out his short sword. He had not yet graduated to a broadsword.

He stood over the kneeling Herrick.

"You heartless bastard!" he snarled.

Herrick turned around and regarded the youngster with the sword in his hand.

"Don't be so bloody daft!" he shouted. "In this state we're in; it's every man for himself! We couldn't carry him! We can barely carry ourselves. It's God's way of helping us two to survive!"

"It was God's way of showing us that we should have helped him!" retorted Andrews, almost shaking with anger.

"Grow up!" growled Herrick. "Leave the sod here, and let's get to safety!"

That proved the final straw for Andrews.

"You would leave me here as well – whether I will be alive or dead!" he shouted

Herrick looked up at the youngster as if Andrews had taken leave of his senses.

"Be sure I would – a soldier has to look out for himself. If anyone or anything is a burden, leave it behind, or it may drag you down as well."

"But he was our friend – you must be sorrowful he is gone from us."

"He is now nothing to me – and nor would you be in similar condition!"

Herrick, still kneeling and attending to his pack, turned his head away. Andrews was sick with disgust – and for a short moment, lost all sense of reason. All he could see was someone he had thought of as a friend showing no sorrow at the death – in fact, relieved that the death no longer proved a burden. His right boot lashed out, catching Herrick on the side of his head. Herrick looked back at the young man for a brief moment before his eyes rolled upwards, and he toppled onto his side and lay unmoving.

Andrews stared down at the still form, picked up his pack, then walked away, back in the direction they had come – knowing that not too far distant was the cottage of the old chap who had sheltered them previously. He didn't look back at the man who had died of cold and the man he had possibly killed. He was numb – in all senses of the word.

Brown's squad, numbering twenty only two days previously, was now far fewer - and one of them was heading eastwards.

Chapter 15

To Sergeant Brown, it was as if the sun had appeared both in the sky and on his fortunes. They approached the small hamlet of Peter Tavy, unsure what they would find there. King's or Parliament's supporters? He need not have worried.

Leaving his men at the roadside, he approached the first small cottage and knocked at the door. Steps approached from within – hesitant and shuffling steps. The door creaked open, and a very old head appeared around it.

"Saw you from afar – coming down from the moor. You be king's men!"

So, thought Brown. Nothing wrong with your eyesight! The face, old and creased with wrinkles, held two piercing blue eyes over a broken nose and a mouth devoid of teeth.

"Yes – we are king's men," Brown acknowledged. "We seek food and shelter as we have survived the sleet and cold."

"If you had been parliament's men, I would have slammed the door on you, old as I am. I have but little here to offer you, but if you go another half-mile down the track, you will find a warm welcome at the hall."

"Who is it that would give us this warm welcome?" Brown was cautious.

"That would be Lady Herriot – widow these ten years past."

That name registered somewhere in Brown's still slightly foggy brain.

"Sir Percy Herriot?" he said.

"The very same, young man. Fought beside King Jamie, he did – and perished up on the border."

"Then I thank you for your help," Brown gave him a cheery wave and went back to his men.

Having told them what he had learned, he led the group further down the track and then in at a pair of very imposing iron gates. A little way down a gravel drive, they were accosted by two men dressed in brown and green. Each held the lead of dogs that stood stock still and fixed their eyes unblinking on the soldiers.

"We have been directed here to Lady Herriot," Brown spoke up, halting his men behind him.

"I see you be king's men," the taller one replied. "Her ladyship will make you welcome. Follow us, and we'll take you to the steward."

Another hundred yards and the Hall came into view – very old and covered in ivy from ground to eaves. They were led around the back and into a courtyard where two young serving women were busy beating rugs suspended on a rope.

Clouds of dust arose from their ministrations with wooden beaters.

A door opened, and a man in his middle years looked out at the newcomers.

"Master Steward," the tall guide said. "King's men directed here for food and shelter."

"Then they are welcome," the man said. He looked back into the house and called for attention. Immediately, he was joined by a man in a white apron and by two more serving women.

"Follow into the kitchen, and you shall be fed. Then we shall see to making you warm and comfortable in the hay barn."

They needed no second bidding and trooped into the kitchen, where the cook and his helpers started to pile platters with bread and cold meats.

"You have our thanks, sir," Brown said to the steward.

"I see you are their sergeant," the steward noted. "Come – bring your platter and tell me your story."

He led the way through the large kitchen and into a small parlour. Brown accepted the offer of a comfortable chair very gratefully whilst the steward went to the fireplace and leaned on the mantle. In between mouthfuls of food, Brown related all that had happened from their time in Bovey. The steward listened in silence, then went to sit in a chair opposite the sergeant.

"Lady Herriot will certainly want to make you welcome in person. She is resting at the moment. But I can tell you what news has reached us. Lord Hopton has been given command now and is ordered to garrison the town of Torrington. All who escaped that terrible affair in Bovey have been ordered there to swell his numbers. We have also heard that Fairfax is gathering a large force near South Molton. The force that defeated you at Bovey is making its way there, or so we have been told."

Brown digested all that.

"That will put parliament within easy striking distance of Lord Hopton," he observed.

"Indeed, it will," the steward nodded. "It would appear that Fairfax is hell-bent on driving the king's army completely out of the West Country. And then only the Good Lord knows what may happen thereafter!"

"Then we must needs hurry to Torrington," Brown stated.

"Not in your present state," the steward raised a slight smile. "You need good food and good rest before you attempt any more marching!"

"Yes, sir – you are right on both counts. We are of little use in our present state!"

Having eaten his very welcome food, Brown joined his men, and they were taken over to the hay barn. In little more than ten minutes, all were fast asleep – warm at last and with food inside them.

They were still asleep in the late afternoon when Brown was woken and taken again into the house, through the kitchen, and into the main hall. There, seated in a huge chair and surrounded by soft cushions, sat a very old and very grand lady. Brown gave a little bow.

"Come nearer and sit down on the stool. My old eyes cannot see you properly from this distance," she commanded.

Brown lowered himself onto the stool and waited.

"And now tell me your story," she ordered.

Brown gave an almost word-for-word repetition of the tale he had related earlier to the steward. The old lady listened in silence as Brown wound up with their arrival at the Hall,

"You say that you were commanded by that fop Wentworth!" she said. "My late husband would not have employed that oaf as a woodcutter – far less as a commander in the field!"

Brown was a bit startled. The nobility, in his experience, never spoke to common people in such a manner about one of their own.

"Now Hopton is in a different class altogether," she went on. "A thinking soldier and a man of integrity. I take it you are going to join him."

"Yes, my lady – as soon as we are in a fit state to be of any use."

"Indeed, you must rest and feed properly first of all. You are welcome to stay here for as long as you deem it necessary."

"Thank you, my lady. We are all most grateful for your hospitality. If we may stay for the whole of tomorrow and the night, then we will indeed be fit to march north."

Having been courteously dismissed, Brown returned to the barn where his men were tucking into bowls of broth and fresh bread. He told them that they would be there for the whole of the next day and night. That news was greeted with grunts of pleasure.

Brown ate his supper in as good a frame of mind as he had experienced for a fortnight or more. And then he started to contemplate the journey they would have to make on foot. He reckoned it to be something approaching forty miles. In good weather and properly supplied, that would take two whole days. If the weather turned nasty, they could be on the road for twice that time. He shrugged, burrowed into the straw, and fell fast asleep.

--------------------- OOOOOOOOOO ---------------------

Sergeant Lovelace and his three were in far worse condition than Brown and *his* men. They had welcomed the change in the weather – had, in fact, almost wept with relief as the sun made its reluctant appearance. A mile to the south of Peter Tavy, they wondered for the umpteenth time what had happened to their messengers. All they could do was track Brown's men.

When they had witnessed the fact that their opponents had turned into the grounds of the Hall, they had retreated south to seek shelter. Although the sun shone down, it was still bitterly cold. They had one small advantage – they were trackers and well used to spending days out of doors. But they were still very cold and hungry.

Garvey, who had another skill, managed to unearth a couple of coneys. These, when the men were well concealed in a small wood, were cooked over a small fire. Lovelace knew that they would never starve – they had skills that few others possessed.

When the sparse meal had been completed, and the remains of the fire damped down, Lovelace gathered the others into a huddle. He had been friends with them for enough time to know that each one had knowledge and skills that were of benefit to the group. He wanted all their views before he made a decision.

"Between me and yonder ash tree, I have no idea at all what is happening between us and the king's army!" he stated. "We have had no reply from our messengers; all we know for certain sure is that we're here in this wood and that a few of the king's men are in that big house. Just where our army is – well, they could be on the moon for all I know."

Ratcliffe, who was prone to sit and ponder things, cleared his throat and offered his thoughts.

"King's men be all going west - or they were when last we had knowledge of them. They are mostly without a horse, so they are on foot – as we are. Tavistock seems the likeliest place for them to gather. Those few we have been tracking are close to the town now."

"They are fewer than before," Garvey noted. "Three fewer."

"And they were three fewer before the storm broke about us!" Ratcliffe went on. "Did they go on some mission, or did they perish somewhere that we did not see?"

"Or did they simply run away?" Lovelace wondered. "Our lads gave them a severe beating back in Bovey. Perhaps the three simply left to go their own way."

Haddock had so far not joined in. He was always the quietest of the four, letting things roam about in his brain.

"I reckon they ran off," he said. "What did that lot all look like, traipsing across the moor and looking like they had lost a groat and found a farthing. No – they ran off, and we saw no hue and cry. Maybe the rest were glad to see them go!"

"So – we reckon that lot down in the big house are making for Tavistock. We have no idea where our lot is. All we can do is to carry on trailing our group and see how many they join up with."

And so, Lovelace had made a decision. In all fairness, it was the only one open to him.

--------------------- OOOOOOOOOO ---------------------

Andrews walked blindly along the track. From the direction of the sun, he was able to work out two things. He was heading roughly east, and it was noon or thereabouts. He was ravenously hungry and very tired. All he could think about was the pathetic bundle that was the dead Porter and the huddled bundle that was Herrick – probably now also dead, and at his hand, or boot, to be more precise.

He dimly realised that, should he continue with the sun behind him, he would continue east, and signs of human life would eventually appear when he dropped off the moor. He trudged on until he simply could go no further. Just ahead was another of those granite outcrops. He would sit for a while with his back to one of them, facing the sun.

Despite his best efforts, he nodded off. Still chilled despite the winter sun, he was also desperately tired. With his pack beside him, and his short sword lying on the grass beside his musket, he simply drifted off into a deep sleep.

At about the time that Andrews started his long nap, Herrick awoke – very slowly and painfully. The first thing he was aware of was a deep throbbing on the left side of his head. After some moments, he remembered that he had been kicked by that wretched youngster – and all because he had told the boy some simple truths.

And then he was sick. He also saw things in a strange way. As he lay there, he tried to focus on a large granite boulder some ten yards off. He closed his left eye, and the boulder was there. He closed his right eye and opened the left. The boulder was there still, but quite a bit to one side.

He hoped that, as the fierce pain in his head receded, his sight would go back to normal. He was sick again soon after. That decided him to lay still and wait for some sign of improvement. He closed both eyes and remained as still as he could.

Inevitably, he dropped off to sleep again. He awoke sometime later to find that the pain was still there – and just as fierce. He repeated the experiment with both eyes and was relieved to see that it was more normal. He still felt terrible. He glanced upwards and knew that there were no more than a couple of hours of daylight left. He needed shelter, at the very least.

It took him minutes to get to his feet – where he swayed about alarmingly. He still had his pack, which he painfully worked onto his back. It never occurred to him to pick up his musket. All he knew was that he had somehow to retrace his steps to find the shelter he dimly remembered from the previous day.

With his head throbbing like a clock with every faltering step, he stumbled off on his return journey. Behind him, the sun slowly set behind a tor. As it did so, the cold intensified. He stumbled onwards, veering to the left and right of the faint track.

Suddenly, he was falling, sliding down the almost vertical side of what the local folk referred to as a pixie hole. He came to a juddering halt as his boots contacted the rocky bottom. In despair, he looked up at the darkening hole above him. He knew immediately that there was no way he could climb back out – not with his head throbbing fit to burst. His only hope was to stay there until daylight – when he hoped his head would be a lot clearer. He shut his eyes and was a bit sick yet again.

Just before the light faded completely, he became aware of rustling above his head. He looked up at the rim of the hole and saw three sheep gazing down at him. One of them gave a bleat. Herrick was certain that it was laughing at him.

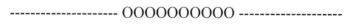
--------------------- OOOOOOOOOO ---------------------

Lord Hopton paced backwards and forwards. The town of Torrington had welcomed him earlier that week. He would have been very happy to have reciprocated that greeting. Having been charged with command of the king's army in the South-West, he was desperate for far greater numbers than he currently had at his disposal.

The fiasco of Bovey back in early January had left him woefully short of manpower. Not for the first time, he cursed at the utter stupidity of Wentworth – now in disgrace somewhere. Whole regiments and their horses had been simply put to flight with almost no resistance. It was, to Hopton, utterly shameful.

All he could do was to set about fortifying the small town as best he could – and hope that Wentworth's men would find their way to him. His intelligence was that Fairfax and his army were heading for somewhere to his east – but were as yet in no position to launch any form of attack. He had time. He also had a dispirited army.

His thoughts were brought to a halt as a junior officer galloped up and came to a stop before him. The young man jumped down and saluted his commander.

"My lord, news of a small host making their way here from Chulmleigh."

"Small host? How small a host?"

"Our outriders reckon somewhere between three hundred and fifty and four hundred, my lord."

"And all on foot, I suppose?"

"So it is reported, my lord."

"Return to the south and bring me the news when you know their real numbers and their condition. Who is leading them? Do you know?"

"I believe it is their sergeants, my lord."

Hopton grunted and sent his young officer on his way. Then, with two of his aides in tow, he made for the tavern in the main square. He threw open the door and stamped across to where a group of senior officers were sitting, warming themselves in front of a blazing fire. Suddenly aware of the presence of their commander, the group sprang to their feet.

"You!" Hopton barked, singling out Sir Stephen Long. "Are you even dimly aware that the remnants of your force are now approaching the town from the south? Are you even dimly aware that they are being led here by your sergeants? Have you no care for them, or are you concerned only with your comfort?"

"Er, no, my lord. I was not aware of that."

"Do you even have a care what befalls them? If you wish to retain any sort of command in my army, you will round up your officers and go and see to their welfare. Get them here as soon as you may – and I want them in fit shape to

150

form part of the defence of the town. Now, get out of my sight and *do something useful!"*

Hopton stumped out, followed by his two aides – who were careful not to let their grins show until they were well behind their commander. He went back to his headquarters and studied maps. He looked up as hooves sounded on the cobbles outside. He saw Long at the head of a group of officers heading south.

"Useless. Bloody useless," he muttered to himself.

Chapter 16

February started much as January had finished – cold winds and clear skies by day and clear skies and frost by night. The town of Bovey woke up each morning to icy roads and wells that had to be broken into by the first to go for water.

Every afternoon, Gil and Ella had been working on the cottage. They sometimes had the help of young Simon. Even Mary had joined the effort until all the walls, both inside and out, had been lime washed.

A proper set of stairs had replaced the shaky ladder, allowing Gil to carry planks of wood up to the larger of the two rooms. He finished making the bed frame and stood back to admire his work. It was large enough and had a straw-filled palliasse, two cushions for pillows, and a feather bed cover.

He looked at it and then looked at Ella.

"No!" said Ella - and fled down the stairs.

Down below, there was a table and stools in the main room, a side table on which would rest their platters – when they had obtained them. In the kitchen a hearth for cooking, a trivet at the side, and a large shelf to hold pots and skillets – when Abel had fashioned them.

Progress had been much faster than either Gil or Ella had imagined. Realistically, the house could be completely habitable in another few days. In a shed at the back of his uncle James' bookshop was the settle that Gil had made. In two more days, it would be Ella's birthday, and Gil planned to set it in the cottage with a special cushion that his mother had embroidered.

Kit and Luke had made the work on the cottage go much faster than anyone had planned. And that was the cause of some consternation in both the Ramsey and Smith households. What to do with the pair now that their supposed help was no longer necessary.

Fit and well-fed, the two had no hesitation in saying that they would make their way back in the direction of their supposed homes. The two families must not trouble themselves further. They had done more than enough.

"That's all well and good," John had replied the previous evening. "But we all know that no home awaits you there. How will you fend for yourselves?"

"We will find work somewhere," Kit assured them. "After all, we're master builders now!"

The next afternoon saw the arrival of two people. The first to arrive at the cottage was Sergeant Franks. Gil eyed him with some disquiet.

"Ah – that's a fine cottage for you and your betrothed. It has been well made indeed!"

"Yes, sergeant – it is just as we planned. And our vegetable beds are dug over again and again – ready for their first planting when the weather warms."

"So, your mother's two relatives will be returning to their homes?"

"They leave tomorrow," Gil answered.

"And so do we," Franks said. "We are called to join our regiment. We will be gone just after daybreak."

Gil did his best to hide a massive sigh of relief.

"Before I leave, I will tell you that I never for one moment believed the story of the two from Dawlish! They are both king's men – but I cannot prove it. Do not even attempt to deny it. But this I will say. When this conflict is over – and over it must soon be – I shall make it my business to return here. If those two are still here, I will pursue them until I have what proof I need. Until then, young man, I wish you good luck with your endeavours."

After he had gone, Gil was eager to get back to his home and report what had been said. But before he could do so, he had another visitor. The bailiff trotted up on his horse.

"That's fine work," he said, looking down at Gil. "Now – that sergeant and his men will be gone on the morrow. So, your two helpers will be no longer needed, I suppose – now that the cottage is nearly completed."

"No indeed, master bailiff. They will also leave tomorrow – back to Holcombe."

The bailiff gave a loud guffaw.

"That's as pretty a tale as I have ever heard," he grinned. "Those two rascals came from the king's regiments that were on the Heath. 'Tis as plain as the nose on your face. They will need a place of safety for some time to come. Tell them to report to the master steward in the morning – rather than send them on a pointless journey towards Dawlish, where they have no home! They have proved themselves able workers. Master steward will have use for them well beyond Parke and its estate. Our master has lands up towards Lustleigh. Some of the properties there needs work done on them. Your two will be safe from prying eyes and will have jobs, food, and shelter."

"Master Bailiff, that is good news! They will be grateful, as are we."

The bailiff gave Gil a cheery nod and rode off. Gil abandoned what work he had intended and ran home to spread the good news. That evening in the house, honey mead was drunk and good health wished. Kit and Luke were mightily relieved that they now had some sort of a future.

--------------------- OOOOOOOOOO ---------------------

The next day, the family waited for the departure of Franks, then sped Kit and Luke on their way. Gil waited impatiently for the end of his delivery, then asked for a loan from Simon. Together, they carried the settle to the cottage and put it before the fireplace, it's back to the front door so that it would shield its occupants from any draughts. The cushion, embroidered with the initials 'G' and 'E' intertwined, sat against one corner. And then, with both families present, he brought Ella to see his gift.

Ella almost shed a tear as she saw what she regarded as the crowning glory of what was to be her new home.

"I'm sure that all of us here would never begrudge you a kiss for your betrothed," Abel boomed.

Ella blushed but reached out for Gil and kissed him as he enfolded her in his arms.

Far to the north, Lord Hopton was again pacing back and forth. In fields around the town, his army was practising and being drilled. He cast a jaundiced eye on Sir Stephen, who was lounging against a post and paring his nails with a short knife. Unable any longer to contain his frustration, Hopton strode over to the man.

"Who is drilling your men?" he asked quietly.

"Why, my sergeants, my lord. Who else would be doing it?"

"You!" shouted the irate peer. "They are your men! You should be training them! You will get over to them now and start practising volley fire by ranks. I shall inspect your endeavours tomorrow morning. Should I find them lacking in proper training, I shall remove you from your command and hand it to someone who has, at the very least, some semblance of duty. Be warned, Sir Stephen – this is your very last chance!"

--------------------- OOOOOOOOOO --------------------

Brown led his remaining men out of the manor grounds. He had personally thanked the Lady, her steward, and the servants for sheltering them and for filling them with good food. Three of his men carried large packs of food to see them well on their journey. At the large gates, he turned to his right and started on the road that would meet up with the way to Tavistock.

Some two hundred yards behind them and hidden from sight in the woods, Lovelace and his three tracked the group.

Nearly half an hour later, Brown came to the junction of their road off the moor and the road that joined the north of Devon with Tavistock, and then Plymouth further south.

Brown turned right again, heading north away from Tavistock.

Watching from their safe distance, Lovelace halted his little group.

"Well, bugger me!" Haddock whispered. "Going north. Now, what do we do?"

Lovelace was in two minds. The obvious course was to follow north to see where the group of king's men were headed – and why. He chose the opposite course.

"We turn south and try to discover why they're not going where everyone thinks they're supposed to go."

Suiting his action to his words, he turned south and went the short distance into Tavistock – keeping in dense cover. About an hour later, he discovered why the group had turned north. Tavistock seemed deserted.

--------------------- OOOOOOOOOO ---------------------

It was about mid-morning when the sheep were counted. The shepherd, a man of middle years, had been shepherding on the moor ever since he had passed his fourteenth birthday. Now in his mid-thirties, he was passing generations of knowledge to his own son. The young lad was nearly ten years of age and had spent the last two years trailing in his father's wake, learning the ways of the moor, the ways of sheep, and how the two things managed to co-exist.

The lad had spotted three sheep standing almost motionless and apart from the bulk of the flock. He went over to hustle them back but stopped in his tracks as he peered down into the pixie hole – much as the sheep had done hours before.

"Da!" he called. His father, being some distance off, didn't hear that. So, the lad emitted his special whistle, and that drew his father's attention. They used that whistle when they needed to get one another's attention – a far different whistle from the many used to control the two dogs.

His father, along with the one dog they had brought for the day, ambled over and joined his son, gazing into the hole.

"Stupid!" was his father's only comment.

"Wonder who he be," his son muttered.

"He is a king's man, that's who he is! Stupid to be wandering the moor all alone like that. Run back to the cott and fetch some rope."

That took over an hour, their cott – a poor thing made of blocks of granite covered in turves and moss – was over two miles from where the sheep had wandered. The lad returned with a coil of old rope over one shoulder. The shepherd took it and put knots along its length, about a foot apart. Put one end over his shoulder and coiled it around his waist.

"Get ye down there and see what's to be seen," he told his son.

The lad used the knots to grasp the rope as he slithered down by the side of the soldier. Herrick had subsided to a kneeling position.

"Cold as ice, da!" he called up. Death int all its forms was hardly unusual on the moor; the lad had tended dead and dying sheep and lambs since a very early age – even the odd traveller who had been misguided enough to attempt a crossing of the moor in poor weather.

"Anything of use?" his father called down.

"Musket, short sword, good boots, purse – nothing more, da."

"Musket be no use – his powder will be ruined, and we have none. A sword is useful, as will boots. What's in the purse?"

"Coin, da."

The boots were prised off the dead and very stiff feet and thrown one by one up out of the hole. The lad took the sword and poked it through his belt; the purse he cut off and stuffed it down his blouse. Then climbed back up again.

Father and son examined the spoils. The purse contained two groats and eight pennies. The shepherd gave a groat to his son and put the rest in his own purse, throwing the empty one back down the hole. The boots would be taken back that evening. The sword had first to be rendered unrecognisable – an easy task. It was placed on a flat granite block, and another smaller one was used to bash out the identifying mark on the blade, just beneath the hilt. It was then pushed through the shepherd's belt.

"We say a prayer over him, da?"

"Suppose we might at that."

Ten minutes later, Herrick was gone and forgotten. Just one more unfortunate who had dared to disregard the moor's eternal rights – and had lost.

--------------------- OOOOOOOOO ---------------------

Earlier that same morning, Andrews had awoken stiff, chilled to the marrow, and ravenously hungry. It had taken him some minutes to realise where he was and the predicament in which he had landed himself. Standing had taken a while, his limbs so stiff that he had to *will* them to move as he wanted. And then, glancing at the sun, set off slowly towards it – east, as he knew.

Ahead of him stretched unbroken moorland, with granite outcrops wherever he looked to left and right. He had been staggering slowly eastwards for about an hour when he was aware that he was slowly descending into a small valley. At the bottom of it, not that far below him, he espied a stream that had strange arrangements of rocks barring its path. Nothing unusual in that, he knew, but these were arranged in almost neat lines across the run of water.

And then he became aware of a group of three men at the most downstream of the little dams. At the same moment, one of the men became aware of Andrews stumbling down the stream. He nudged his colleagues, who also stared at the ragged young soldier.

On the far side of the stream was a large hold dug – an excavation that had taken days to accomplish. Andrews arrived at the stream between two of the small dams and knelt, preparing to cup his hands to get a drink.

"Not there, you girt fool!" came a shout.

Andrews looked sideways at the three men who were walking towards him.

"Drink upstream well past the first stopper!" came the voice of another of the men. "We start washing the spoil here – it be full of tin, or that be our fond hope!"

So, thought Andrews, these are tin miners. He had never seen one before. They looked and sounded like any other man he had met.

"What be a young soldier doing wandering the moor? And a king's man by the look of ye. And looking half starved!"

The third man went back to where they had been standing and brought an old pack out of which he took one of the slightly hard loaves and a small wedge of cheese.

"Now – you sit there and eat and tell us what and why!"

Andrews fell on the meagre food and started chewing. It was washed down with clear water from upstream. Slowly, he recounted to them his story, starting with his view of the disaster of Bovey. He recounted the flight under his sergeant up onto the moor and how three of them had broken off to go their separate way. He made no mention of the death of Porter nor of his attack on the miserable Herrick – just that he had become separated and had decided to make his way back.

He slowly removed his short sword and tossed it onto the tough grass well out of his reach. He wanted the men to see that he posed no threat. He also laid aside his musket and opened his powder horn.

"Wet and of no use at all!" he muttered.

"So – now what for ye? You tell of parliament's men putting king's men to flight – and you be a king's man. Where are both armies now?"

"I last heard tell that King's men were to gather over west to Tavistock. Where Fairfax and parliament's men be, I have no idea. Which favour you? King or parliament?"

The three looked at one another and started to roar with laughter.

"Makes no difference to us!" one of them said, wiping tears of mirth from his face. "Both need tin; both need what tin can do for them. Let them fight one another to a standstill for all we care! We will still search out the tin; we will still take the tin for assay; we will still get a coin for the tin; we will still eat."

"But what for you?" asked another. "You are dressed as a king's man. No matter where you go, folk will recognise you as such – and some may well not like you for it. Best come back with us, rest up and eat. Then add your young strength to ours and dig for tin."

That, to a defeated young man, seemed like the answer to his prayers. Later that day, he went back with the miners to another nearby valley where about twenty of them had built a small village of stone huts. Two old women were labouring over a large cauldron heated by a fire that had been set between large rocks.

The stew went down well, followed by flat loaves of bread that had been baked on hot stones. What was in that stew, Andrews neither knew nor cared. It could have come from four-footed or feathered animals. It was hot and filling. He slept that night on a flat pile of long, dried grasses. Under his old blanket, he slept easily for the first time in days.

-------------------- OOOOOOOOO --------------------

Things had not gone well for Sir Stephen Long. For a start, he bitterly resented the demands placed on him by his new commander. He was much more used to the gentlemanly conduct of his previous 'boss', the now disgraced and dismissed Wentworth. Under that aegis, the senior officers left the day-to-day running and training to the sergeants, who were, in Long's opinion, far nearer in status to the common soldier. Senior officers were for leading into battle. At other times, they were expected to act and comport themselves as gentlemen – not as mere senior soldiers.

His reluctance was mirrored in large part by that of his soldiers. He had harangued them and offered nothing but disparaging remarks as they went through the drill of firing by rank.

The object of the exercise was very simple – to present the enemy with an almost continuous barrage of musket fire. The soldiers were mustered in three ranks, with good spaces in between both ranks and files. The leading rank would present and fire, then retreat through the two behind them to start loading again. The second rank, now the first, would present and fire, retreat, and so on. Thus, an orderly retreat was slowly and inexorably achieved.

Lord Hopton arrived on horseback at mid-morning, accompanied by his two aides and his senior master of musketry. Long presented his small regiment for assessment.

"Proceed!"

The ranks went through the drill, although not a shot was fired – it being thought prudent not to waste valuable powder and shot until needed. All went well until the first rank was again at the front. They had mostly not gone through the drill of charging, rodding, filling, and priming. Some had, but not many. The resulting 'clicks' of hammers meeting pans were ragged and took a considerable time. Those who had fired immediately retreated through the ranks. The others followed when they were ready.

By the time all three ranks had managed to complete two rounds, the result was a tangled mess, not helped by Long's screams of abuse. His junior officers, following the lead of their regimental commander, added to the chaos with screams of their own. Hopton had seen enough.

"Cease this racket!" he bellowed. "Who is the senior sergeant?"

Hooper looked at Franks, who had recently arrived.

"I am, my lord."

"Name?"

"Hooper, my lord."

"Sergeant Hooper. Drill again – and this time, thoroughly. I will see it again after dinner. Sir Stephen – attend me at my headquarters."

A rather disconsolate Long trailed after Hopton and reported as ordered.

"That," Hopton announced, "was an utter disgrace. I believe I told you to drill your men in that exercise."

Long had had enough time to think up a plausible excuse.

"The men are near rebellious, my lord. It would not surprise me if that was all done for a purpose."

"And that purpose being what exactly?"

"To make me appear less than adequate to you, my lord!"

"That was apparent to me some days ago. I needed not that exercise!"

Hopton drummed his fingers on the desktop. "No – there can be no more excuses. You are dismissed. What I shall do with your soldiers, I have yet to determine. I have no further use for you. Leave!"

That afternoon, Hooper was able to demonstrate that the small regiment *could* carry out the exercise in an orderly manner. All Hopton could do was to find some officer capable of taking command – not the easiest task!

--------------------- OOOOOOOOOO --------------------

As the light faded, Gil barrowed the last of his cut logs to the cottage, set them into the covered wood store, and took sufficient of them in so that he could light the fire to start to dry out his new home.

A short while later, a good fire was drawing nicely. He deliberately threw a damp log onto the top and went outside to view the top of the chimney. To his immense satisfaction, smoke started to emit from the chimney and from nowhere else.

He would spend the night on the floor by the fire but not in the upstairs bed. That would be kept unused and tidy for his and Ella's first night together.

Work was finished at Kingsbridge – the bridge was now fully repaired and strong. Buskin and his mates, finding themselves unemployed, spent a final night together in a tavern. In the morning, they would all go their separate ways, discarding uniforms as they went.

No more soldiering for them.

Chapter 17

Gil awoke several times in the night. The floor was hardly conducive to restful sleep. By dawn, he woke for the final time and placed turves carefully over the fire and then went home to deliver the bread. He would make sure he had a more comfortable resting place for the coming night.

Before going back to the cottage, he borrowed two sacks and filled them with straw. They would at least afford his hips relief from the hard floor. Satisfied, he went back home to help with chores – cutting wood, measuring flour into the bins, sweeping the yard.

Three more nights would, he believed, warm and dry the cottage.

--------------------- OOOOOOOOOO --------------------

Kit and Luke soon settled into their work up in the small village of Lustleigh – there was plenty of work for them to do. Forewarned by the steward, the local reeve had showed them into a disused and somewhat dilapidated cottage. In return for food and lodging, they were to renovate that cottage and then start on another two that were in similar condition.

Timber, lime, nails, tools – all were provided for them, and they set to with a will, knowing they were indeed lucky to have found so good a retreat.

"Wonder who is to have this cottage?" Kit said on their first morning of work.

"Some lucky family, I suppose. The faster we do it, the sooner we lose this place and have to move into another broken-down lodging!" Luke replied.

"But we cannot linger over the work. It will surely be noticed. We had the best move forward with it - but do it carefully so that there can be no complaint. This is too good a billet for us to lose," Kit decided. Luke could do nothing else but agree.

And so, a very well-refurbished cottage was started, earning them praise from the villagers and from the reeve himself.

One of the local maids, the daughter of a woodsman, made a point of passing the cottage far more often than her duties required. She had noticed Luke the first day the two had arrived. She was fifteen years old and had bright copper hair in abundant waves.

Luke had noticed – he would have had to be blind not to do so. By the third day, they were exchanging smiles. By the fourth, smiles were accompanied by waves.

"For the love of heaven, speak to the maid!" Kit growled as the girl disappeared into her own home. "At the very least, ask her name!"

"Oh, I dare not. Her father wields a mighty axe as he sets off for work each morning."

Kit was the one who made the move. As the girl went past the first time the next morning. He leaned out of the window and called out softly.

"He is called Luke," he grinned.

"I am called Meg," she replied, making sure she looked straight ahead and not at the open window.

"There!" Kit poked his mate in the ribs as the girl moved out of earshot. "She is named Meg. Now, what are you going to do about it?"

"I have no idea," Luke admitted his face a picture of indecision.

"Every day, she walks past here with that basket over her arm. What you must needs do is find out where she goes and for what purpose. Tomorrow morning, leave here before her and hide down the path. I will make enough noise for two."

As luck would have it, February was as fickle as it usually was – and it poured with rain, a vicious, cold rain that kept all sensible people indoors. Some unfortunate souls, like cattlemen, shepherds, and woodcutters, had no choice. Meg apparently did, and there was no sign of her all day. Luke moped around and buried himself in limewashing the interior walls.

It was well into the afternoon before the rain let up. Luke was just about finishing the wall under the main window and was on his knees below the sill. The window was ajar so that fresh air could circulate but not wide enough that rain could enter.

"A good day to you, Luke," came a soft voice.

Luke bobbed up so quickly that he bumped his head on the inside projection of the stone sill. He was just in time to see Meg passing around the corner and out of his sight.

"God's bunions!" he swore, rubbing his head and glaring at Kit, who was doubled up laughing.

--------------------- OOOOOOOOOO --------------------

Ella had spent some afternoons with Gil's aunt Avril – possibly the most knowledgeable person in the village where plants and herbs were concerned. Rows of seeds were in paper packets, each one labelled in Avril's neat hand.

By the side of the table stood a bucket containing that newcomer to the vegetable patch – the potato. Left alone for a couple of weeks, each one had sprouted many little shoots.

"I have never grown a crop of them myself," Avril said. "But I do believe that you plant them shallow and then heap the earth up into a mound above them."

"They are strange things," Ella remarked, picking one up and examining it. "Mother has given us them to eat once before. She boiled them in water, then cut them open and served them with eggs. They tasted nice with egg but had little taste without."

"They will also take much of your ground. So, you will have to make a decision on whether or not to plant them. Perhaps a few as a test?"

In the front room of the house, James was attending to a customer who was complaining of stomach cramps. He advised a concoction of crushed arrowroot immersed in weak ale. Having crushed some to powder, he sold the packet to the customer and came back into the back room. He ran his eye down the seed packets.

"Cabbage, kale, onion, garlic, leek, carrot, parsnip, turnip, peas, beans – a veritable feast for any kitchen," he laughed. "Are the beds ready yet?"

"Oh, indeed they are," Ella replied, nodding. "Not only dug and manured but marked out with sticks."

"And have you yet seen Reverend Forbes to settle the date?"

"No, alas. Master Garlick reports that he is still attending Prince Charles but is expected back in two or three days. Gil celebrates his birthday next month on the third day of March – so Master Garlick has written that in and has already published the banns."

"And do you look forward to your marriage to my nephew?"

"Oh, without question. If it were tomorrow, I would be dancing around the room!"

"Have you ever considered how lucky you be? Common folk like us can marry who we want. Those more nobly born have to marry where they are bid!"

"And just to increase wealth! That always seems to me to be no basis for a life together! I marry Gil because I love him – and he loves me – or so I do believe."

"That young man would cross the seven seas for you, silly girl! He loves you, and it's plain for all to see."

Ella went quiet for a while, hugging herself and happy that all would be well. Back at her home, she was quietly singing to herself as she helped prepare supper for her parents and young brother. Simon, now as tall as his sister and weighing almost twice as much, came through from the smithy and made a grab for a pastry, only to receive a rap on his knuckles from a wooden spoon.

"Your hands be filthy with the coals from the fire!" he was told by an irate Ella.

174

"Tis my own muck and will go in my own mouth!" he retorted.

"You wash first – then you may eat."

"And I suppose you will bar me from your own kitchen when you and Gil are wed."

"Only if you try to enter with the day's muck on you!"

"Yes, mistress. Certainly, mistress," he grinned, dancing out of reach of the wooden spoon.

And that brought Ella up with a jerk. Not so long from then, she would indeed be Mistress Ramsey, her hair covered and mistress of her own home. No longer young Ella, blacksmith's daughter; Mistress Ramsey, wife of Master Gil Ramsey. It was a slightly sobering thought.

--------------------- OOOOOOOOOO ---------------------

Lovelace peered through the fronds of bracken that grew in profusion along both sides of the lane. He seemed to have spent the better part of the last year peering through fronds of bracken, low bushes, through dense packed trees. What sort of a life is this for a grown man, he thought? I might just as well have been born a deer or a brainless sheep!

He wriggled back to the small clearing where his three men were lying down and trying to keep warm. Never without food of some sort, they were moderately content.

For three days, they had trailed after the sergeant and his remaining men, having no other real option open to them.

"Not far from the town now," Lovelace told them. "There seem to be no side paths for them to follow – so it's Torrington, or so it would seem."

"How far more?" Haddock grunted, looking closely at the sole of his right boot. It was wearing thin in places.

"No more than two miles – or that's how I reckon it."

"Then what?"

"The good Lord above only knows," Lovelace replied, shrugging. "Right – enough of lying here. Up and away!"

The four started out yet again, keeping within the bracken. They eventually stumbled across a deer track that went parallel to the path. Garvey, who was leading, regarded the imprints in the soft earth and counted one stag and five hinds. His mouth salivated at the thought of so much venison.

An hour later, he held up a hand to halt progress. He crouched down, his three colleagues immediately melting into cover to left and right. He crawled back to Lovelace.

"Looks like they've arrived," he whispered. "I can see the town about another mile distant. Our lot just got stopped by an outpost – maybe twenty or so royalist dragoons."

Lovelace digested this information, then silently signalled the other two to close on him.

"Torrington it is, then," he spoke very quietly. "Seems to me that this is where they are in numbers."

"That's all well and good," Ratcliffe muttered. "But what do we do – where do we go?"

"We get right into a deeper cover for a start," Lovelace decided. "Now we know there is a big gathering here, and there is little else we can do. So, we rest up, then go south until it be safe to head east again. We be bound to come across our lot sooner or later."

"You reckon so?" Haddock was sceptical. "South be the moor!"

--------------------- OOOOOOOOOO ---------------------

Sir Thomas Fairfax read the letter for the third time. It had been hastily scrawled by one of his agents and sent south by fast messenger. On the western outskirts of Exeter, his army was ideally placed to react to the latest intelligence. He called his senior commanders. He waved the crumpled letter aloft.

"It would appear that the king has sent troops south from Oxford," he announced to the assembled officers. "That can mean only one thing – they intend to meet with Hopton and join forces. That I will not allow! Their journey is at least three times the journey we must take to keep us between them and Hopton. We will head for South Molton. That is near enough to Torrington. We will be ideally placed to stop any such meeting – or to march on Torrington itself."

By the next morning, the parliamentary army was well on the road north-west. By noon, outriders had passed straight through Crediton and were well on the way towards Chulmleigh.

By nightfall the following day, Fairfax had settled his army around South Molton – much to the consternation of the local inhabitants, who viewed this New Model Army with apprehension – and locked themselves in their homes.

--------------------- OOOOOOOOOO --------------------

Hopton, meanwhile, was doing his level best to garrison Torrington. The had about 2,000 Cornish troops and 3,000 others gathered from Devon, Dorset, and Somerset. He set some to erect barricades on the south and west of the town.

One of his officers, charged with supply, decided that the church of St. Michael was the ideal place to store the many barrels of gunpowder. Brushing aside the horrified remonstrations of the local vicar, he had his sweating soldiers pile over 80 barrels of powder along the side aisles. He then arranged soldiers to man the supply lines to the forces defending the barricades. Militarily expedient it might have been. Sacrilegious it most certainly was. The vicar rallied support from the town burgesses - but all were ignored.

-------------------- OOOOOOOOOO --------------------

By the middle of the second week of February, the weather had again decided that it had not finished with winter – it started to sleet again. The inhabitants of Bovey shrugged their shoulders and got on with life, thankful that it was not going to bury them in deep snow.

The previous autumn's harvest had been good, so there was sufficient food to last until the better weather allowed more to be either produced or bought in. John and Evelyn were concerned that the mill might run out of grain – no grain, no flour for bread making. They were assured that there was enough grain stored to last at least another three weeks. After that, it was in God's lap!

From the back of his plot, Gil gazed out at the Heath to his south. Little sign remained of the rout of the royalist forces or of the fact that some hundreds of troops had camped there. He turned back to look at the vegetable beds in their neat rows. The beds had been turned again to benefit from overnight frosts – it helped to break up the soil. Why this should be, he had no clear idea but trusted his Aunt Avril and Ella – who had been learning assiduously all winter long.

The Reverend James Forbes had returned to the parish the day before and had asked Gil and Ella to meet him so that he could discuss the wedding ceremony – which was due to take place the day after Gil's birthday. That would be in twenty-two days, Gil reminded himself.

He knew that Ella, her mother, and his own mother had been busy making the wedding dress – and had forbidden him to even ask about it, never mind look at it. Gil had taken a suit of his best clothes to old Mistress Wilkins – the local seamstress – so that she could make sure that they were sound in hem and stitching. Every night, he took out his best-buckled shoes and polished them. They were now almost painful to look at, being polished like a pair of mirrors.

The cottage was certainly ready for its new occupants. All the internal plaster and limewash had dried out, as had the timbers. Some of those had dried out a bit too fast and had necessitated new pegs to be fashioned and driven in to hold joints together properly.

He went home for a wash before calling for Ella. Hand in hand, they walked up to the church, only to be glared at yet again by Hubert and Mercy Green – who were out for their daily walk. Those two walked a good two feet apart, dressed soberly in black from head to foot. The sleet had given up for the day an hour before, allowing Ella and Gil to arrive at the church cold but dry.

"That is sinful behaviour!" Hubert had muttered to his wife as the two young people passed them with barely a nod in their direction.

"Sinful and brazen!" Mercy agreed with a sniff. Hubert walked with his hands clasped behind his back. Mercy walked with hers clasped in front, almost in an attitude of prayer.

Gil and Ella did nothing to lighten the situation by looking at one another and bursting out laughing.

Just out of earshot, Gil turned to Ella.

"They have no children, do they?" he said.

"I wonder why that is?" Ella giggled.

They entered the church and made their bows towards the altar. Long gone were the days of genuflecting and making the sign of the cross.

"Aha, here are our two lovebirds; come to see an old man," the Reverend Forbes rose from where he had been sitting in the front pew, reading a passage from Leviticus. He was wondering if it could be used as the basis of a sermon but had decided that it was far too obscure. No – it would be back to Exodus.

"Come – sit with me here," he said, shuffling along the pew. He was a round and jolly man in his fiftieth year. He was happiest when conducting marriages and baptisms; saddest when conducting funerals. He was pious and respectful when conducting morning service, almost rapturous during evensong when his choir raised their voices in sweet harmony.

He briefly outlined the marriage service, with which both young people were already familiar. Then turned to other matters.

"I'm recently returned from the Prince of Wales," he informed them. Gil and Ella already knew this but waited respectfully for him to continue. James Forbes was loquacious – but one had to wait for information as he was also long-winded.

"The situation is bad, very bad," he went on. "All seems confusion. The king's forces are in disparate places and poorly led by all accounts. However, His Majesty has great hopes that his force sent south from Oxford will join with the Lord Hopton. He has great regard for Hopton, although I hear that the Lord Grenville is not best pleased."

"Does that mean that a great battle will be fought?" Gil asked.

"Almost certainly," Forbes nodded, setting his jowls quivering. "That scoundrel Fairfax will not sit by idly and let the two forces gain the ascendancy. It is to be regretted that Fairfax is a crafty general and employs excellent tactics. He is served by able commanders. Would that we had such expertise!"

"Surely the king cannot be utterly defeated," Ella was aghast at the thought.

"That is not the way of things," Forbes shook his head, setting his jowls wobbling yet again. "Fairfax and Parliament under Pym require the king to agree to what is tantamount to a sharing of power. If the worst were to happen and the king's forces defeated, they would renew that demand – and it is one that His Majesty simply cannot contemplate. He will insist upon his divine right, as God's anointed sovereign, to rule absolutely – and without yea or nay from parliament!"

There followed a minute or two of silence before Gil asked what might happen when the king refused to comply.

"I dare not contemplate," Forbes said quietly. "Things cannot continue as they are with a steadfast demand from parliament and a steadfast refusal from the king. Somehow or other, the two sides must reach a compromise. I pray for that daily!"

"Then so shall we," Ella said, suiting the action to words. She fell to her knees and whispered a silent prayer. Gil, not quite as committed to religious observance, joined her. Forbes sat silently, his hands folded, and his eyes shut. He did not like what he saw in his mind's eye.

Chapter 18

The next day, there was a meeting in the village square. In cold, hazy sunshine, most families were present as Rev. Forbes, and the Bailiff broadcast the news – or the news as they understood it. The address was listened to in near silence.

There was still no news of the Lord of the Manor – Lord John Vickery. Some supposed him to be with the king's army somewhere; others were convinced he was with Parliament. One other notable absence was the Member of Parliament for the area – Sir John Northcote. But, as he was known to be a supporter of parliament and its views, he was not missed.

Also absent were Hubert and Mercy Green. They were notorious for their anti-royalist views, being strict Puritans. They had often been heard condemning the king as 'that vile pope's puppet'.

Whilst the vast majority of the village supported the king as their rightful ruler, they wanted no truck with Catholicism. It was widely held that the queen, Henrietta Maria, was urging her husband for much closer ties with Rome – and she was hugely unpopular as a result.

After the vicar and the bailiff had answered questions to the best of their ability, the meeting broke up into smaller groups. The Ramseys – John, Evelyn, James, Avril, Gil and

Mary – joined up with the Smiths and Master Garlick, the churchwarden.

"Please – come and accept our hospitality," James urged. "For a start, we shall be out of this cold wind!"

"And I have made a batch of my sweet pastries," Avril added as an extra inducement.

The interior of the apothecary's house smelled equally of sweet herbs like mint and rosemary but also leavened by the more bitter ones of mallow. Nevertheless, it smelled wholesome and welcoming as the large group settled around the blazing fire – the senior members on settle and chairs, the more junior on stools.

Avril bustled in from the kitchen with a pewter platter piled high with pastries that she had stuffed with damsons and plums – the previous season's fruit that had been preserved in stoppered jars. James made himself useful by filling tankards with ale.

"These are delicious," Master Garlick said around a mouthful of pastry. "But how have you sweetened them – damsons can be sharp to the taste."

"Honey – just honey," Avril replied. "But what of the news we have just heard. Can it be that parliament wins this terrible conflict?"

"My dear," Old Garlick replied, "parliament won this conflict a while ago. They have proved themselves invincible in both battles and stratagems. The talk of further battles is futile, for parliament will win them without question. No, that conflict is over and settled. What is not over and settled is the manner in which the realm be governed. The king's position is weak, having lost the armed dispute. But his insistence on his right to govern by divine authority is not diminished by the slightest degree. He will certainly insist on that right – to govern unopposed as Almighty God's anointed sovereign."

"That, I have never been able to reconcile," James shook his head. "Yes, he received that anointing at his coronation. But he is just a man like any here. Does he truly believe that he rules in God's name?"

"Yes – that has always been his insistence."

"Then why has he sometimes called a parliament, albeit of short duration?"

"That, I cannot answer," the churchwarden admitted.

"To present his decisions in a public manner?" Abel suggested. "He is my sovereign lord, and I support him – like all here. Parliament has presented him with many grievances – grievances that I know have wide support. To refuse even to countenance that a mere one of those grievances may have merit is surely to inflame matters more than they already be!"

"Does he truly believe that God has given him wisdom in his rulings? That he may never be judged wrong by mere mortals? That anyone who dares question him is guilty of some sort of heresy?" Gil thought aloud. "If so, then he sets himself equal to God – and that cannot be right!"

The discussion went on far into the afternoon. It went on until Abel could contain himself no longer.

"I need my dinner," he demanded. "We are never going to find an answer – and I am starving with hunger!"

That met with universal approval. Gil and his family went home, as did Abel and his family. Master Garlick accepted an invitation to dine with James and Avril – during which the matter was turned over until no conclusions were reached, the lamps had to be lit, and Garlick went home.

"Young Gil made a telling point," James said to his wife as they ate a quiet supper.

"He sees our king sitting upon a throne in heaven. Surely, that cannot be what the king truly believes," Avril replied.

"This is all going to end badly – parliament now enjoys such a position of power that they are not going meekly to surrender that power to a king that they regard in such poor light."

"I fear you have the right of it," his wife nodded. "Come, let us spend the evening on other matters – or this one will surely drive us both to distraction."

--------------------- OOOOOOOOOO --------------------

No such matters of kingship or politics invaded the thoughts of Luke, starting work on the next cottage. Weather conditions had frustrated his plans to follow and, hopefully, speak to the daughter of the village woodcutter. Sleet, bitter winds and thick frost had intruded into his and Kit's plans.

And then, a miracle of miracles, a day dawned bright and cold. Surely, Luke reasoned, Meg will now resume whatever mission takes her away from the village. He crept out of the cottage and secreted himself behind a large clump of hazel, waiting for the girl to pass by.

He could not see back along the lane into the village – nor the path immediately opposite his hiding place. But he could see the path beyond the first bend. His heart skipped a beat as a slim figure, topped by a blaze of auburn hair, and carrying a large empty basket, emerged into view. He waited until she had passed around the next bend before silently following. He dodged behind a large tree and watched the girl take a side path into the woods. Surely not, he pleaded – surely, she was not going to meet with her father!

He followed as carefully as he could, turning into the side path and along the first two twists and turns. Without warning, he found himself in a clearing, Meg standing in the middle of it and looking directly at Luke with a cheeky grin on her face.

"Well, Master Luke. This has taken you some time, has it not?"

"You knew I was following you?" Luke stammered.

"Certainly, I knew. I was brought up by a woodsman. I know the sounds of the woods – and yours are not one of them!"

"Please, I mean you no harm – I just wanted to speak with you," Luke was worried that his stealth could be misinterpreted.

"If I had thought you had evil intent, I would have borrowed a knife from my father. I know you and your friend to be king's men – or that you *have been* king's men. So, Master Luke, what speech would you have with me?"

Luke shrugged with a hopeless gesture. "Now that it comes to the point, I have no clear idea. I just wanted to be in your company."

"And why would you want the company of a woodcutter's daughter?" Meg was provoking him unmercifully.

"Because you are very beautiful!" Luke blurted out, going red with embarrassment.

"And because of my beauty, you believe my conversation would be just as interesting? You may find that my looks hide an empty head!"

"You are mocking me!" Luke stamped a foot in frustration.

"Nay, Master Luke. I am intrigued. I thank you most sincerely for your pretty compliment. Now – before my walk is rendered without purpose, come with me, and I'll satisfy your curiosity."

She turned her back and walked on, back through the wood to another, larger clearing. Luke trailed in her wake. Meg stopped before a stand of elm trees and set down her basket. From it, she took a small tool and started peeling bits of bark, taking each piece and placing it in the basket at her feet.

"There is a wise woman in Lustleigh – and she makes concoctions for people with rheums and other ailments. The bark of elm is something she uses – and I come here to gather it for her."

"Oh!" was all that Luke could muster. He had never heard that elm bark had any use other than to protect the trunk of a tree.

"And now you know the purpose of my walk. You may tell your friend so that two curious minds, rather than just one, may be put to rest. Surely, there is no other reason for your pursuit?" Meg was taunting him again.

Luke, had he been a mere child instead of a grown man, would have hopped about in frustration.

"You know full well there is another purpose," he stated. "I need to know you better – to become your friend. I am smitten with you – and you know it!"

"Again, Master Luke, you flatter me. So, if the weather be kind, you might want to meet me here again on the morrow. I would know more of you – where you are from and what your intentions are now that you have most obviously finished with soldiering."

"Then I will most certainly meet with you here, should the weather permit. And now I must needs get back, or Kit will be working all alone – and he will not be best pleased!"

"Until the morning, then, Luke."

"Aye, Meg. Until the morning."

Kit pestered him unmercifully until Luke had given him a fully detailed account of his little adventure.

"She is as intrigued as you be," he remarked. "Else, why should she want to enquire more about you."

"That, Kit, is my fondest hope!" Luke grabbed up a saw and set to with a will.

Preparations for the defence of Torrington were almost completed. The wooden barricades to south and east were high enough to permit defenders to fire above them but stout enough, the defenders hoped, to withstand an assault.

The morning of the 14th of February was overcast with the promise of cold rain – or so the local inhabitants believed. Away north of the moor, they were well used to being on the receiving end of the lashing rain that battered the moor in winter – not as bad as on the high moor but bad enough to be lashed by the storm's northern edge.

Rumour was rife in the small town that parliament with its army were fast approaching from the east. Like all townsfolk that were garrisoned by an army of any colour, they feared for their lives and their livelihoods. In addition, they were incensed that their church had been used to store many barrels of gunpowder – not only for its desecration of their church but also for the danger it represented. The inhabitants of Torrington were not happy.

In similar measure, the king's army garrisoned there was also far from happy. If the rumours reaching them of the danger coming from east of the town proved to be anywhere near accurate, they were either going to be very hard-pressed – or in mortal danger.

Lord Hopton was similarly unsettled by the rumours – substantiated in part by scouts that reported back at regular intervals. But, unlike a great many of the men he commanded, he was not daunted. His duty was clear – hold the town and try to meet up with the king's men, now reported to be advancing southwards through Gloucestershire. He would not waver.

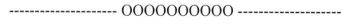

Not that many miles to the east of Hopton, the parliamentary army, some 10,000 strong, bypassed the settlement of Umberleigh and made camp for the night. It was Fairfax's intention to send a probing force to find out the strength of the opposition. If the next day proved fair, he would follow his plan. He gathered his generals and drew them into conference – so that all knew exactly what part they and their soldiers were expected to play. Night fell, and the clouds gathered – not the best omen for the following day.

Driving rain put paid to the plan. All morning it sheeted down from the west, making life miserable for potential attackers. The defenders in the town fared a bit better, having access to shelter of some form or another.

Fairfax sat quietly in his tent. He was in no hurry. The plan was good. All it needed was for Almighty God to smile dry weather on North Devon – and he was prepared to wait for that gift to materialise – as surely it must.

By nightfall on the 15th, the rain ceased as suddenly as it had begun. Fairfax sent for Cromwell and gave orders for the probing force to start forward before dawn.

-------------------- OOOOOOOOOO --------------------

Tin mining on Dartmoor had been going on for centuries – and had imposed certain routines on those who engaged in it. Rain, the heavier, the better, was looked upon as a blessing rather than a curse. It loosened the ground, making it far easier to excavate the rocks – once it had ceased.

Andrews had quickly been assimilated into the little village – joining the most unskilled of the teams – those whose job it was to dig out the rocks and the loose stones. He arose from his straw pallet every morning as the dawn broke, ate a meagre breakfast and set out with the team to where the more experienced miners had designated as the site to be dug.

It was hard, unremitting work and required stamina as well as brute strength. But it allowed him plenty of time to think. Could he endure life up on the moor and become a miner? Could he simply walk away and find employment somewhere else? Could he abandon the moor and find the king's army so that he could take up the life again that he had been accustomed to?

If the third alternative, where would he find the army to join? The last he knew of them was that Tavistock was the intended meeting point. But that had been many days ago. It would also require a long walk across the moor. Even if he managed it, would they still be there? People there would probably be able to tell him where they had gone. No – there were far too many unknowns for that to be a feasible option.

Anyway, he had neither musket nor sidearm, his uniform abandoned for a borrowed set of clothes more suited to the work of mining.

A life spent up on the moor was hardly attractive. Despite the fact that he had been accepted and allowed work in return for food and shelter, he slowly accepted the fact that it was not for him.

That left him with only one option – to depart and seek a life elsewhere. But where? His home was many miles and many weeks of walking away. His thoughts turned to the last village he had known – Bovey. Whilst encamped on the Heath, he had thought it a peaceful and prosperous little place. Added to that was the fact that it was staunchly for the king. Yes, he decided, levering a stubborn rock from its bed, he would make his way back there. He would keep back some bread and cheese every day until he had enough for two days' rations. The drink was no problem – the moor was riddled with rivers and streams. All he had to do was to walk south to the unmistakable double outcrop of Hay Tor, then follow the track east, down off the moor, and there would be Bovey Village.

He was not fool enough to think this would be easy. It was still winter – cold and unpredictable. But if he started off in dry weather, he should at least make Hay Tor. And then it was all downhill. East would be Bovey; south would be Ashburton. Either would do. He was young, fit and strong. Work should not be hard to find.

The first probe at the defences of Torrington proved to be anything but easy. Musket fire from over the barricade proved a fierce deterrent. Cromwell, commanding the probing force, changed tactics and concentrated on one point. He called up more troops and soon managed to force a gap through which hundreds of soldiers poured. Fairfax ordered many more into this rather restricted bottleneck. In the town itself, with parliamentary soldiers in vast numbers, it all became concentrated in a small area.

The push of the pike was the only sensible tactic in that tight environment. Such tactics end with a struggle of attrition – who had the greater numbers? Who had the greater force of pike? Fairfax did – and inexorably, during the early hours of the battle, Hopton's army was pushed slowly and remorselessly backwards.

Around the periphery of that sweating men, others were using muskets and carbine to winkle out smaller pockets of resistance. The struggle very slowly approached nearer to the church.

After three hours, Hopton's army was in a hopeless situation. Many already lay dead or dying from the push of the pike. Many more had been taken, prisoner. The church was now impossible to reach so that supplies of powder could be brought out to the retreating remnants.

Nobody ever admitted to being responsible for the decision to force the captured soldiers into the church. Possibly a junior officer somewhere thought it a good idea – a safe place to quarter them – and easy to guard. Whoever it was, over 200 king's soldiers were packed into the church, with a few of Fairfax's soldiers' mounting guard on them.

Nobody ever found out where the errant spark came from. It could have come from anywhere – a musket or carbine, a stray spark from a burning building. But one spark was all it took.

Without any warning, there came a thunderous explosion as over eighty barrels of gunpowder blew up as one. The church literally disintegrated. The prisoners died; the guarding soldiers died; many townsfolk died or suffered horrendous injuries. The area around the church was bombarded with falling debris – falling from a great height. Stone, wood, and lead rained down and took many more lives and crushed limbs.

Fairfax himself had a very narrow escape as a large piece of debris thudded into the ground, literally two feet away from his horse, nearly unseating him.

It was literally the last straw for Hopton's army. They fled the town and ran for the border with Cornwall.

The battle of Torrington was over by nightfall on the 16th of February. It had, unlike Bovey Heath, been a fight between armies. Bovey's had been a rout.

--------------------- OOOOOOOOOO --------------------

That night, Sergeant Hooper took a final look at the jagged cut in his left arm. A piece of wood from the church, a piece no longer than his thumb, had embedded itself in his forearm. He had pulled it out, wrapped a piece of cloth around the wound, placed the splinter in his pocket, and then carried on leading his men in harrying men of the king's army.

Now, in the relative peace of the night, he unwrapped the small wound and saw that it was still just that – a jagged tear with no signs of festering at its edges. It would heal. He took out the splinter and looked at it. It was of oak and could have come from any source - a beam, a pew, even a part of the lectern or rood screen. He neither knew nor cared. But he would keep it as his own souvenir of the battle.

Only one of his men had perished. Crushed by a large piece of falling masonry rather than by any enemy act. Two had been injured. One lay with bandages swathed around his head – a much larger splinter had gouged a furrow through his scalp. Another was with the surgeons having the shattered remains of his lower right leg removed – shattered by a musket bullet.

Fairfax was content – it had been a great victory. He had simply put aside any memory of the falling debris that could so easily have killed him. He wondered where his opponent was at that moment. Hopton would, he knew, never abandon his men. Therefore, he would be somewhere near the border with Cornwall – perhaps already mustering the remains of his decimated army somewhere like Launceston or Callington.

He allowed himself a grunt of satisfaction, knowing that royalist resistance in the West Country was as good as over.

Chapter 19

News of the battle spread far and wide and surprisingly quickly. It spread west with the fleeing royalists – and with the detachment of parliamentarians who were pursuing them.

It spread south down to Lydford and Tavistock – thence to Plymouth as a few disheartened royalists fled down that way and back to their homes. It spread north – and had not far to go to reach Bideford and Barnstaple.

It reached west of Torrington a bit more slowly – backwards due east, South Molton and Crediton were already fully aware. To get down to places like Bovey, Newton Abbot and the coastal towns of Teignmouth and Paignton, there were only two routes – down the east of the moor or across it.

The news reached Bovey two days later when scouts from Fairfax paused there on their way to seek out possible royalist troublemakers. Having rested their horses and eaten a silent meal in the tavern, they were soon on their way again, leaving a shocked village digesting the news of what seemed to them a tragedy.

Soon after the scouts' departure, people started to gather again in the street.

"Can it be really so?" was the general feeling. Most now accepted that the struggle for supremacy was as good as over. Hopton, their great hope, set to surrender to Fairfax. Prince Charles possibly fled abroad somewhere – nobody either knew whether this be true or not and, if true, where he might have gone.

The King was beleaguered in Oxford, and the Scots were poised for yet another foray into the North Country. Bovey, like many a town and village, was subdued and not a trifle fearful. Would parliament seek reprisals on those places that had declared openly for the king?

Into this subdued village came a covered cart pulled by a large horse who, by his very gait, seemed to mirror the misery of the people talking in subdued voices.

"Pots to mend. Kettles to mend." Came a deep voice from the man seated at the front. Intermittently, he rang a handbell between his announcements.

"Who be this fellow?" one matronly woman asked of her neighbours. "Not our usual tinker, that's for sure."

"Heard tell old Billy took sick some weeks ago," the neighbour replied. "Took sick down Totnes way. Whoever this may be has either taken Billy's business or has seized his opportunity."

"Miserable-looking devil, whoever he may be," the first woman noted with a grunt.

The man brought the large covered wagon to a halt at one side of the small square, climbed down and set chocks of wood before and after the wheels. From the back, a younger man climbed down. He paused and lifted down a little girl of about four or five years of age. The young man then lifted down a box of tools, a wheel with a hand-turned grindstone and an iron contraption with a large metal mushroom atop. It would be used to provide an anvil to support the inside of a dented or bent pan so that a hammer could then even out the imperfections.

Despite the unwelcoming glower from the older man, many Goodwives scurried to gather their pots, cauldrons and other implements that had suffered the inevitable dents and small holes and tears.

Young Mary, who had accompanied her mother and father to the square to seek opinions from their neighbours, walked over to the little girl, who was skipping up and down with a red ribbon.

"Hello," she said. "And who may you be?"

The little girl looked up at the friendly face. She had the face of a little cherub surmounted by a mass of blonde curls.

"I am Nell – and that's my dada," she pointed at the young man.

"And I be Mary. Is the other man your grandpa?"

"Yes, he is, but the father of my wife," the young man looked up.

By then, the first of the women from the village was clamouring to have a big dent in her blackened kettle eased out.

"Rocks on the trivet," she said. "Rocks dangerously."

The older man grabbed the kettle and handed it to his son-in-law with a grunt. The young man fiddled with the open top of the kettle over the metal stand and positioned it inside the centre of the dent. Taking a ball pein hammer, he started gently to tap out the dent. He gave a grin to his little daughter and started to knock gently in a steady rhythm. Little Nell began dancing, keeping in time with the hammer.

"Tis a game we play," the young man said quietly. "My wife died giving birth to my little angel – so she never knew her mother at all. We find happiness where we may."

Mary, ever the sensitive member of the family, heard this, and a tear of sorrow came to her eye. She went back to her own mother and father and relayed it to them.

"Tis sad but not unusual," her mother nodded. "Birthing is as dangerous for a mother as it is for the babe. That young man tries his best to be both mother and father, seemingly."

By then, the earlier gathering had dispersed. By the time the sun was dipping below the western hills, there was still a large queue for the tinker and his operation.

"All must now wait for the morrow," the older man announced. "What light is left to us is not enough to see by."

Mary, who had returned with a badly dented pan, went over to Little Nell.

"Do you sleep in the wagon?" she asked.

"Aye," replied her father. "We have beds and blankets. The winter is almost ended; praise the Lord. In the warm weather, we put the beds outside and sleep under the stars."

"I counted over thirty stars last time," Nell announced. "And the moon, of course. One of the stars was very bright. Dada said it was a doggie called Sirius! It didn't *look* like a doggie!"

"My uncle James will know all about it," Mary said confidently. "Uncle James knows everything!"

"That, young Mary, is a gross exaggeration – and well, you know it!" came a voice from behind her. She whirled around to see her uncle standing with her aunt. Both had come to watch the operation.

"Well, you *do* know an awful lot!" Mary insisted.

James squatted down beside little Nell.

"When you look at all those stars, you will see that they are in groups that make kind of shapes. Those groups are called constellations. That bright star is in one of those called Canis Major. Now, Canis is the Latin word for dog. The star itself is indeed called Sirius, as your dada told you."

"Oh!" Nell looked as puzzled as before. "Why do you know everything?"

"That's my niece being kind to an old man," James laughed. "I know *some* things. Only God knows everything."

"But why would He make a star and call it a doggie?"

"He certainly made it – like he made everything we can see. But *we* called it Sirius."

"But why did we call it that? Is it after a doggie called Sirius?"

"No – it was named Sirius many, many years ago. The word Sirius comes from a similar Greek word that means bright and shining."

"There!" Mary said. "I told you Uncle James knows everything!"

Little Nell frowned, obviously attempting to store this somewhat arcane knowledge in the recesses of her young brain.

"May God keep you this night," Mary said, preparing to go home.

"And may He shine his brightest light on you and yours!" the young man replied with a grin.

In the hour before dawn the next morning, Andrews – a late soldier for the king – crept out of the small building where his bed was laid. Fully dressed and with a rough

205

woollen cloak about his shoulders, he picked up the small sack in which he had stored quarters of loaves and pieces of cheese. Both were stale, but that couldn't be helped.

Picking a silent path between the huts, he set off as quickly and quietly as he could. He had kept his ears wide open during his work with the miners. He had been able to learn that the village of Manaton was about four miles to the east. From there, he would need to head south towards Widecombe and Hay Tor before turning east again to descend from the moor to Bovey.

One hour later, with a westerly wind blowing behind him, he saw the sun slowly appearing to his front. It was a very dim sun, obscured by heavy clouds. But he was happy. The westerly wind was speeding him on his way – or so he believed – and the sun told him he was heading in the right direction. He started to whistle quietly to himself.

A while later, he prudently skirted around the stirring village of Manaton. He was not at all sure where they stood in relation to the miners. Some were violently opposed to mining, whilst others accepted it. He sought a path going south – or southeast. Not finding one, he put the dim sun in front of his right shoulder and walked on, mindful of watching the ground carefully. One stray foot into a bog or a deep hole could bring his adventure to a premature end.

He walked past a set of small, standing stones, wondering who had thought to put them like that in the first place. Finding a large granite outcrop, he stopped and ate the stalest piece of bread and the hardest piece of cheese from his small sack. A few hundred yards further on, he came to a little stream from which he slaked his thirst.

A little way further on, he came across a faint track. Checking that the sun was almost level with his left shoulder, he followed the track. He headed south confidently. Looking up, he could see that the track led down into a deep valley. Somewhere down there, he knew, lay the village of Widecombe.

Raising his eyes to the far side of the valley, he became aware of a large double granite outcrop. It was as if two giant teeth were taking a bite out of the grey sky. That, he knew for certain, was Hay Tor. Reach that, he said to himself, and the track would lead east off the moor and end up at Bovey.

He marched onwards and gently downhill. He whistled a bit more cheerily.

Sergeant Brown raised himself on one elbow and looked around the large room. The surgeons had taken over two of the local inns. One, they had used for amputations; the other for injuries that did not require amputation. Brown resided in the second of those, his head and upper left arm wrapped in clean linen. He counted himself very fortunate.

In the second wave of assault on the barricades, he had been in the middle of his men. The two on either side of him had not been fortunate. One had been almost decapitated by a wildly swung broadsword; the other had received a musket ball in the chest that had almost blown a lung in half. Brown had almost dodged a pike thrust at him. It had glanced off his helmet and made a furrow down his left arm.

When he had eventually been able to remove his pot helmet, he became aware that the side of his head was bleeding. The pike blade had dented the helmet and had dragged the dent down the side of his head.

All around him, lying on blankets on the floor, were men in the far worst case – and most were royalist soldiers. The man to his immediate right was moaning. He had been shot in the stomach and was obviously not going to last much longer. Some in the room were already dead. Brown levered himself upright and managed to get to his knees.

"That is not a wise move," he was told by a voice from the doorway. "You have a head injury and should rest."

"I also am responsible for my men," Brown countered. "And I must see to them."

"I guarantee that you will not make it to this door!"

"Bollocks!" Brown growled under his breath. He put out one hand to the wall to steady himself as he rose groggily to his feet. He let go of the wall and took three unsteady paces towards the door. The world suddenly tipped sideways and then started to revolve. Brown slumped to the floor in an untidy heap.

"I told you what would befall you!"

Brown swore, then managed to crawl back to his blanket. As the world steadied again, he looked up into the plump features of a matronly woman whose apron and sleeves were a mess of dried blood. She carried another blanket in her hands which she rolled up into a bolster, knelt down at Brown's side and helped him as he raised his head. The bolster was laid under the back of his head, and he lay back feeling nauseous.

Strong and capable hands unwound the linen to expose the wound to his head and arm.

"The arm will heal all by itself," she announced. "I shall put more salve on it later. But the wound to your head is a different matter. That is what made you swoon. Head wounds take time and rest. So, sergeant, lie back and let the Good Lord work His magic on you in His own time."

The linen was wrapped around his head and arm.

Brown lay there cursing but knowing that the woman, whoever she was, had the right to it. He would have to be patient – and that was never one of Brown's talents.

--------------------- OOOOOOOOOO ---------------------

The queue that formed at the tinker's wagon was smaller than it had been the previous day. The young man, as cheerful as ever, mended and polished with his usual good humour. Little Nell played around the wagon with a small dog that had managed to escape from a nearby house. The older man mended holes in pans and pots with never a good word for anyone. He snorted at each new job and grunted as he took coin on completion of the task.

By early dinner, the last of the customers had been satisfied. The two men started to load up their tools and equipment as Nell bade a sad farewell to her latest four-legged friend. A fair-sized crowd gathered to see the tinker off. The horse was fetched from the stable where he had spent a comfortable night – and was attached to the wagon.

The wooden chocks were removed from the wheels, and the older man climbed up to his seat. Little Nell poked her head out of the back of the wagon, ready to wave goodbye. The whip was cracked, and the wagon lurched forward. Unfortunately, the younger man was not yet completely over the tailboard – and fell to the cobbles, where he landed on the back of his head. Those nearest to the incident heard the ominous crack.

"Dada!" Nell screamed, trying to climb back down.

Young Simon dashed forward and caught her before she joined her father on the unyielding cobbles. The old man hauled on the reins to stop the wagon, climbed down and stalked back to survey the damage.

His son-in-law lay motionless, and his little daughter, released from Simon's grip, kneeled at his side. She said nothing, nor did she wail. She just knelt there as tears flowed down her face.

Avril, acknowledged as the best person to assess the damage was called from the apothecary shop. She hurried over and knelt by the other side of the young man.

"Do not move him!" she ordered.

"Nay – get the fool up!" snarled the old man. He went to put his boot into the ribs of the young man but was hauled aside by Simon. Although still very young, Simon was in the mould of his father and was as strong as an ox.

By then, more of the village had come to see what was happening. Abel joined his son as the old man again attempted to rouse the stricken fellow with the toe of his boot.

"Mistress Avril says he is not to be moved," Simon told his father. Abel simply placed one massive hand on the old man's shoulder.

"Take heed of what's said," he said quietly. "Mistress Avril will know what is best."

"And what is best for me?" shouted the older man. "I need that young layabout to work – and we have other places to be. I say you load him into the wagon, and we shall be on our way!"

"And that could well be the end of him," Avril countered, looking at the pale face on the ground. "What is needed is for a large board or a door. Then we will gently place the young man on it and take him to our shop, where we will lie him down to rest. Until he wakes, I will not know what is best for him."

As a couple of the men hurried to the carpenter's home to borrow a board, Nell stroked her little hand down her father's face.

"Wake up, dada – please wake up," she moaned.

"He is sleeping," Avril spoke gently to Nell. "He needs to sleep for a long time so that the Good Lord may work his blessings on him. I promise that my husband and I will look after him and tend his wounds as best we are able."

"Will you take the girl and look to her needs?" Mary asked the older tinker.

"Her? Of what use is she to me?" the tinker looked at her in amazement.

"Of what use? *What use?*", Abel shouted, his face an inch from the man. "She be your blood and kin, you vile turd!"

"Blood and kin, is she? Well, so she may be. But she is still of no use to me!"

"Then she shall come and bide with us," Avril countered as the two men came back with a stout wooden board. "She shall be with her dada and will help us bring him back to her."

Avril supervised as Abel, Simon, and the two others gently lifted the young man onto the board. Picking Nell up in her arms, she led the way to her shop.

In the parlour behind the shop, the young man was laid down gently on his board on the floor. James had brought down a spare palliasse which he laid by the far wall. The unconscious man was very gently transferred to the palliasse, and the two men took the board back to the carpenter. James took hold of Nell as Avril knelt by the side of her young father. Ever so carefully, she took his head in both hands and slowly rotated it back and forth. And then she felt down the neck.

"I cannot find any break of the skin – hence no bleeding," she said quietly, almost to herself. "I also find no grating of bones. But he is deep asleep. Mayhap that is best – that he sleeps for as long as he may."

James set Nell down. She immediately went to kneel by her father's head and started gently stroking his face. Avril and James looked on, then glanced at one another. No words were needed.

"Nell," Avril said quietly. "Would you like to stay here with us whilst your dada sleeps? We can put cushions by his side for you so that you may talk to him. He might hear what you say, though he will not answer for quite some time."

A little tear-streaked face looked up at her and nodded.

"Yes, please, mistress," she murmured.

"Then it is settled. You will stay here with us and eat when we eat. Now, you must keep up your strength so that you can be by his side. I have some nice raspberry wafers for you to nibble on until it is time for our supper."

She was relieved to see the little mite start on the wafers. What she and James needed to do was to keep up her spirits whilst endeavouring to nurse the poor young man back to health. But secretly, Avril was not at all sure that would happen. She had some knowledge of human anatomy, and that knowledge told her that the brain within the skull was damaged. How damaged? Only time will tell. She offered up a silent prayer for the man and the little girl.

Meanwhile, the tinker drove his wagon to the far end of the village street, where he again stopped it, set the chocks under the wheels and unhitched the horse yet again. He went to the tavern for ale and something to eat.

Word had spread of his treatment of his son and granddaughter. Glory, who first saw him enter, went straight to the back room where her father was tapping a new barrel of ale.

Dick Allen, with Sal, his wife, by his side, went straight to the tinker.

214

"We have no use for you here. You will not be served."

"My coin is as good as any man's," retorted the tinker.

"That it may be. But we have no use for you here – as you have no use for that sweet little mite. Now, leave before I have you thrown out!"

"And if I refuse to leave?"

"Then every man and woman here will assist in tossing you in the nearest midden!"

Scowling and muttering dire imprecations, the man got up from the bench and left. He would have to make do with stale bread and water that night."

Chapter 20

Garvey and Haddock were nearing the town of Ashburton, coming down from the moor. Before setting off a few days earlier, Lovelace and the three soldiers/trackers had decided that it was pointless following the king's men any further towards Torrington. What they needed to do was to bypass that town and then head east to where they were confident they would find General Fairfax and the bulk of the army.

Having slipped south of Torrington, they ran into driving sleet. That had made them seek shelter in the densest wood they could find. Mercifully, the sleet stopped after a few hours, leaving them in the darkest of nights. Even their woodcraft skills had been rendered useless. They stayed where they were until the first light the following morning.

Lovelace led them back to their original track, heading east towards High Bickington. But only a mile beyond Torrington, they almost ran into a royalist outpost. Unusually for the four, they were caught completely unawares. Lovelace could not believe that he had been so careless. He was normally brilliant at melding into whatever countryside he passed through.

At a shouted challenge, the four melted into the nearest cover they could find, then ran as fast as possible away from the outpost. Lovelace, followed by Ratcliffe, disappeared into a little valley and fled eastwards. Garvey and Haddock chose a slightly different path and almost stumbled into a shallow stream that was tumbling over rocks. They instinctively followed the course of the water and then, hearing no sounds of pursuit, slowed and made their way into a stand of stunted oaks.

By the time they emerged on the other side, they were over four miles from where Lovelace and Ratcliffe had continued on their way eastwards.

Haddock stopped at the edge of the trees and looked east and then south. The view to the east was blocked by an extensive forest; the view south revealed the northern slopes of the high moor, some miles distant. He sat down and shrugged off his pack.

"Time to take stock!" he said, taking out the remains of a coney they had cooked over a small fire the previous day. He broke off a leg and handed it to Garvey. He ripped off some cooked flesh and started chewing. Neither said a word for a while.

Putting on his pack again, Haddock looked down at his mate.

"This be a daft mess," he ventured. "Dick and Hugh be miles away – probably."

Sam Garvey shrugged. "Not sure I want any more of this," he grunted. "Wandering hither and yon, tracking

king's men. Bloody, cold and wet all the time. What say we head south and find some nice, warm billet?"

"Warm billet sounds good. But where do we find one? There be none hereabouts with king's army scattered all over the county!"

"All fighting is in the north of the county," Garvey countered. "We know south of Devon is free of the enemy – so why don't we head there?"

"We might be hunted down and shot as deserters; that's why not!" Haddock replied.

"And we look like soldiers?" Garvey pointed at their rustic dress – all dark greens and browns to blend into the countryside like all good woodsmen and trackers.

"Well, no – we look like any woodsman," Haddock was forced to acknowledge.

"Then I'm for heading south and finding that warm billet and proper food."

Somewhat reluctantly, Haddock nodded.

"But we have to cross the moor to get south – or go west again and back down through Tavistock."

"That journey is too long. Over the moor is best."

Against his better judgement, Haddock had agreed. And four days later, they walked down into the stannary town of Ashburton, tired and very hungry.

--------------------- OOOOOOOOO ---------------------

Sergeant Lovelace, having managed to rejoin Fairfax's army, was separated from Ratcliffe – signalling the end of that quartet. He was kept back from the front line of the battle – his skills were being kept in reserve.

When the last of the royalist army had fled Torrington, he was ordered to track one group that was thought to contain at least three of the most senior officers. He recruited a couple of soldiers that he had previously worked with and set off towards the border with Cornwall. Sneaking across the bridge at Gunnislake in the dead of night, the three of them made for Launceston.

--------------------- OOOOOOOOO ---------------------

Ratcliffe was a part of the second wave of parliamentarians to eventually break through the defences at Torrington. He was well beyond the church, pursuing with his company a group of royalist soldiers who were desperately seeking a way out of the town.

His long pike had been discarded when the shaft had been smashed by a blow from a sword. With his own sword in hand, he and his colleagues were fighting almost hand-to-hand in an alleyway when the church blew up.

219

Every man in that alleyway froze. It was as if the last trump had sounded. Some fell to their knees; mouths open in horror. Others simply turned about and fled for their lives. Ratcliffe didn't move fast enough. A small piece of masonry plummeted down from the sky and smashed into his back between his shoulder blades. He collapsed in a heap.

That evening he woke up and found himself lying on a blanket. He peered around a large room filled with others like himself. There was a lantern burning at each end of the long room. He groaned as he tried to lever himself up. He managed to get as far as one elbow, noticing that another man was doing the same almost opposite him.

"You and I seem the only ones awake," the man said. "What injury have you suffered?"

"That, friend, is what I would dearly like to discover," Ratcliffe answered. "All I remember is feeling a mighty blow on my back just after there came a great explosion."

"The church blew up, or so it would seem. Gunpowder was stored there."

"I was past the church," Ratcliffe remembered. "I had entered an alleyway and was fighting with sword in hand – and then it seemed that the world had suddenly ended."

Sergeant Brown and Ratcliffe, neither noticing in the gloom that they were of opposing armies, also remained blissfully unaware that they had been less than two hundred yards apart many days before at Bovey Heath.

Ratcliffe slumped back down on his blanket, noticing that there was a tingling all the way down his right hip and leg. Brown also laid back down, waiting for the room to stop spinning.

--------------------- OOOOOOOOOO --------------------

James and Avril took turns sitting with Nell and her father. The young man neither moved nor made any sound - except for his regular breathing. Avril took the regularity of breath as a hopeful sign. Not long after Nell had been urged to lay down beside her dada, Avril had been aware that the little girl was also not moving. Now and again, there came a sniff.

Avril allowed an hour to pass, hoping that the little girl would eventually drift off from sheer exhaustion. Creeping over, she saw a tear-stained face peering up at her.

"My dada won't wake up," Nell snuffled.

"No, my sweeting – he is sleeping and slowly mending," Avril bent down and picked Nell up in her arms. She went back to her chair, cuddling the little girl to her.

"Shall you help to make him better?" Nell whispered.

"Aye, my pet. I shall do all that I can. Now – why don't we say a prayer together to the Lord Jesus – He will surely help us."

Nell closed her eyes tightly shut. With one little hand clasping Avril's arm, she started her own prayer.

"Lord Jesus, please make my dada better. Please let him sleep, and please let this kind lady mend him. Thank you, Amen."

Avril felt a huge weight of responsibility settle on her shoulders. This beautiful little mite was pinning all her hopes on her. What if she failed? What if her father should never wake again? She lifted Nell so that her curly head rested above her shoulder and into her neck.

"Hush, little one. Sleep now like your dada. Trust in the Lord Jesus to make him better."

A few minutes later, she was aware that Nell had indeed dropped off into an exhausted sleep. She dared not move for fear of waking her back into her living nightmare. Instead, she began thinking about what hers and James' life would have been like if they had been blessed with such a lovely child.

Some hours later, James came down to take his turn. He went immediately to the young man, noting the evenness of breath. He turned and saw his wife smiling at him from her chair by the fire, one little girl clasped firmly to her.

"Are you able to move without waking her?" he whispered.

"She is deep asleep, so it might be done."

"Why do you not take her up to our bed and settle down with her? I shall keep watch over her father."

It took minutes for Avril to stand without moving her charge. She went to the stair and climbed carefully. In the bedroom, she gently laid Nell on the bed and then lay down beside her. Eventually, holding the little girl close, she drifted off to sleep.

Downstairs, James settled himself in the chair. He looked over at the young man.

"We still do not know your name," he said quietly.

Garvey and Haddock had spent a very comfortable night in the stables of an inn. The previous evening, they had passed a smallholding just to the north of Ashburton, at a bend in the River Dart - and had used their considerable skills to 'win' a chicken, which they had removed to a safe distance, killed, plucked and roasted over a fire that was hidden from view by a stone wall. And then, they approached the small town from a different angle and sneaked into the stables.

They were woken just after dawn by the cheerful whistling of a stable boy who had come to feed the three horses that were being looked after for guests at the inn. The young lad first became aware of the presence of two interlopers when he had finished filling each of the small troughs with water. Looking to his right, where hay was stored on a platform, he became aware of two rather grubby and unshaven faces peering at him. Haddock was the first to react.

"Fear not, lad," he said quietly, holding out two hands to demonstrate the absence of any weapon. "We came up from the south yester eve and, having no coin for a bed, crept in here for sleep and warmth. All we seek is work."

The youth recovered from his initial fear as Garvey also added his two empty hands for inspection.

"If it's work ye seek, then you will find plenty hereabouts," he said. "Many have gone to fight, and it is not known when they may return."

"From the south, we have not heard of too much fighting," Garvey added his voice to the proceedings, continuing the lie. "But we came through Totnes and heard of fighting at Berry Pomeroy."

"Some say that the castle there is ruined," the lad nodded. "Let me feed these horses and come away in. Mistress may have work here for you."

Brushing hay and straw from their clothes, the two men followed the lad into the back of the inn, where a large woman in an apron was supervising two young girls who were chopping vegetables to add to a huge pot. She looked around and glared at the lad.

"Why do you bring vagrants into my kitchen?" she demanded.

"These be two seeking work, mistress,"

Haddock put on his most earnest face. "We be not vagrants, mistress. We be woodsmen seeking work. Our master went to fight, taking most with him. That was four weeks past – and not a sign of them. So, we had to leave as mistress were too distressed to manage."

"That is all too common a happening!" the woman nodded. "I thank the good Lord that my man be too old for such capers! So, ye be woodsmen, be ye? Then see to my woodpile – there be lots of logs to split and store. Do one hour of that, and I shall feed you heartily."

"Then that same good Lord will smile his thanks on you, mistress," Garvey knuckled his head. The two of them went out and surveyed a large pile of thick logs. The lad went to a small shed and brought out a large axe and a hefty billhook. Although woodsmen by profession, the two were not, and never had been, engaged in felling or coppicing. They were woodsmen trackers. But they did know how to split logs! They set to with a will.

One hour later, the boy came to summon them inside, where two steaming bowls of thick stew waited for them – along with hunks of fresh bread and cheese.

225

"You have well earned that," the woman gave them a cheery grin. "Do the same after you have eaten, and a late dinner shall be yours."

"We thank you most gratefully, mistress," Haddock replied, spooning stew into his mouth. "Do you know of work we may do when we have completed your task?"

"Tis possible," she said, furrowing her brow. "One of the guests be travelling eastwards and may have need of guarding on his journey. He was saying that just yester evening. Stay you here and eat, and I shall ask for you."

She came back as the two were finishing their stew. She brought with her a man in his middle years, well dressed and wearing a tall, feathered hat even indoors.

"You be seeking work?" he said in a deep, rumbling voice.

"Indeed, we be, master."

"I leave here on the morrow for Exeter but shall break my journey at Bovey, where I have business with the lord's steward. I have certain things with me that I would not wish to be taken from me."

"You wish us to guard you and your goods, master?"

"But first, I need to know your allegiances. Be you for the king or for parliament?"

Garvey, ever the quicker thinker, replied almost immediately.

"We be for neither king nor parliament, master. We be just simple woodsmen, happy to leave such matters to others."

The man stayed where he was, fixing the two with a frown of concentration. Then, with a grunt, he made them his offer.

"On the morrow after breakfast, I shall leave with my cart. Be ready to accompany me. Cut yourselves good staves. I have pistols for my own safety."

"We both thank you most heartily, master. We shall be ready."

The man gave another grunt and went back to the main part of the inn.

"Thank you, mistress," Garvey said, remembering that it was she who had brought it all about. "And now we shall fill your wood store."

---------------------- OOOOOOOOOO --------------------

James came awake with a start. It took him a few seconds to realise that he was sitting in a chair before a fire that needed bringing to new life and that a badly injured young man was lying on a palliasse by the far wall of this room. His first job was to blow life into the embers and then feed small logs onto them. Within minutes, the logs had caught, and a cheerful fire was crackling away. And then he went over to see how his patient was faring.

It was as if the young man had not moved a muscle since the previous evening. He lay peacefully on his back, Covered and warm with a blanket. His chest rose and fell rhythmically, slowly and with only the slightest sound. James reached a hand and placed his fingers gently against the neck – as he had often seen his wife do. He felt a pulse that was also steady if a trifle weak. The skin was warm to the touch but without any sign of fever. So far, so good, James thought. He got to his feet and crept up the stairs and peeped around the door.

His wife was sleeping soundly, as was the little girl clasped tightly to her. Like Avril had done the previous night, he wondered what it would have been like if that little girl was indeed their child. He gave a sign and went downstairs again to warm some ale with a poker thrust into the fire.

He put on his warmest coat and went outside to await his nephew Gil. Gil's handcart was still a few cottages up from the apothecary shop, but Gil, seeing his uncle, walked down to him.

"How is the poor man?" Gil asked, handing James two loaves – their regular delivery.

"Exactly the same as when he was brought here. He is deep asleep, breathing well and warmly. Your aunt said that the longer he sleeps, the better his chances. But she also said that, should he sleep beyond today, he might be in deep trouble."

"And how is that sweet little soul?"

"Also sleeping – fast in the arms of your aunt Avril."

"Then our prayers will be for them both," Gil said and continued with his deliveries.

James went back indoors and added more wood to the fire, withdrew the poker and thrust it into his pewter mug of ale. There came a hiss, and a load of bubbles as the ale was warmed. James risked his wife's wrath and broke off a heel of one of the new loaves, crunching his teeth through the new crust with pleasure. His brother and sister-in-law were indeed masters of bakery, he thought.

"And you never thought to bring me some new bread," came a soft voice from the stairs.

"I saw you asleep with Nell – so I didn't wake you," he answered, somewhat guiltily.

"She is still fast asleep," Avril descended the stairs. "But I had better get back to her, or she might panic if she wakes all alone and in a strange place."

She filled another mug with ale, warmed it with the poker and, taking the remains of the first loaf, went up again to make sure her little charge was safe.

A short while later, she came down again with Nell clinging onto her skirts. Nell went over to her father and looked down at him.

"Dada still asleep," she said, looking up at Avril.

"Yes, Nell. He's still asleep, and with the help of your prayers, he's slowly mending. Now – I think you must be hungry. How would you like some porridge with honey?"

For the first time since the previous afternoon, one little face brightened into something approaching a smile.

"Yes, please," she said.

--------------------- OOOOOOOOOO --------------------

Abel Smith put down his hammer and cast a look at the iron spade he had been fashioning. In between his jobs for paying customers, he had been making a set of tools for Gil and his daughter Ella. He walked out to the front of his workshop to get a breath of cold, fresh air – he had been by the furnace for the last two hours.

Hands-on hips, he breathed deeply, filling his lungs with cold air. He slowly became aware of muttered swearing up the road to his right – just in front of the church. The old tinker was coupling his horse to the cart and making a poor job of it. He held the doubled-up reins in one hand and was thrashing the flanks of the horse.

"Simon – come and help me here," Abel called over his shoulder and started striding up to the tinker. He grabbed the arm that was holding the reins and pulled them away from the tinker.

"You leave me be!" snarled the man. "Tis my horse, and I'll beat him if I choose."

"Then you be as big a fool as you look," Abel snorted. "Simon – hold the shafts steady, and I'll get old dobbin here into proper position."

Within minutes, all was done. Abel stood at the head, stroking the horse's nose to calm him.

"And now you be on your way?" he asked in a deceptively mild tone.

"Aye – I have work to do at Chudleigh," the tinker replied, preparing to mount the cart.

"And you would leave the lad and his little one to fend for themselves?"

"They be no use to me now!"

"Hear that, Simon – one young man and a little girl be of no use to him anymore!"

"Aye, father, I heard that."

"And what would the name of that young man be? We know little 'un be called Nell."

"Him? That's Hal Dawkins – he that wed my daughter."

"And Hal Dawkins and his daughter Nell be of no further use?"

"Nay – I'm now better off without them."

"Yes – we understand that," Abel replied, still talking quietly. "Now let me tell you where we are in this village. If you leave here and abandon them, never let us see you here again. For, if you do appear again, I will twist your head from your shoulders and let the lads play football with it."

"And I shall be glad to help," Simon added equally quietly.

"Then, the devil takes you and your village," the tinker snarled, cracked the reins and set off.

Abel and his son watched as the cart disappeared around a bend.

"Be you away to the apothecary, Simon. Tell them the name so that they know who resides with them. And bring me the news."

"Aye, father." Simon set off down the village. Now all would know who lay injured.

Brown woke up feeling much restored. The injured who were awake and able to eat had been fed the previous evening and also that morning. He looked across the room and saw that the man he had spoken to was also managing to sit up, propped against the wall. Brown very tentatively stood up and was mighty pleased to note that the place no longer went around in circles.

"Now, let's see if I can make the door," he called across. He took small steps at first, then larger ones as his confidence returned. He went through the door in search of a privy.

Ratcliffe had watched Brown – knowing that the sergeant was definitely a soldier for the king. He laid back down and sighed. During the night, two more of the injured had died – and had been carried out. Only one of the rest was truly awake – and he was alternately muttering to himself and shouting for someone called Garton. He's obviously out of his wits, Ratcliffe thought.

Brown walked confidently back in – looked across at Ratcliffe, then came over to sit against the wall.

"My part is done now," he said. "All the way from Bovey to Torrington – and all in vain."

"You were at Bovey?" Ratcliffe said. "Yes, I was there also."

Chapter 21

Late that afternoon, Avril made one of her regular checks on the young man. He had been sleeping all that day peacefully, his breathing regular, his skin just warm to the touch. She slowly stood back up again and went out of the back door so as not to disturb James in the shop. He had little Nell sitting on the high stool and was showing her the row of pots in which he kept medicinal herbs.

Avril walked slowly up the village street until she saw young Mary coming down towards her, a basket on her arm.

"Aunt Avril – why are you out without cloak or shawl? Tis not yet warm enough."

"Aye, Mary. That I know. Will you take a message for me to Reverend Forbes?"

Mary immediately frowned. "Is the poor man not improved?" she asked.

"Nay – not improved. Ever since he fell, he has been breathing quite deeply and regularly. But now his breath is shallow. I do not like it, and I think 'tis time Reverend came to bless him – just to be safe."

"I will go right now," Mary said, turning around to walk back up the street.

Avril hurried back and went in as she had left, around the back. Taking a warm cloak down from a peg, she hurried out again to await her niece. She had not long to wait. Mary came back with Reverend Forbes at her side.

"Mary tells me you worry for the young man," he said.

"Indeed, that is so. Not once has he woken or uttered any sound, but he breathed regularly and kept warm. I went to check some minutes past, and his breathing was not so regular and was not deep. And he uttered little moans."

"Then it is wise to prepare," Forbes said. "How fares the little maid?"

"We have been keeping her busy with other things in the shop. She helped me make some gingerbreads. James is showing her all the herbs."

"It would be as well to keep my presence from her. Is there aught of interest that Mary might take her to see?"

"Indeed, there be, reverend," Mary replied. "There be new lambs on the heath."

Mary went straight to the shop and started the small stratagem.

"Would Nell like to come with me to see the new lambs?" she said, knowing full well that it would be something most little girls would never pass up.

Nell looked up at James. James cast a look at his niece, who was nodding with a serious face.

"I think that would be a lovely thing to do, Nell. Let us make sure you are wrapped up against the cold."

He rummaged under his counter and found a small blanket that he sometimes used to place over glass jars of herbs to keep the summer sun from the contents. He wrapped it around Nell's shoulders.

"There – warm as a coney in his warren," he said. Mary had intended to walk with Nell but couldn't resist lifting her in her arms.

"We shall be back soon, Uncle," she said, indicating with her head that he should go into the back.

As the two left the shop, James went into the back parlour to find his wife entering via the back door with the reverend. He immediately went to the young man and placed his hand gently on the chest.

"Aye," he said. "That is a wise thing to do."

Forbes knelt by the palliasse, joined by Avril and James. James took his wife's hand in his and joined in the prayers. The first prayers were for the recovery of the young man; the rest were for his peaceful entry into heaven.

Forbes left soon afterwards, not wanting Nell to see him there less she worried that something was amiss.

"Whilst there be life, there be hope – that is what we must keep saying to Nell," Avril said as she thanked the reverend.

A short while later, Mary brought an excited Nell back. She looked much better with rosy cheeks from the cold wind. She was bursting with news, and that gave James an idea.

"Nell – why not be with your dada and tell him all about the new lambs? He may be deep asleep, but he may hear you. If he can indeed hear, he will be cheered to hear your voice."

Nell jumped at the suggestion. She very gently laid herself down beside her father and started telling all about the new lambs – how some were taking milk from their mothers and how some were jumping up and down, testing their long legs.

James looked down at the two and said nothing. Mary grabbed her aunt's hand and drew her out into the backyard. Tears were falling down her cheeks.

"May I run home and see my mother? I feel that I cannot leave that little soul – and I might help to entertain her."

"Bless your kindness, Mary – your uncle and I would be glad of your company."

--------------------- OOOOOOOOOO --------------------

Trooper Andrews was tired. He looked back behind him at the setting sun, then looked to his front. The tower of Bovey church was visible in the valley below him. He was nearly there, and he reminded himself. No need to seek a place to pass the night in the open air. He would instead seek a warm barn – and there were bound to be barns aplenty in and around the village.

He had just enough stale bread to see him fed until the morning. He walked on a bit faster, wanting to spy out the land before the light was gone. A little later, he stopped and saw a possibility. Beyond the church in a large field, he had espied a tumble-down barn. He would make for that by a circuitous route. Surely, there would be old straw into which he could burrow!

He managed to reach the barn just as the last of the light faded. It was indeed a wreck, some of the upright timbers missing, leaving a part of the roof sagging sadly downwards. But, the joy of joys, at the far end, was the straw. It was piled up and looked a bit mouldy. But it was like a palace to the young trooper. He put his near-empty sack down, crawled to the straw, and sat down to eat the last of his bread, then rolled the empty sack to poke it under his belt.

And then, with a sigh of relief, he burrowed deep into the straw and immediately fell deep asleep. For the first time in many a long day, he was happy.

--------------------- OOOOOOOOOO ---------------------

A few miles to the north of where Andrews slept, Kit Warden was a far from happy man. The work on the cottages was nearing completion – and he felt that he had done most of it himself. That, had he thought clearly, was an exaggeration – Luke Farmer had certainly pulled his weight when he had been there!

Farmer was, Warden muttered to himself, utterly smitten with the copper-headed Meg. On three of the past four days, he had met up with her and had helped her gather not only elm bark but bay leaves and the strangest little mushrooms he had ever seen. And then, that very morning, he had dared to plant a chaste kiss on her cheek.

Her response had surprised him. Instead of being either outraged or coy, she had faced him and pressed her lips hard on his, drawn back and giving him a broad wink. The farmer had been almost beside himself as he walked back alone to the cottages.

All that afternoon, he had waxed lyrical and without pause until, in sheer exasperation, Warden had told him to shut up before he died of boredom.

"To hear you, one would believe you the only one on God's good earth to have kissed a maid!" he snarled. "You have told the story twenty or more times, and my ears are now shut. So may your mouth be!"

Luke Farmer was a deeply worried young man.

"The work here is nearly finished," he said. "How may I stay here when they have no further need for us?"

"You cannot!" Warden told him. "So – you will have to put the delightful Meg to the back of your mind. We must move on."

"That I cannot do!" The farmer was adamant. "I must go to talk to the woodsman. I shall be honest with him about my feelings for his daughter."

"Then I shall need to borrow a cart to take away the parts of you that he leaves unchopped!"

"Tis a risk I have to take."

"Then may the Good Lord have mercy on your soul. For my part, I shall move on – maybe back to Bovey. The fuss will have died away by now. Luck may be on my side, and I shall find work there."

The two rolled themselves into their blankets and went to sleep.

--------------------- OOOOOOOOOO --------------------

Late that same afternoon, the bags containing Hal's and Nell's belongings found their way down to the apothecary's shop. Nell had spent more time lying down by her father's side, telling him all about the lambs she had seen frisking about.

At one point, young Hal had muttered something, and Nell had called out, but by the time James and Avril arrived, he had gone silent again.

During the day, Avril had been wetting the young man's lips with weak ale. She knew the dangers of a body being without the liquid but had no idea whether any of it had found its way down his throat. When the bags arrived, she delved into the one containing Nell's things and found two more little dresses, a small night shift, and a bundle of underclothes. As well there was a wooden doll and a little wooden cross.

"Shall we get you into your night shift?" she asked when their supper was eaten.

"May I sleep in your bed again?" Nell asked shyly.

"We shall cuddle up and be as snug as two little bugs," Avril stated.

"And I shall keep watch over your dada," James assured her.

Nell went over to Hal, knelt down, and planted a kiss on his forehead.

"Sleep tight, dada – and please get better," she folded her hands together and made a small prayer.

Avril looked at James with tears in her eyes but quickly wiped them away as Nell stood up. The two went upstairs and were soon asleep.

James made sure the fire was well supplied – and that it was safely inside the stone fireplace before wrapping himself in a blanket and making himself comfortable in the large chair.

Twice during the night, he woke up, certain that the young man had spoken. But as he went over to check, there had been no change.

"Wishful thinking?" he muttered to himself, settling back in the chair.

He finally awoke well before dawn. He unwrapped himself from the blanket and put more wood on the fire, then went over to young Hal Dawkins. He knelt down and pressed his finger into the neck, as he had seen his wife do.

The first thing that registered was the temperature of the skin – it was cold. And then, search as he might, could find no pulse in the neck. He bent down to the mouth and placed his ear as close as he could. He found no trace of a breath. He sat back on his heels and started a prayer for the young man – and then another heartfelt one for the little girl.

He had heard the story – Nell's mother had died in childbirth. Now, she had been abandoned by that despicable old grandfather and had lost the one person who had been the mainstay of her little life. How, he wondered, could this be allowed to happen? How, he also wondered, could he deal with telling Nell that she was now all alone in the world? He stayed kneeling by the side of the young man, wondering what was left for her.

He crept up the stairs and peered around the open door of the bedroom. One little blonde, curly head was pressed into the neck of his sleeping wife. He must have made a faint sound as Avril woke up and peered at him. He looked at her and shook his head.

"He is gone?" she whispered.

"Aye – sometime during the early hours."

"Then he is surely resting in Christ's arms – for he deserves no other!"

James nodded and stood where he was.

"And now, how do we tell that little mite? Tell her that all she had in the world is gone from her?"

Nell stirred and looked up at Avril.

"Is it morning?" she asked sleepily.

"Nay, my sweet – 'tis still night," Avril told her.

"Is my dada awake, then?"

James decided to do the only honourable thing. He went to sit on the bed.

"Nell, your dada has gone to Jesus. He will not awake now."

Nell's mouth dropped open, and then she gave a soft moan before tears began flowing down her cheeks. Avril just held her close, rocking the little girl gently in her arms.

Looking out between the slats of the shuttered window, James had the start of an idea. He went in search of a thick blanket and gave his wife a nod. He gently prised Nell away and wrapped her in the blanket and carried her to the window. Opening the shutters, he spoke as gently as he could.

"Nell – can you see that bright star?" he asked.

Nell searched the night sky and wriggled one arm free of the blanket. She pointed.

"Yes – that's the brightest star of all. Somewhere up there is heaven."

"Is that where Jesus is?"

"Yes – we are told that Jesus is with God his father up there in heaven."

"And will my dada be there with them?"

"Yes, he is sure to be – and is looking down at his little girl and telling her that he is now safe and happy – and that you are safe and will always be loved by those who care for you."

He stood there for some time with Nell in his arms and Avril by his side. Nell was still looking at the bright star when it slowly faded as the sky started to lighten.

"Can I talk to dada every night when the star shines?"

"Aye – we will make sure you may."

James and Avril shared a long look – a look that needed no words. They would love and care for that little soul – no matter what obstacles might be put in their way.

Chapter 22

Kit Warden walked all through the early part of the night. Having decided to go, he wanted to make as soon a start as possible – and that meant leaving with a full stomach. A soldier learns to take whatever he may, when he may. It was with some misgivings that he left his friend Luke Farmer. He had a nasty suspicion that the woodcutter would not take very kindly to Luke's approach concerning his daughter. However, he bade his friend goodbye and good luck, slung his pack on his back, and set off as the light dimmed.

He knew that his journey would take him no more than two hours to cover the five miles to Bovey. He was not at all sure what welcome he would get when he made his presence known. After all, he admitted to himself; it was the kindness of Bovey that had sent him to Lustleigh in the first place. But he reasoned that, as the work on the three cottages was now complete, it made some sort of sense for him to return to see what else may be on offer.

Passing down the lane that served the small hamlet of Hawksmoor, he had to brave the fierce growling of a large dog that was chained outside one of the cottages. The last thing he would ever do was to take any notice of the brute. He knew, as did any countryman, that to acknowledge any animal, either by word or eye contact, would make further contact inevitable. So, he simply ignored the dog and walked on. The growling subsided, then stopped altogether.

A bright moon, the same that had illuminated the stars for Nell, bathed the village of Bovey so that he was able to turn aside from the road and skirt the houses to the north. Pausing as he came behind the church, he saw beyond it was a large field and a broken-down barn.

"That looks like my bed chamber," he muttered to himself and made his very careful and silent way there. As he arrived at the gaping doorway, he became aware of the sounds of someone snoring.

"So, it would seem I have to share," he said to himself. Out of the bright moonlight, he waited for a few minutes for his eyes to adjust to the gloom within the old barn. At the far end was a large pile of old straw; at the right side of that pile was a pair of boots. Silently, he loosened his pack and set it down on the left side of the pile. Equally quietly, he burrowed into the straw and drew the pack after him. Within a few minutes, he added his light breathing to the soft snores.

--------------------- OOOOOOOOOO ---------------------

James posted a short, written notice in his shop window – to the effect that he would not be opening that day. Having done so, he left Avril talking quietly to Nell and made his way up the village street first to the church. Reverend Forbes lived in a small house just to the side of the Church of Saints Peter, Paul, and Thomas.

"Your presence here, Master Ramsey, can mean one thing – and it is not good news I'll warrant,"

"No, reverend – it is indeed the worst news. The poor young man died during the night and is now still resting where you saw him."

"Have you told the wee mite?"

"Aye – and it was not the easiest thing I have ever had to do. I must confess that I took some liberty with Almighty God. It would seem that young Hal Dawkins would tell his daughter about the stars – and she is quite taken with them. Last night, the sky being clear, I showed her what her favourite star – the one called Sirius in the constellation of Canis Major is. Bless her; she seemed convinced that it is called after a dog!"

Forbes smiled his understanding.

"Aye – I can see how a little mind may confuse the two," he said.

"Nell asked me if that was where Jesus was in heaven – presuming that He would only want to be where the brightest star shone in the night sky – and, if that were so, was her father already there with Him. What could I say but, yes – he most certainly was – and that he was safe and happy. He was looking down at his little girl and telling her to be happy as he was. Did I commit a sin?"

"Sin? No – you committed an act of love and kindness."

"Reverend, what to do with young Hal? May he be buried hereabouts?"

"That is the least we may do for him and little Nell. Now – how to arrange matters. I will send Sam Fewings down with his cart so that the body may be brought to lie here in the sanctity of the church. But – how to do this without Nell being made wise?"

"Oh – that is a simple matter. I shall call in on my brother and borrow young Mary. She can take Nell for the morning – whilst her dada, as she called him, is brought here."

"That is well thought. Mary is kindness itself."

"Reverend – one other matter. Avril and I, as you well know, have never been blessed with children – despite our longing for even one. What would be the judgement of the church were we to take Nell into our home and bring her up as if she were our daughter?"

"The judgement of the church would be that you and your wife were doing no more than Our Lord commanded when he told us that if you do to the smallest child, you do it to Me. Well – not in precisely those words – but the meaning is clear. But what of her grandfather?"

"That devil abandoned his ailing son and his little granddaughter when he left here to go about his business. I cannot contemplate what sort of life Nell would have with him!"

"But in the eyes of the law, the grandfather has, and will always have, a claim to her. Not that I would ever want that to happen, but he would have the law on his side."

"Aye – that we know full well! But Avril and I are determined in this. We will give Nell all the love and care that she rightly deserves – and we will have the support of this whole village!"

"Then some good may come out of all this tragedy. You may count on my wholehearted support. When the Lord Vickery returns – as he surely must sometime soon – he needs to be appraised of your action. He will also offer you his support, or I seriously misjudge him!"

James bade farewell to the Reverend Forbes and hurried across to the bakery, from which tantalising aromas of freshly baked bread were wafting down the street.

Mary, stacking loaves on the shelf in the front shop, looked up as her uncle came in. From his expression, she guessed his news.

"Little Nell has now lost everyone?" she said, tears already forming.

"Aye – she has, and in the early hours. I took her to see her favourite bright star, and she believes that is where her dada is with Jesus in heaven. Mary – would you come down and take the little soul for a while? Sam Fewings, the sexton, will be down to collect the body and take it to the church. I have already seen Reverend Forbes, and he will say the funeral for him, and he will be buried in the churchyard."

"Aye – I will take her again to see the lambs. Perhaps one or two will be with the shepherd, and she can hold them."

John and Evelyn, wondering what was keeping Mary so long, came into the shop and had to be told the sad tale.

"Then Mary must do what she can to help the wee mite. What is to happen to her?"

"Brother – Avril and I will take her and give her the home that she has never had."

"And a loving home it will be," Evelyn laid her hand on James'. "Mary – you get to Nell, and I shall mind the shop."

Mary dusted flour off her apron, fetched her cloak, and went with her uncle down to the apothecary shop, but via the back where Avril was sitting with Nell on her lap, making sure the little girl had some sweetened porridge inside her.

"Nell – my uncle has wondered if you would like to come with me to see the new lambs again. It may be that one or two may need feeding – and you could help do that."

Nell was dressed in one of her other clothes. Avril found her little warm cloak and clipped it around her shoulders. Nell, not having said a word, went to Mary, who lifted her up and carried her through the rear door and went to see the lambs.

Avril looked at James, went to him, and put her arms around him as James told her what was planned to happen and that Forbes had, in as many words, given his blessing.

"Then Nell will bide with us, and she shall have our love and care," Avril said.

Kit Warden was the first to awake. He spat out a piece of straw and sat up, making more noise than he should have, but for that moment, unaware of where he was. He soon found out as there came a startled oath from his left and a young, tousled head emerged.

"God's toenails," the head gasped. "You gave me a fright. I did not know I shared my bed with another!"

Warden, senior to Andrews by some years, was first to get to grips with the situation.

"And who may you be, and why be you here?" he asked.

"Then I shall ask you the same question – as I was here before you!" Andrews retorted.

"Aye – I suppose that's fair," Warden nodded. "I have been working at Lustleigh – repairing cottages. My work is finished. I came here to seek what else I may do. So – that is my story – what be yours?"

That put Andrews in a bit of a fix. His story was that he had deserted from the king's service, had probably killed one man, and had fled. Instead, he offered a more recent account.

"I was working with the tin miners up on the moor – and tired of it. I came here like you to seek more pleasant work."

"I hear there was some sort of battle fought here," Warden hadn't a clue why he brought up the subject. He was very surprised at Andrews' reaction- the young man looked startled and turned his face away.

"Had you any part in it?" Warden made an educated guess.

"Yes – I had some part in it," Andrews turned to face him. It would be a relief indeed to share his knowledge – for it was burning a hole in him. "I was not a quarter mile from here and saw it all."

"But you were not in the thick of it!"

"Nay – my sergeant and my group were hidden in a wood down to the left of the heath. We saw what happened, how our army was put to flight, with little resistance offered. We made our way west afterwards and crossed the moor. I became separated from my sergeant and turned back. I was found by the tin miners and given work and shelter."

Andrews was still not able to talk about his and Herrick's leaving of the unit – nor of his own probable killing of Herrick.

Realisation slowly dawned on Warden. He had always been right behind Sergeant Brown and with his mate Farmer. He had never had much to do with the younger members of Brown's men. Something registered with him.

"You be one of them that followed that idiot Herrick!" He grinned. "What happened to him and the other whose name I forget?"

"Porter."

"You three went off into the mist!"

"Aye, we did – and more fools us. We became lost soon after and wandered around for hours. Sometime after that, we became so cold that Porter could go no further. He died – just went to sleep and died. Herrick, may his soul rot in hell, just said 'twere a good thing, as Porter would have held us up. I kicked his head and left all on my own. I probably killed him!"

"Then, no more than he deserved! A soldier never abandons his mates! So, here we are after all that has happened – two soldiers for the king with no master!"

--------------------- OOOOOOOOOO ---------------------

Garvey and Haddock had walked the five miles to Bovey. Armed with stout ash staves, which they had cut themselves, they kept company with the travelling merchant on his wagon. The man, sitting in splendour way above them, had spoken hardly a word on the journey. By the time the small group arrived over the bridge by Bovey mill, the two were still none the wiser as to the 'valuable' contents of the wagon. Maybe, they surmised, they were better off not knowing.

The merchant drew the wagon to a halt and reached into his purse. He handed Garvey, who was the nearer of the two, a small handful of coins.

"Your task ends here," they were told. "I shall carry on to Chudleigh Knighton."

"Then, God speed you, sir," Garvey said but received no reply. The wagon slowly disappeared around the bend to the right past the village square.

"Do we eat and sleep warm tonight?" Haddock enquired.

"Aye – enough for three nights and three dinners. It seems a year since we were here with Sergeant Lovelace and Ratty – down in that wood."

"'Tis only just over six weeks!"

"One thing we must bear in mind," Garvey warned. "This be a village strongly for the king. We must guard our tongues if we want to find work."

"Aye – that we must. But what work can we seek – not much call for woodland trackers hereabouts!"

They trudged up the village street, past the square, and headed for where they knew the tavern to be situated. They arranged beds for that night, then sat down for bowls of thick stew and a mug of ale. They were struck immediately by the air of quiet despondency until they realised that a royalist village had little to celebrate.

Luke Farmer also had little to celebrate. Despite his quiet determination to speak to the woodsman father of Meg, the man in question had not been seen for some days, apparently deep in the woods thinning out a stand of beech trees that were needed for chair and table legs. With almost no coins in his purse, he stayed put in the final of the three cottages, pretending to make small repairs. Soon, he knew he would have to go to the reeve and declare that his tasks were completed. He had told Meg of his intentions and had been heartened by her response. Meg also brought him bread and cheese – but did so when nobody else was looking.

Mary arrived at the bakery in time for their late dinner at just after noon. Nell had insisted on walking with her but held her hand firmly all the way.

"Look who I bring to share our dinner," she announced, going through the shop into the back room.

"Why – bless my soul – if it be not Princess Nell!" Evelyn gasped - and gave her a deep curtsey.

"Indeed, it most assuredly is," John played his part by bowing almost to the floor.

Nell looked startled but then caught on and gave a strained smile.

"I'm not a princess," she almost giggled.

"But to us, you most certainly be a princess," Evelyn insisted. "Now, come you to the table and eat, as you must be hungry. And then tell us all about the lambs."

Perched on a thick cushion atop a stool, Nell spooned thick pottage into her mouth. All three were glad to see her eating and calm.

"I had a little lamb taking milk from me. He was warm and soft," she announced.

"But I thought little lambs took milk from their mothers," John prompted, knowing exactly why this had been necessary.

"His mama had three lambs – and she can only feed two!" Nell stated – as if to say that *everyone* knew that!

256

"You will live with James and Avril," John said. "James be my brother, and he and Avril have no children. They will care for you and give you a safe home. And you can come here to see us whenever you wish – and to the smith, next door as their daughter is to wed our son."

"They have a son as well – he's called Simon. But he's a young lad – and boys be silly things!" Mary grinned.

"My dada was not silly!" Nell was quite shocked at the idea.

"No – your dada was a wise and clever man," Mary was quick to appease her. "Boys be silly things and only learn not to be silly when they grow up. Girls are never silly!"

"Girls can be very silly," came from the doorway. Gil stood there, having just come back from his new cottage. "Hello, Nell – my name is Gil, and Mary be my very silly sister!"

Nell, totally unused to a full family life, relaxed a bit more in the company of a family that was obviously settled and happy with one another. She dug her spoon into the pottage and ate another mouthful.

Chapter 23

That evening saw the very belated return of Lord John Vickery. He arrived cold and wet, having ridden many miles with a few of his armed retainers for company. The first thing he did was to summon his steward and senior servants, the bailiff and old Master Garlick – who had fought beside Vickery years before. It was the last day of February, and the weather was wet and blowing a minor gale.

In the main hall of Parke House, a large fire blazed in the massive hearth, the lanterns were lit, and the whole room was bathed in the flickering light. Lord Vickery, ignoring his normal chair at the dais, stood by the stone mantle and looked over the small gathering.

"The king's cause was faltering some month ago," he said, his face drooping with fatigue. "Now, that same cause is lost and gone. Three days passed, and Fairfax attacked them at Launceston – those meagre remnants that remained. I have to tell you all that they have been soundly beaten. Not just beaten, my friends, but put to flight. His Grace, the Prince of Wales, accompanied by some of his senior officers, fled to the Isles of Scilly. The Good Lord only knows when we may see him again – even *if* we see him again. Those men left standing have fled to the furthest corners of Cornwall, though I suspect some have managed to get back into Devon."

Peter Cove, the bailiff and the senior of all the rest present, raised a hand.

"My lord, where does this leave us here? Indeed, where does this leave all those other places up and down the country who were, and still are, faithful to our king?"

Vickery, setting his pewter tankard down on a side table, gave a wry grimace.

"It leaves you, master bailiff, exactly where you were yesterday and for all those months before. You go about your business and live your lives as usual. The king – I am led to believe – is still at Oxford. Surrounded by the last few who remain loyal to him. The Scots, seeing one of their own Stuarts in distress, mass on the border. Whether or not they attempt to march south in support, I know not. But – rest assured – Master Fairfax and Master Cromwell will not tolerate that, should it happen. Master Pym has the Commons firmly under control – as he has had for many a month."

"Will nor parliament attempt to wreak vengeance on those places like Corfe and Exeter and Berry Pomeroy – which already lay in ruins?" old Garlick asked.

"I have given much thought to that, as you may imagine. I have had ample opportunity to dwell on such matters on my ride here! No – I do not believe they will. And here is my reasoning. Master Pym and his parliamentarians – they are not fools. Fairfax alone has proved that beyond any shadow of a doubt. They need all to carry on with business because they need taxes. Without that money, how shall they pay that new army? Without that new and effective army, how may they impose control? No – all of you should be safe from anything other than harassment. Some of my brother lords, on the other hand, may well suffer some retribution."

"And the king, my lord? What of him and his rights?"

"Indeed – what of him and his rights?" Vickery gave a bark of laughter. "We have a king who is king in name only. He has three options. One – he surrenders to parliament and accedes to their demands; two – he attempts to raise further support; and three – he flees to France, to Scotland, to anywhere who will have him. The first – acceding and bending the knee to parliament is so abhorrent to him that it will not happen. The second – raising support from whom? The Scots? They are a heathen bunch but know they will stand little chance against this New Model Army. The third – flee anywhere. Who will take him? The Scots know he will be pursued. The French – well, that perfidious lot would probably *sell* him back to parliament."

"But that leaves only stalemate," Peter Cove objected.

"No, master bailiff – it leaves one other outcome. The capture of the king and his virtual imprisonment. And that, I fear, is what is about to befall him. Our illustrious Prince of Wales, his cousin Rupert, his other high-ranking supporters – all are gone, fled to safety or fled in disgrace. His one commander worthy of the name – my Lord Hopton – either already has – or will soon – surrender to Fairfax. The likelihood is that he will abjure the realm – either that or suffer lifelong imprisonment."

"Lord John," old Garlick was the only man in the village who was able to get away with such a form of address. "If, as you say, Pym and his henchmen are able to capture the king – what then? Demands? Threats? Forced abdication?"

"Demands certainly! Threats? Threats of what? Regal emasculation? The queen to be sent away? I suspect that it might well start with the pretence of negotiation. But Charles will never negotiate with those he sees as his subjects! I see only months, maybe years, of turmoil. Not directly for you down here, but for the king and the governance of the country."

"That lack of governance will impact each and every one of us," Peter Cove objected. "Maybe not directly, as you say, my lord, but indirectly as parliament imposes whatever laws and restrictions it feels appropriate."

And on that very unsatisfactory note, the meeting broke up. By morning, the whole village knew of the news and of their lord's thoughts and predictions.

--------------------- OOOOOOOOOO ---------------------

Nell had woken up during the night – still not used to being in what was, for her, a strange house. James and Avril had put a small palliasse on the floor in their own room. They planned to make the smaller bed chamber fit for Nell when she had settled in further.

The first that James and Avril were aware that Nell was awake was when they heard a little sob. James propped himself up and saw a diminutive figure in a white night shift peering out of the window into the darkness.

"What – not asleep, Nell?" He called out softly.

"I can't see the star!" came a muffled sob. "I want to talk to my dada."

James slipped out of bed and went over to the little girl. Gently, he lifted her up and held her close.

"You can't see the star because there are lots of clouds. Believe me, Nell; the star is *always* up there shining bright. Sometimes, we just cannot see it. But it most assuredly is there."

Nell stopped sobbing and buried her face into James' neck.

"Is my dada still there as well?"

"Yes – he is there; the star is there. Listen – can you always see the sun? Of course, you cannot. On many days there is a dark cloud, sometimes a white, fluffy cloud – but the sun is still there. That is exactly the same for the moon and the stars. If there be clouds, we can't see them – but they are always there. So, whether there be a cloud or clear sky, you can always talk to your dada – for he will be there to hear you."

"Will he hear me, really?"

"Nell, my sweet, who do you say your prayers too?"

"Jesus."

"And can Jesus hear you?"

"I think so."

"And can you see Him?"

"No – nobody can see Jesus. He's up there in heaven."

"And where is your dada?"

"Oh -if he is with Jesus, then he can hear me as well!"

"Exactly. Whether or not you can see that star matters not. So, offer your prayers to Jesus and talk to your dada. It's all really one and the same."

And may the heavens above forgive me this subterfuge, James said to himself as he felt the little girl relax. He planted a kiss on the blonde curls and laid her back down on her pallet, covered her with the blankets, and went back to bed. Avril leaned towards him as he climbed back into bed – and gave his hand a squeeze. Both of them heard a little girl whispering quietly, then silence as she dropped off to sleep again.

The first service to be held in the church that day was the funeral of young Hal Dawkins. It was attended by many of the villagers – with three notable exceptions.

Mary called down for Nell as soon as work in the bakery had finished. She brought with her young Hob – the bailiff's little lad who was a messenger and odd job boy at the estate. Hob, like Nell, was an orphan. He had been the only child of one of the estate gardeners. The man's wife had died soon after Hob had been born – and the gardener had died when Hob was just six years old. The bailiff and his wife had taken young Hob into their home and had cared for him. Hob had joined two other children, a boy of ten and a girl of thirteen. At twelve and fifteen, the two were now employed in the mansion. Hob, a mere five years older than Nell, was irrepressible – he never walked but ran. He climbed trees, scrumped apples, and was regularly into some mischief or other. He was the finest and probably the fastest messenger.

Mary, an empty basket on her arm, had been only too willing to keep Nell from what was to be a very sad day. She had forewarned Hob not to even mention the fact that Nell's dada was being buried.

"Say one-word amiss, and I shall see you beaten with a large stick!" she had warned.

"I'm not stupid!" Hob poked out his tongue, then dodged as Mary took a swipe at him.

"No – that is one thing you are not," Mary agreed. "Cheeky, as fast as a hare, you may be. But you be not stupid. We will take Nell into the woods and search for young elm trees. My aunt Avril needs slivers of bark for one of her preparations."

"What? Elm bark? That would choke you if you tried to eat it!" Hob observed.

"It is ground down and mixed with water to spread on burns and skin injuries," Mary explained. She was learning fast from both aunt and uncle – and absorbing knowledge like a sponge.

Sometime later, Mary heard the bell from the church ring and knew that the body of Nell's father was now in his grave – therefore, it was safe to return. But instead of going straight back to the apothecary's shop, she diverted to the estate to make sure Hob got there properly – and didn't scamper off to do whatever mischief he may have planned.

Then, having delivered Nell and her basket back to her aunt, she walked back up the village to her dinner at the bakery. She would be back again for her training as an apprentice that afternoon.

"Chip will be making a small cross for the grave," John told his daughter. "He will carve the name into it and also say that he was father to Nell. I have no idea when Nell should come and see it!"

"Not for some time, certainly," Evelyn nodded her agreement. "She needs to settle in with James and Avril, make some friends with the village children, and be a happy little girl again."

"I have had an idea," Mary spoke up between eating slices of pork and fresh bread. "When 'tis May time, can Nell not be our May Princess? I know we do not usually have one – and that it is Primrose's turn to be May Queen – but who is to say that the Queen may not have a princess as well?"

Mary had been May Queen the previous year. Primrose, daughter of the saddler, was to take her turn as May Queen. The year before Mary, Glory from the tavern had been May Queen.

"That is a splendid thought," Evelyn remarked. "It will achieve two things – make Nell feel special and also make her a part of the village. What flowers shall adorn that curly head?"

"Something blue," Mary said at once. "Her eyes are the same colour."

"We shall make sure the idea is acceptable to one and all," her mother stated. If she, her husband, and – above all – Abel backed the idea, who would say her nay, she thought.

Luke Farmer was slowly getting towards his wit's end. Day after day, he had made almost no progress with the last cottage until he realised that he could hang it out no longer. And then his prayers were answered – the woodcutter returned to his cottage for his midday dinner.

Do not disturb his meal, Luke warned himself. Let him eat his fill, drink his ale, and relax into a good and friendly mood. He had not seen Meg that day – presumably, the wise woman had enough of her supplies. He wondered what else Meg may have been doing.

And then, well past the dinner hour, he summoned up his courage and went to the woodcutter's cottage and knocked on the door. After a few moments, Meg answered it and gave him a big grin. She stepped aside so that Luke could enter the main room of the cottage. The woodcutter sat in a large chair by his hearth, his feet up on a stool and a large pewter tankard of ale in his hand. Luke also noted that the huge axe was leaning against the wall.

"And who may you be?" came a deep, bass voice from behind a bushy beard.

"Er – my name is Luke Farmer, Master Woodcutter."

"Oh – you be one of the two mending cottages for the bailiff."

"Aye – and the work is finished. My friend has already gone back to Master Bailiff to see if more work can be had."

"Heard tell you were with king's army. Is that so?"

"Aye – we were at Bovey and then trailed over the moor to try and join up again with Lord Hopton."

"From all I hear, 'tis as well for you that you failed to do so. Hopton suffered badly at Torrington – and again at Launceston. So, how come you arrived here again?"

"We had nowhere else to go. We became separated from our sergeant, then walked back across the moor as we had no idea where else to go."

"And now we come to the big question, Luke Farmer. Why be you here talking to me? I have no work for you – nor do I have means of getting work for you with anyone else."

Luke took a deep breath. Then completely forgetting his carefully prepared speech, simply blurted out.

"Sir, I have been keeping company with your daughter Meg. I do believe she is of like mind. I wish to pay court and seek your blessing."

"Keeping company, eh? And I wonder what lies behind those two words."

"Nothing untoward, I promise you, sir. I have respected Meg in every way."

"Yes, I know all that," the woodcutter grunted. "Do you believe that a simple woodcutter has not eyes to see? My Meg has told me of your liaison – and that you have shown her every respect."

Luke gave Meg a startled glance. She replied with another of her wide grins.

"You seem to be of good character – so I'll make a bargain with you, Luke Farmer. Get you gone back to Master Bailiff and obtain good and honest work. Then you may come back here and pay court to my Meg."

"Then I thank you, sir – it is all I ever wanted. I shall do exactly as you say and will return here with my honest intentions as bright as they are now."

"Good. Then be off with you,"

Luke made his farewell and, giving Meg a huge smile of relief, returned to the cottage to pack his meagre belongings before reporting to the reeve.

Meg sat on a stool by her father, who was laughing quietly.

"So, my little Meg – you have turned a head, have you?"

"Aye, father. I love that man and would have him for my husband."

"If he proves honest and trustworthy, then you may have him."

Meg went outside into the overcast day and did a small jig. She hummed happily to herself as she fed the few chickens behind the cottage.

Luke hummed to himself as he walked the few miles back to Bovey. He needed to meet up with Kit again. Two stood a better chance of obtaining work than one on his own.

Just over a mile southwest of Bovey Tracey was the little village of Brimley. On its northern edge stood Brimley Court, virtually unoccupied for some years following the death of the last member of the family that, for the previous century and a half, had been tenants of the Vickerys – who were, in turn, tenants in chief of the king.

The previous day had seen the arrival of a formidable lady – one Lady Violette Charlton, a distant relative of the Courtney family – a family that had been prominent in Devon for many years. Her husband, Sir Gaston Charlton, had died just before the previous Christmas. Being childless and without any near relatives, Lady Violette had decided that the squalor of London was not for her any longer. The large house was sold, and her agents instructed to find her a suitable small estate somewhere rural and peaceful. She had arrived with her own steward, her own cook, her personal maid, and two old retainers.

The first sight of her new home had not filled her with great joy – she had been downhearted at the very look of the place. However, being of a stoic disposition, she immediately dismissed the caretaker and his wife.

"You have kept the rain from the upper rooms," she snorted. "But that is all I may say for your guardianship. The rooms are filthy and the grounds in disarray."

"My lady," her steward stepped forward. "Give me a week, some good people to work, and you may not know the place."

"Thomas – I know I may leave all in your capable hands. Now – my requirements for the rest of today are simple. I need fresh water for washing, a change of clothing, some plain food to eat, and a dry bed in which to sleep. Tomorrow, we make a start in earnest."

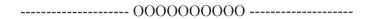
--------------------- OOOOOOOOOO ---------------------

Sergeant Brown was almost fully recovered from his injury. Ratcliffe was so fed up with lying on a rough pallet that he ignored all advice and started walking around the large room. In the intervening days, five more of the badly injured had died, leaving only Brown, Ratcliffe, and two still unconscious patients in the room. The landlord of the inn, his patience near breaking point, had been given assurance that his premises would be returned to him in another couple of days.

Being a sensible chap, he recognised that the parliamentary officer left in command of Torrington – or what remained of it – needed no show of temper or bad manners. He simply thanked the officer and waited patiently to resume his life.

Brown had heard all about the final defeat at Launceston and knew that there was no unit left for him to join. There was only one option left for him – to go home.

Ratcliffe *did* have the option to join up with parliamentary forces. However, he had simply had his fill of traipsing around the countryside like a fox stalking his prey. He and Brown had become almost friends – unlikely as that would have seemed a few weeks before. When they both related their stories and swapped reminiscences, they came to the conclusion that continued enmity was pointless, indeed utterly futile.

On the day that Brown shouldered his pack with his few possessions – his armaments having been confiscated – he first sat down beside Ratcliffe on a bench outside the inn.

"Off home, sergeant?" Ratcliffe said, prepared to say farewell.

"Aye – the Lord alone knows what I may do when I get there. Beg to be allowed back into my father's house, I suppose."

272

"Have you work to go back to?"

"No – I have been a soldier for the king ever since I was old enough to carry a musket. How about you? Have you anything to return to?"

"That is doubtful – as doubtful as my managing to get back to my home, which is far from here in Hampshire."

"But that is not so far – if you can obtain a lift with carts or wagons every now and again."

"And of what use would a woodsman tracker be in Hampshire?" Ratcliffe laughed.

"As much use there as anywhere else, I would imagine," Brown slapped him on the back. "See here, my parliamentary friend – we both start off by going south and east. Why do we not at least start off together? With your tracking skills and my skill with a slingshot, we will never starve!"

The unlikely pairing set off that afternoon – heading first for South Molton and then planning to head south down the east side of the moor towards Brown's home in Trusham.

Chapter 24

The third day of March was marred by only one thing – cold, persistent rain that seeped into every nook and cranny from the western tip of Cornwall to the start of Savernake Forest. Later in the day, Salisbury Plain would feel its clammy embrace.

In the bakery, everything started off as normal. The bread was baked, deliveries made, and damp villagers came to the shop. But then, an hour and a half before the noontide dinner, the whole house bulged with visitors and well-wishers. Gil, still in his flour-whitened apron, sat somewhat bemused by the constant stream of villagers he had known all his life who came in steady stream to wish him a happy birthday.

Old men slapped his back, and old women kissed his cheek; younger men grasped his hand and drank his health; younger women and girls fawned at him. His own mother, father and sister dispensed ale and pastries to one and all. But the guest of honour was Ella, to whom he would be married the next day. She arrived from the smithy with her father, mother and brother. Dressed simply in everyday clothes, Gil wondered not for the first time what good sprite had blessed him with such luck – Ella, despite her sombre dress, looked as pretty as any picture.

"Right, lad," Abel boomed for all to hear. "Make the most of your time with Ella, for in one hour, she will return home with Glory and Primrose for the company – and you shall not set eyes upon her until she arrives at the church porch tomorrow morning."

Gil felt that this was all a trifle unreal. Here he was, a baker's son and probably nobody in particular, being feted as if he were himself a noble prince – and a noble prince set to wed a beautiful bride. His soon-to-be brother-in-law, young Simon, saw to it that Gil's pewter mug remained filled with ale. Mary, his sister, also kept her eye on that mug, determined that her big brother would not fall into a drunken stupor. Gil, as she knew full well, was not like some of the young men – determined to get drunk at the slightest provocation. In fact, she admitted to herself, Gil was sometimes far too sober and sensible for his own good.

As the crowd slowly dispersed, all that was left were his family, along with James, Avril and little Nell, plus the Smiths. Little Nell had been hugged by nearly everyone and was sat quietly on Mary's lap, still bemused by the fun and laughter that had been like nothing she had ever experienced. For a whole hour, she had not once thought of her grandfather or even her dada.

And then Glory and Primrose had come back to collect Ella.

"Say farewell to your betrothed," Abel ordered.

Gil stood up and went over to Ella. He took her hands in his and kissed her somewhat chastely.

"Until the morrow," he whispered.

"Until the morrow," Ella whispered back, then planted her mouth firmly on his, turned and walked firmly out of the room, her two chaperones giggling behind her.

"And now we eat," Evelyn stated. She, Mary, Avril and Faith started bringing in cold meats, vegetables, bread and a thick gravy. Avril perched on a stool at the table with little Nell on another stool by her side – Nell being boosted with cushions.

Mary, ever conscious of others' feelings, watched with a smile as the little girl dipped her spoon into her bowl and ate as heartily as anyone else around the large table. Nell would thrive in this village, she thought.

"This time tomorrow, you shall be wed – a husband with a wife to cherish, a home to safeguard, and a business to grow," John put his arm around his son's shoulders. "Are you ready for such responsibilities?"

"Aye, father – ready and eager. It is all I ever wanted – and Ella is all I ever dreamed of marrying."

Abel drank deeply from his mug of ale and put it firmly down on the table. "Some fathers will be nervous for their daughters. But I am not. Faith and I have known you all of your life and know you will be a good and faithful husband."

"Aye, sir – so I shall."

Faith, never the one to say very much in company, simply gave Gil a smile and turned to her son.

"Simon – you will cease to keep filling Gil's mug with ale. Despite what those scallywag friends of yours say, 'tis not right!"

"But mother, 'tis fun!"

"Hear what your mother says," Abel gave him a punch on the arm that had Simon wincing.

"Aye, father."

"And now 'tis time for us ladies to go attend the bride-to-be," Faith stated. "And we have a small surprise for little Nell – as she shall play her part as well."

Nell looked a bit startled, but Avril put her hand on Nell's.

"It is a special part, and you shall be very happy with it. You be a part of this family now – and we all love you."

The three women, Mary and Nell, all took their leave – going next door to keep company with Ella and her bridesmaids. Faith had one parting shot.

"Simon – remember well what I said!"

"And that does not apply to the rest of us," Abel grinned, reaching for the ale jug.

"Indeed, it does not," John agreed, holding out his own mug. James looked on with a happy smile whilst Simon begged for a refill.

--------------------- OOOOOOOOOO --------------------

Thomas Carpenter, steward to Lady Charlton, was in his element. Charged with getting a large house and grounds in order was something he relished. Being a literate and numerate man, his first task was to list all the jobs that needed doing – both within the house and without. Having done that, he then attached the names of the servants who should attend to those tasks.

Within the house, thar was a simple business – the two maidservants and odd job man they had brought with them would suffice for the cleaning and polishing. However, there were other tasks of a more professional nature – broken bannisters, cracked ceilings and missing glass – these all needed the services of people not readily available to him.

The outside was another matter. Painting, woodwork, not to mention the gardens, all needed more staff – and he did not have them.

Thomas was in his fifty-eighth year, the son of a London innkeeper. He had escaped what he saw as a sterile occupation by begging lessons from various other shopkeepers. By the age of ten, he could read whole books and write detailed essays. He could calculate bills and add up accounts.

"Bloody nonsense!" his father had damned such knowledge. "Of what use be they to an innkeeper? All you will need is the ability to brew good ale and wield a large stick to control troublemakers."

"But, father, do you not want to know what your profit is?"

"Go and look in the strong box. If there be piles of coins, I'm doing well. If not, then I must need to charge more. 'Tis all I need to know!"

Thomas simply left one day after his fifteenth birthday. He sought work in a large house as a junior page, worked his way up to senior page, and then by the age of twenty, was under steward. He had joined Lady Violette's household as her steward at the age of twenty-eight – and had been with her ever since. Her household became a watchword for efficiency, prudent housekeeping, and excellent service.

He sought out Lady Violette and found her in the upstairs gallery marking out where pictures were to be hung.

"I need to consult a local source to find how I may employ suitable persons, my lady," he said. "May I have your permission to speak to Lord Vickery's steward?"

"That is well thought," she answered, peering down from a stool. "I have heard that he is well thought of. You have my permission."

Carpenter needed no second bidding. He went to the stables and ordered his own mount saddled, then set off for the very short rude to the Parke estate. Trotting through the large entrance gates, he marvelled at the acres of neat grass and shrubs. That is what Brimley shall look like, he promised himself.

He stopped at the house that was a short distance up the driveway, dismounted and tethered his mount to a post. He was about to knock when the door opened, and a large man in everyday clothes came out.

"Ah – a stranger," he greeted Thomas. "A good day to you."

"And to you, my good man," Thomas replied. "I am seeking the steward. Is he within?"

The man gave a beaming smile and decided it was time for a little joke. He desperately needed something to smile about.

"Indeed, he is. Pray to follow me within."

He opened the door and ushered Thomas into a room where a busy man sat at a desk, penning a note on a piece of paper.

"Someone seeks you, master steward," the large man said.

"Thomas Carpenter, steward to Lady Charlton," Thomas held out his hand to his counterpart.

Luke Barton stood up and shook the man's hand, then looked at the large gentleman.

"Is there anything else, my lord?" he asked.

Thomas blanched, then folded himself into a deep bow.

"My lord, I crave pardon," he stuttered.

"Pardon is readily granted," Lord Vickery said. "And how is the redoubtable Lady Charlton?"

"Up to her elbows in dust and cobwebs, my lord."

"Yes – that sounds fairly typical. I leave you with Master Barton here. Any help the dear lady requires shall be hers for the asking." Lord Vickery closed the door behind him, still chuckling.

"Please – take a seat and tell how we may be of service," Barton indicated a chair.

"It is people I seek, Master Barton. We have arrived with housemaids, our ostler, a handyman, and of course, my lady's maid. Where may I obtain the services of good and reliable staff? I ask, as we are strangers in this county."

Barton sat back in his chair, preparing to break what he believed would not be welcome news.

"Would that I had spare staff to help out," he said. "Some went months past to serve the king – and have yet to return – even if they are able to do so. The village is likewise bereft of such persons. But now that the fighting is over – at least for the time being – I would expect that there will soon be many men seeking work. I shall direct any I think suitable to Brimley."

"Then that is all I could ask. I thank you for your time."

Thomas rode back to Brimley to give Lady Violette the news. Bad news that there was nobody immediately available; good news that there could well be in the near future.

"Then we shall have to make do ourselves. Hand me that hammer," the resourceful lady replied.

--------------------- OOOOOOOOOO --------------------

It had taken Brown and Ratcliffe two days to walk the twenty-seven miles from Torrington to Whiddon Down. Michael Brown had chosen that route after thinking about and dismissing others – it was more direct. From Whiddon, he intended to walk down to Chagford and Moretonhampstead. Then he would cross east towards Trusham.

So far, he and Hugh Ratcliffe had been unfortunate in getting lifts from merchants with carts. Unsurprisingly, travellers were wary of picking up anyone unknown to them; the north of Devon was swarming with ex-members of the various king's armies – all looking for lifts. There had been many cases of merchants being beaten and left at the roadside, their horses and carts stolen.

Brown, quite naturally as a virtual prisoner of war, had been obliged to leave all his weaponry behind. Ratcliffe, being ostensibly a member of the victorious parliamentary forces, had left with his short sword and pistol. The pistol, being a canny individual, he had sold to the first person he met on the road. He had neither powder nor shot anyway.

The first thing they did when they got anywhere near a stand of trees was to use Ratcliffe's short sword and fashion a couple of staves. With this in his hand, Brown immediately felt about twelve inches taller – and more complete. All they had used the staves for was walking, but it still felt a lot better than having nothing with which to defend themselves.

They had managed to feed themselves without too much trouble. Ratcliffe, the stalker, had found the animals – coneys mainly – and Brown, with a crudely fashioned slingshot, had brought it down.

"Pity we were not able to stay longer," Ratcliffe observed as they sat in a small wood eating roasted coney again. "Too early in the year for other prey – hedgepigs be good eating, and they be still asleep – lazy buggers!"

That was a new one on Brown. "Hedgepigs?" he asked.

"Aye – hedgepigs. Find some mud and pack them into a big ball of the stuff, then get a good fire going and poke the thing deep within. Then, when it be cooled, break open the clay. All his prickles come away with the clay shell. Tastes good!"

Brown was secretly glad that it was still too early in the year for that to be even attempted. They doused their fire and got back on the road, having to climb onto the moor to get to their next destination, the small stannary town of Chagford.

They were just in sight of the church tower when three ragged individuals leapt out of the trees on the right of the road. Each had a stabbing dagger in his hand and circled the two travellers. Brown and Ratcliffe had spoken about this possibility – and had planned their response. They immediately stood back-to-back, their staves grasped in front of them. One of the attackers, bolder – and as it turned out, more stupid than his friends – immediately ran at Hugh Ratcliffe, his dagger ready to thrust upwards. Ratcliffe swung his stave upwards from near ground level and with considerable force. The man gave a piercing scream and staggered to the side of the road, his hands grasping himself between the legs.

"One down – two to go!" Ratcliffe laughed. "He'll not be pleasuring the ladies for a week or more!"

Seeing what had befallen their comrade, the other two concentrated on Brown, allowing Ratcliffe to turn and stand by his side. Brown turned his stave and held it as he would have held a pike. Its reach was considerably longer than an arm with a short dagger. He patiently awaited his chance.

The attacker nearest to him danced sideways and made a feint with his dagger. What he got in return was the blunt end of a hefty stave straight in his left eye. He dropped without a sound.

The third attacker fled. Brown and Ratcliffe looked at one another and swapped broad grins. Ratcliffe went over to the groaning man, who was being spectacularly sick. He swung his boot into the side of the man's head, and the man simply passed out.

"King's men and parliament's men," Brown chortled. "Together, we make a good team!"

"Aye, that we do," Hugh grinned. "Onwards, brother!"

By nightfall, they were on the northern edge of Moretonhampstead, their journey almost over.

--------------------- OOOOOOOOOO --------------------

Ella spent the first two hours that night tossing and turning in her bed. She was both excited at the prospect of her marriage – eager and happy to become Gil's wife – but also apprehensive at what she would have to endure. Her mother's advice was still fresh in her memory. The pain of the first encounter would be real, as she had been told. But the joy thereafter will be worth every twinge. Eventually, just as the moon emerged from behind a blanket of clouds, she fell asleep.

Gil dropped onto his bed. For the first time in his life, he experienced the weird sensation of a room slowly revolving around him. Simon had chosen to ignore his father's instruction and had kept Gil's mug filled throughout the early evening. Shutting his eyes did little to stop the sensation. Instead of seeing the room gyrate, he felt himself slowly turning through a complete circle. Those last two mugs of ale had tasted different – very nice, but different. Little did he know that his young neighbour had topped each of those mugs with honey mead. Gil did not feel sick; he felt rather deliriously happy. All he could see with his eyes firmly shut and his body revolving was Ella's face – her dimples, her mass of chestnut hair, and her deep brown eyes. He fell asleep soon after – with a sigh and a smile on his face.

Nell, down the street and in her small bed, gazed up through the window at a bright star. Night-night, dada, she whispered. She fell asleep with a sigh of contentment. For the first time since that awful day, she had no fear of the future- somehow knowing she was safe. She had loved the little dress that had been made for her – and that she would be a part of the wedding celebration. Never having experienced real family life, it was all new and exciting. But above all else, she felt safe.

Lord John Vickery went to bed that night feeling far from happy. His ordered world was collapsing around his ears. The unquestioned rule of the king was severely threatened – more than ever now that his forces had been not only beaten but scattered. He turned his attention once more to the letter that had been placed on his desk by his clerk. It was a plea from James and Avril Ramsey – a plea that they be allowed to absorb one Nell Dawkins, an orphan, into their household. He had made enquiries and had been told the story of this unfortunate little girl. He also knew the apothecary and his wife – and thought highly of them. With a grunt, he picked up his quill, dipped it into his inkhorn, scrawled the word 'approved', and then signed it with his usual flourish. At least, he thought, some tiny spark of good may come out of this wretched day. His clerk would see it on the morrow and would have it conveyed to the Ramseys. He reached for his wine glass, emptied the fine Bordeaux down his throat, and then went to bed.

Just before dropping off to sleep, he wondered whether he was legally allowed to 'approve' this adoption. He knew that Reverend Forbes had 'sanctioned' it – but what was the true legal position? Sod it, he muttered to himself. My word is still law around here – but for how much longer?

--------------------- OOOOOOOOOO ---------------------

At Brimley, Lady Charlton blew out the last of the lamps that illuminated the main hall. She, her personal maid Lily, and the two housemaids had spent all day cleaning and polishing. One room at a time, she had ordered. Tomorrow, the kitchen and scullery, she had ordained – much to the consternation of the cook and the scullery maid who thought these rooms their own empire. They knew better than to remonstrate with their mistress.

The old lady climbed the stairs to her bed chamber – all that had been accomplished there was that her bed was aired and the blankets spread. She dismissed Lily.

"You look as tired as I feel," she said, with a rare turn of appreciation for a servant. "Get to bed and be ready for an early start in the morning. Kitchen!"

She undressed herself – another rarity – shrugged into her night shift, knelt at the side of her bed and closed her eyes.

"Lord – I give You thanks for my day. I wish You to grant me the same success on the morrow – and for many days thereafter. I ask that You pour everlasting damnation on Masters Pym, Fairfax, and Cromwell – and all the other villains who wreak havoc on this poor land. Amen."

She climbed into her bed, blew out her candle and immediately dropped off into a deep sleep.

Chapter 25

John and Evelyn were the first to see the sunrise on the day of the wedding. Not only had they baked enough bread for their customers, but they had roped in young Simon to do the deliveries. Mary, having attended the shop, then posted a notice in the window to the effect that they would be closed for the rest of the day. This angered only one person – the irascible Mercy Green. She arrived five minutes after Mary had shot the bolt on the door.

Following persistent hammering on the door panels, John went out to see who was creating the racket.

"Ah – Mistress Green," he sighed. "We are closed for my son's wedding. We will be open again as usual on the morrow."

"And in the meantime, we are deprived of our daily bread – and all because those two shameless young people have decided to end their shame with marriage!"

"I hope, Mistress Green, you are not implying anything improper of my daughter," came a voice from just behind her. She spun around to find the enormous figure of Abel Smith glowering at her.

John gave his neighbour a big grin. He was going to enjoy this confrontation.

"She wears her shame for all to see – holding hands and kissing before the whole world!"

"You, Mistress Green, are a foul-minded wretch – as is that weed of a husband of yours. The old habit of ducking a scold in the pond may well have to be brought back. The whole village would be happy to see you punished thus."

"Indeed, we all would," John nodded. "It would be so well attended that we might even be tempted to charge admission."

"Now – be off with you, and never again let me hear you speak ill of my Ella."

He bent down and placed his bearded face an inch from the sour countenance of the woman.

"BOO!" he shouted. Mistress Green turned pale, gathered her skirts in one hand and fled.

"And now to more pleasant things," John said. "Abel – you will take a glass of mead?"

"Aye, John – it would be my pleasure."

Gil awoke with his head, not in its usual place – or so it seemed to him. His mother banged on his door and cried out that if he wanted to break his fast, he should get downstairs. He slowly swung his feet onto the floor and stood. He was pleased to see that the room stayed stationary. He discarded his night shift and struggled into breeches and a shirt. His appearance at the table caused some merriment.

"Dear Lord above," his father laughed. "Outside with you and duck your head in the cold trough. Simon – as you were probably the cause of this, you may see it done."

Gil reappeared some minutes later, water streaming down his head. He had to admit that he actually felt considerably better for that immersion. Simon, laughing at his friend's discomfort, climbed onto a stool and attacked a still-warm loaf. He slathered butter and honey on it and took a huge bite.

"And now you may join my drunken brother in the trough," Mary giggled. "You are covered in honey!"

Simon poked his tongue out at Mary and took another massive bite. Gil ate slowly and sparingly, even adding water to his breakfast ale. He did not want to take Simon to task as the lad would be helping out at the bakery for the next two days.

Old Will Garlick, the churchwarden, supervised the decorating of the church. Sam Fewings, the sexton and two other members of the parish had volunteered to assist. Early spring flowers – mainly primroses, snowdrops and narcissus – were woven into boughs of yew and box. The porch was garlanded in ribbons of yellow and green. Reverend Forbes prepared his very brief sermon and opened the bible on the lectern to the appropriate verses.

In the tavern, all was being made ready. Tables were covered in linen cloths; pewter was polished; yellow bows of ribbon were tied to the beams; the top table had two large chairs at the centre with cushions and more yellow bows. Two new barrels of ale were tapped and set on their slanted trestles. Jugs of claret were filled.

--------------------- OOOOOOOOOO --------------------

In the back room of the smithy, all male personnel were banned for the rest of the morning. Faith – mother of the bride; Evelyn – mother of the groom; Mary and Glory – bridesmaids; Nell – special bridesmaid; and Ella – the bride; all were in the usual lather of preparation. Worried exclamations were punctuated by outbursts of giggling.

The two mothers were ready first – dressed in their very best apparel. Mary and Glory were next – both in dresses of primrose yellow and wearing little chaplets of flowers around their heads. Little Nell, excited as never before in her short life, was pampered and put into a matching yellow dress. Instead of flowers, she wore a band of light blue ribbon around her blonde curls – and carried a posy of small flowers. Ella wore a dress of emerald green and had a circle of green ribbon and white narcissus flowers on her chestnut hair.

"Well – we look fit to attend the highest court in the land!" Evelyn exclaimed as she surveyed the group.

Ella sidled over to her mother. She was getting a trifle apprehensive – she was still shy of her sixteenth birthday. Faith took her hand and whispered that all would be well. Ella, slightly comforted, still had a little fit of butterflies.

--------------------- OOOOOOOOOO ---------------------

Gil, resplendent in a white hose, brown breeches, ruffled shirt and short cote, looked down at his buckled shoes. His face, distorted, looked back at him from within the deep shine.

He joined his father and young Simon – plus his Uncle James and Aunt Avril.

"Do I look correct?" he asked hesitatingly.

"You look perfect," Avril assured him. "Ella will hardly know you."

"You look like one of the king's pages," Simon grinned.

"Take no notice of that young oaf," Abel grunted. "He would not know a well-dressed page if he stumbled over one!"

"'Tis time we left for the church," his father reminded everyone.

With the exception of Abel, they all made their way up the street to the church – where they waited on the porch. Abel went back to the smithy to wait for his daughter. He would take her hand in his beefy arm and walk her to the church.

---------------------- OOOOOOOOOO --------------------

Gil stood nervously on the porch, looking down the street for a first glimpse of his bride. He shifted his weight from foot to foot until Reverend Forbes laughed and told him to relax.

Abel, dwarfing his daughter at his side, came slowly up the street. Immediately behind them came little Nell, followed by Mary and Glory. As they drew nearer, Gill couldn't help a short gasp as he caught sight of Ella. To his eyes, there had never been, nor would there ever be, a more beautiful bride.

"You, young Gil, are a very lucky man," Forbes muttered.

"Aye, reverend. I know that full well," he muttered back.

The pair were joined by hand on the porch as had been the custom for hundreds of years. Forbes led them through the marriage ceremony and declared them to be man and wife. He then led the wedding party into the packed church, where they were greeted by the choir singing and the congregation smiling as they slowly processed towards the rood screen where two kneeling stools awaited them.

The service was short, the readings appropriate, and the sermon mercifully devoid of any mention of the issue – a fact that made Ella, for one, very grateful. And then it was time for them to process down the centre aisle to the subdued clapping and broad smiles of all their friends.

They led the way to the tavern, where they were received graciously and ushered to their seats at the top table. They were toasted in wine and then joined everyone in eating a fine meal of a spiced soup, roasted capons, various vegetables and plates of marchpane and candied fruits. And then Abel raised his voice and stood.

Nell, sitting on Avril's lap, looked in some awe at the massive blacksmith. She had revelled in her part and had eaten probably too much marchpane. Despite a slight queasiness, she waited breathlessly for what was to come next.

"My friends and neighbours," Abel started off. "Today, you have been with us all as our little girl enters marriage and womanhood. No longer a little daughter, but the wife of our neighbour Gil – the son of our own dearest friends. It is customary for the father of the bride to utter threats of dire retribution to his newly acquired sin-in-law – treat her badly, and I will visit the hounds of hell upon you. With young Gil, Faith and I know that such threats be unnecessary. Gil will guard his new wife with his life, will love and honour her as we have all just heard him promise. This poor country be in turmoil and sadness. But today, this little part of it bears witness to great joy and happiness. We are most grateful that you all are here to share that joy. So, raise your glasses and wish long life and happiness to our Ella and her husband, Gil."

The toast was drunk, and Abel sat down to great applause. Gil swallowed nervously and stood. Ella looked up at him and gave him her special smile, then took his hand in hers. Thus fortified, he began.

"Master Smith – I thank you most sincerely for that. In response, I tell you all that the vow I made before Almighty God I shall keep until the day that one of us is called to Him. Reverend Forbes said to me as Ella came up to the church that I was a lucky man. I am indeed the luckiest of men. Was there ever more beautiful a bride?"

He was interrupted by a barrage of applause and not a few whistles. Ella blushed furiously - but was quietly delighted.

"Like my now father-in-law, I thank you all for coming to witness and enjoy the day with us. And now I ask that you raise those glasses again to the health of my sister Mary, her lifelong friend Glory, and the newest and sweetest member of our family – little Nell."

The toast was drunk, and Gil was loudly cheered and applauded as he regained his seat.

"May the heavens be blessed that I did not falter," he whispered to Ella.

"Husband – you were magnificent," Ella blushed at the words.

"Wife – you are a prize beyond compare," he answered. "I love you."

"And I love you," was the reply, accompanied by a kiss – that was duly noted and applauded.

Dick Allen, the innkeeper, his wife Sal and their son Zachary, along with the three tavern maids, started clearing the floor for dancing and general merrymaking. The usual musicians from the village – drum, pipe, lute and viol – tuned up and started a round.

Formal dancing soon gave way to spirited jigs. The afternoon sped past as ale was tapped, more food consumed and lanterns lit.

--------------------- OOOOOOOOOO ---------------------

Sergeant Lovelace now had a new job. He had done particularly well at Launceston, leading a small squad that managed to breach the royalist defences, then taking more than thirty of them prisoner. For some reason that he was never to understand, he had then been teamed with Sergeant Franks. Not that he objected to the man; the two of them hit it off almost immediately. Franks had the greatest respect for Lovelace's abilities, whilst Lovelace admired the organising skills of Franks.

The two sergeants were given command of a team of eight soldiers and ordered to ride to Bovey. There, they were to set up patrols and, in the words of their captain, 'to keep a weather eye on the buggers'.

Similar teams were sent to Torrington, Barnstaple, Totnes, Tavistock, and as far south as Kingsbridge. Lovelace and Franks had argued over which route to take. Lovelace was quite vehement.

"I've seen as much of that bloody moor as I ever want to!"

"Then, we have to go south down the western edge, then east along the bottom," Franks countered – "and that's almost twice the distance."

"Which would be the faster route?" their captain asked.

"If we run into foul weather, then the longer route would be faster. If the weather remains fair, then over the moor," Franks answered.

"And who's to forecast the weather over the moor? I, for one, cannot!" Lovelace snorted.

The captain thought for a moment, then made his decision.

"Be ready to leave at first light. If the weather be fair, then over the moor you go. If the weather be foul, then head south and go a long way."

Lovelace went to bed that night, praying hard for rain and mist. His prayer must have been answered as when the sun arose on the ten soldiers, and there was a dank mist that obscured the distant hills.

On the afternoon of Gil's and Ella's wedding, the small troop rode through the main street of Ivybridge. They had taken three days to get that far. One more would see them arrive at Bovey.

Franks had spent some time on the journey telling Lovelace and the eight mounted troopers all he knew of their destination. He remembered it well and had drawn his own version of the houses and fields. By the time they all arrived, each man would have a good knowledge of the layout and the people who lived there.

He particularly remembered the two 'relatives from Dawlish'. He still didn't believe a word of that story. He wondered whether he would find them still there.

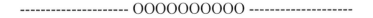

--------------------- OOOOOOOOOO ---------------------

As the sun set, Ella and Gil walked down to their cottage. Most of the party revellers accompanied them – some offering ribald advice, others embarrassed by it all. Ella gripped Gil's hand and tried to hide her apprehension. Gil also tried to hide *his* apprehension.

What, he wondered, if they were not suited? What if he disappointed Ella? What if Ella disappointed him? He stole a glance at his young bride and told himself not to be so stupid. At his side was a very beautiful young woman, a very beautiful young woman he had loved for many years past. They had their own small home in which to start their life together. They even had the beginnings of their own business to grow into something special. They had advantages granted to a few of their class.

When they reached the door to the cottage, it was opened by Hob. He had been given the job of lighting the fire, storing a supply of wood, and making sure everything was in order. He slipped out and went to stand beside Simon. He was shaking with mirth. Simon looked hard at him.

"What little surprise have you left for them?" he whispered.

"Shall not tell you," Hob whispered back. He crept around the press of people and ran back to his bed in the bailiff's house, still shaking with laughter.

"May the Lord bless this house and those who dwell within," Reverend Forbes gave a blessing.

"And all the little ones who come hereafter!" one wag called out.

Abel stood and addressed the throng.

"Let us all leave them in peace – I am thirsty and am returning to the tavern. Who shall come with me?"

That started a minor stampede back up the street, leaving Gil and Ella in the open threshold.

Gil led Ella into the cottage and closed and bolted the door. Then he took Ella into his arms.

"And now we are alone," he said softly. "My beautiful wife and I have all our lives before us. Let us begin as we mean to go on."

He kissed Ella softly, took her hand and led her to the bottom of the stair. Ella gulped and followed him up and into their small bed chamber. The bed had been made, and petals were strewn on the cover and the two pillows. Gil went to bed and pulled back the cover. Ella gave a startled shriek.

There, in the middle of the bed, was a dead frog.

"I shall personally flay that Hob within an inch of his miserable young life!" Gil roared, taking one stiff leg and hurling the corpse out of the window. He turned around to find Ella sitting on the edge of the bed, tears rolling down her face. She was laughing helplessly.

If she had but known, that start to their married life would have been a blessing. It relaxed her almost completely. One further thing helped her relax even more – Gil was kind and gentle. Nestled in one another's arms, she knew that she was going to enjoy her life.

"I love you, husband," she murmured sleepily.

"I adore you, my beautiful wife," he replied.

--------------------- OOOOOOOOOO --------------------

Hob's first job the next morning was to run to the apothecary's shop with a message. He kept mumbling it to himself as he ran – anxious not to get it wrong, as the bailiff could get angry if he either forgot or ended up relaying a load of garbled nonsense.

By the time he arrived, James was opening the shutters and getting ready for the day ahead. He looked up to see one young lad, hardly out of breath and standing on one leg.

"Good day, Hob. What may I do for you? Some salve for your bunions? An ointment to promote hair on your bald head?"

"Nay, Master Ramsey. I bring a message for you. My Lord Vickery presents his compli – things, and may you and Mistress Ramsey and little Nell attend upon him this morning at eleven of the clock."

It had all come out as very nearly one enormous word – but James got the drift of it.

"Please take back a message that we shall be honoured to attend his lordship at the appointed hour."

Hob stood still, mumbling it to himself at least ten times. Then, without a word, he turned tail and scooted off.

James hurried in to tell Avril.

"May this be good news," she uttered a small prayer.

"Amen to that," James nodded – and went to find Nell.

 --------------------- OOOOOOOOOO --------------------

Franks, Lovelace and the eight mounted troopers arrived in the village square just before eleven o'clock that morning. Word spread throughout Bovey so that, within ten minutes of their arrival, nearly all the inhabitants knew of it. Their first job was to unload the panniers and set up tents beside the mill – in exactly the same place that Franks had occupied previously.

"As you are the one already known here, may I leave it to you to announce our presence and purpose to Lord Vickery – assuming he be here," Lovelace suggested.

"Aye – as soon as we be settled, I will do exactly that. But let us have our dinner first."

"Then, whilst you be away, I shall detail the first of the patrols."

It took very little time for the tents to be erected and the bed rolls installed. Dick Lovelace stood at the side of the mill and gazed down the heath and off to the left where he and his trackers had been concealed. It seemed a lifetime ago. His reverie was disturbed by Franks calling the troopers together.

"You all know why we have been sent here," he said. "We are here to be vigilant – looking out for anything or anyone who may pose a threat to us and our victory. Pay special attention to any gathering – especially in that tavern. We are *not* going to be welcome visitors. We may be cursed, even spat upon by some. We do *not* respond to anything like that. We ignore it. We keep our discipline at all times. We go about in pairs, never alone. Many people will talk openly about a new muster for the king. It will all be bombast and piffle. But there may well be some small planning acts of mischief. Be silent, watch and listen – do not react in any way. Have you all understood that?"

A chorus of 'yes, sergeant' greeted his speech. Being wise, Franks knew that not all his men would be silent when the insults started. Some would react – and react violently. He would then have to exert even stronger discipline.

"One further thing," he added. "The womenfolk are to be respected. If I hear of any misbehaviour in that respect, the culprit will be flogged – before the assembled village!"

Lovelace nodded at that. "I shall be the one wielding the whip – and I'm very good with one of those," he growled.

---------------------- OOOOOOOOOO ---------------------

James and Avril set off, having closed their shop for an hour or more. Nell walked beside Avril, clutching her hand. As they came level with the mill by the bridge, James called across to Franks.

"Back again, sergeant?"

"Yes, Master Apothecary – back again," he nodded.

It took the three about fifteen minutes to get to the bailiff's house at Parke. Hob was hovering on the doorstep, muttering to himself.

"Off with another message, Hob?" James grinned.

"Aye – one for Master Garlick – but I have no notion what it means," Hob replied, again standing on one leg.

"As long as Master Garlick knows its meaning, you need not worry."

"Aye – but I'm not sure such will be the case. Means nothing to me!" the lad grumbled. "Might as well be in foreign!" He turned and scampered off. Nell looked after the lad as he shot through the open gates.

"Hob never walks!" she stated. "Why is he always running?"

"Ah – Hob be a messenger. He believes that the faster he gets where he needs to go, the more he will remember the message. He thinks that if he goes slowly, there will be more time for him to forget."

"He should write the message on paper!" Nell stated.

"Not everyone knows their letters," Avril reminded her. "Your dada taught you well – and we shall certainly continue as he did. By the time you be Hob's age, you will be the best-lettered girl in the village."

They were shown into the parlour, where Lord Vickery and the bailiff were waiting. James and Avril made their bows. Nell bobbed her curly head.

Vickery handed James the letter he had sent, seeking permission to absorb Nell into their family.

"Master Ramsey, Mistress Ramsey – here be my approval, signed and sealed. I have not an idea whether or not I have the right to do so. Reverend Forbes has given his approval on behalf of the church. It may well be that it is not entirely within the letter of the law. But as long as I remain Lord here, my rule stands. Young Nell could not be in safer or more gentle hands."

"Thank you, my lord," James gave another small bow. "We will indeed treat Nell as if she were our own. We are truly grateful."

"Then I shall instruct my reeve to enter Nell as a member of your household."

James and Avril walked back home with Nell between them.

"Whatever else befalls this poor country," Avril said quietly. "This be the best thing that may come out of it all."

Chapter 26

Kit Warden had reason to offer a short prayer of thanks as he and young Andrews walked down through Bovey that same afternoon. They were on their way to seek work at the Parke estate. They had just passed the shoemaker's shop – a shop that displayed the proud sign, 'Josiah Grubb – Shoemaker' – when Kit happened to catch a glimpse of a tall figure emerging from the side of the mill.

"Bugger! Satan's codpiece!" he muttered, dodging immediately behind his young companion.

"What? Who?" Andrews was a bit startled. His new friend had always seemed imperturbable.

From behind, Warden steered young Andrews towards the shoemaker's window, where he stared with apparent fascination at a pair of shiny, buckled shoes.

"Down by the mill," Warden hissed. "We heard that the sods have set up patrols in towns they believe to be harbouring the likes of us. Well, that fellow is called Franks – and we ran into him when we were here before. He will recognise me for sure."

"So?" Andrews pointed out the obvious. "If he was here before, he would recognise many people. What is so special about you?"

Kit steered Andrews back up the street, making sure that Franks was already disappearing over the bridge towards the crossroads.

"I told you about my mate Luke and me. Well, we were hidden after that disaster on the heath by the baker and his family. To keep up the pretence, we said we were distant kin of the baker's wife – from Dawlish. I *know* Franks knows we were lying. I have no desire to reacquaint myself with the bastard!"

"Yet he did not apprehend you," Andrews again pointed out the obvious. "He cannot have had proof of his suspicions – and he still cannot."

"I still dare not let him see me – or see my mate Luke. I must get word to him."

"I thought you said he was at Lustleigh."

"Aye – smitten with a girl with the most glorious head of red hair you have ever seen."

"Then let us get there and warn him."

"You will come with me?"

"Where else would I go? We are not yet desperate and can spare a couple of days more."

The pair walked back up towards the church, turned left along a path that skirted Bovey, and joined the road north – back the way Warden had come. Two hours and five miles later, they came to the small village only to find the last cottage worked on was locked and silent.

"Only one thing for it," Warden muttered, making for the woodcutter's house.

Meg answered the door and gaped at Warden.

"Why be you back here?" she asked.

"Looking for Luke. I expected to find him here."

"Then you be days late," she gave them her big grin. "My Luke be gone to find honest employment."

"Your Luke?" Warden was a bit startled. "He spoke to your father, did he?"

"Aye – and stated his pure intentions. I told my father I would have no other than Luke. He was told that if he gained honest work, he would have me for his wife – so he left."

"Where was he headed?"

"Why – towards Bovey. Where else?"

"But I have been there for days now and have not seen him. Is there anywhere else he might go?"

"Well, not north to Chagford. Chagford be all mining folk. It is possible he be gone to Chudleigh, but he never said anything about it. He may have heard about Brimley, I suppose."

"Brimley? What would he hear about that place? 'Tis very small."

"My father has heard that there be a new grand lady moved into the big house. There would be work there as it has been empty and neglected these three years past."

"How would we get there? Not going back through Bovey?"

"Why? You been chasing the ladies and have aroused the ire of a husband?" she giggled.

"Nay – there is a sergeant there – a parliament man – who I need to avoid. As does Luke."

"Then 'tis simple. Take the track that winds south, and that will take you to the River Teign. You can cross it and head south still until you cross Haytor road. Not far beyond that is Brimley. If you see Luke, tell him his Meg sends a kiss."

Warden gave her his thanks and a promise to deliver her message – if he was lucky enough to meet up with his friend. The two set off, ignoring the track that led east to the Bovey road. By nightfall, they had crossed the river and were sheltering in a wood. They knew they would reach Brimley well before noon the next day.

-------------------- OOOOOOOOOO --------------------

Gil had woken up long after the sun had risen. Their bed chamber was fitted with shutters, so the weak sun had not filtered through enough to rouse him earlier. He slowly became aware of Ella sleeping next to him. He lay there watching her breathing and, not for the first time, offered up a prayer of thanks. He must have stirred because a pair of deep brown eyes opened and looked back at him.

"Good morning, husband," she whispered.

"Good morning, wife," he whispered back. He couldn't help himself as he wrapped his arms around the beautiful young woman and kissed her tenderly.

"Love me again, Gil," she whispered.

Half an hour later, they were both shaken apart as a hammering came on their front door. Gil slipped out of bed with a muttered curse and threw a loose robe around his body.

"Daily bread delivery!" Simon was there holding out two fresh loaves – a broad grin on his face. "A good night, brother-in-law?" he sniggered.

"I thank you for the bread – now bugger off!" Gil gave his newly acquired relative a cuff around the head. He closed the door and looked back to where Ella, in a robe of her own, was descending the stairs.

"Was that my cheeky brother?" she asked.

"Yes – and asking personal questions."

"Yes, he would. Now on with my wifely duties. I shall make up the fire and prepare breakfast for my lord and master."

"Nay – I shall tend to the fire. The breakfast I leave in more capable hands."

"'Tis very late for breakfast," she gave Gil a cheeky grin.

"Aye, I know 'tis very late. But breakfast it shall be. I shall take my new and beautiful wife to the tavern for supper, so all shall see I am the luckiest fellow in all of this county."

Ella busied herself in the small kitchen, preparing porridge that she would make with milk and honey. She cut the new bread and spread butter, then filled two mugs with watered ale.

"A meal fit for a king," Gil said, regarding the fire he had lit.

"A king with ash and muck on his hands – not fit to sit and eat with his queen!"

"As my lady wishes," Gil went to rinse the ash and smuts from his face and hands.

"As it be Saturday tomorrow, and I do not go back to delivering bread until Monday, shall we set to with some planting of seeds?" he suggested.

"Aye. And I also have a suggestion. May we fetch Nell to help? It is just one more way to make her a part of this village."

"That, wife, is a good suggestion. If we can help make her happy and content, then we will have done all we can."

Ella cleared the breakfast away and went to sit on the settle. She gave Gil a smile.

"'Tis many hours until supper," she declared. "Try as I might, I cannot think of any way we may pass the time!"

Gil chased a laughing Ella back up the stairs.

--------------------- OOOOOOOOOO --------------------

Michael Brown and Hugh Ratcliffe arrived dusty and tired in the village of Trusham. Brown, who had not been back to the place of his birth for some years, gazed down the little main street. The inn looked the same, as did the row of cottages on either side. The cottage last but one on the far right was the place he had been born and had lived the earliest years of his life. It looked very different.

Brown would be amongst people he had known – all without exception royalist sympathisers. Ratcliffe was nothing of the kind. But the two had developed the firmest of friendships, helped in no small measure by their fight with the three footpads.

"I shall say that we met by chance on the way here," Brown told him.

"And I shall say that I be a woodsman without any loyalty to anyone but myself – seeking honest work from whoever may offer it."

Two old men were sitting on a bench outside the inn. One looked up with milky eyes as he heard the sound of approaching footsteps. The other also looked up and gave a shout.

"Michael Brown!" he gasped. "Many a long year since you were here."

"Aye, Cackle – 'tis many a long year. And with old Fish as usual."

Cackle gave vent to a laugh that had earned him his nickname fifty years before.

"I be nearly blind now," the other old chap said, almost with a touch of pride. "You be back to find your folks?"

"Aye – and seeking work," Brown nodded. "The king, bless him, has no further use of my services."

"Then you be disappointed," Fish said. "Your father passed into God's care not twelve months since. Your mother could not manage by herself and followed him two months after."

"But what of that useless brother of mine?"

"Him?" Cackle snorted. "Left soon after and has not been seen since."

"So, cottage be yours, young Michael. Has stood empty since young Alec left. Though what state it be in, I know not."

Brown soon found out. Thick dust covered every surface; dampness and mould grew in corners and up the walls. There was still a trestle table, two chairs and a settle in the main room. The small kitchen was almost empty, apart from two old and battered cooking pots. Upstairs, the two small rooms were even more damp than downstairs. The large bed was a mass of mould. Ragged holes let in light – and obviously rain - through the thatch.

"I be the woodsman," Ratcliffe said. "I will get wood and start a fire. That must be the first thing to do – get some warmth into the place."

"And I have never forgotten how to wield a broom – my mother had me doing that as soon as I could handle it."

By nightfall, there was a fire slowly warming the main room, which had been swept and dusted.

"Tis a good thing I still have a coin for food," Brown stated as they made their way to the inn for stew and ale.

He was greeted by many old friends from his past. He told of his experiences in the king's army. Ratcliffe sat quietly and repeated his own story of being an itinerant woodsman. As the floor of the main room in the cottage was clean and warm, the two of them rolled themselves into their blankets and went to sleep. Just before he slept, Brown spared a thought for his parents. He had been gone so many years that he could only just recall their faces. His brother, on the other hand, he would never miss. A sneak thief and habitual liar, he had never been one of Brown's favourite people.

--------------------- OOOOOOOOOO ---------------------

Gil escorted his new and blushing wife into the tavern. They were met by cheers, whistles and catcalls.

"Ignore those unmannerly oafs," Dick Allen said, taking them to a small trestle table near the fire. "Believe me; most are seething with jealousy. Now – Sal has beef and onion pie with leeks. This comes with the compliments of all of us."

Zachary, acting as potboy, came across with two pewter tankards and a jug of ale. He gave a nudge in the ribs to Gil and a leer for Ella.

"You still be not big enough for a spanking over my knee," Ella told him loudly so that most could hear her. Zachary went red and scurried back to the kitchen.

There came a sudden influx of customers. First came James, Avril and Nell – followed by the Smith family, the Ramsey bakers, Reverend Forbes, old Garlick, Sam Fewings and his aged wife, Peter Cove, the bailiff and his wife, plus Hob.

317

"Friends," James called out so that the chatter stilled. "We are here to celebrate Nell being a part of our family. His Lordship has joined Reverend here in agreeing to it. So, join us, please."

Roars of cheering and tankards were raised. Cries of 'Welcome Nell'.

"There," Avril bent down to her new charge. "You be amongst friends – everyone here be happy for you."

Abel grinned at Avril, took little Nell in his enormous hands and sat her astride his shoulders. He took her on tour around the large tavern. At every table, he stopped so that its occupants raised glasses or tankards and shouted, 'Welcome, Nell'. By the time they arrived back at the starting point, Nell was helpless with laughter. Abel reached up and swung her down again. He held her at shoulder height and kissed the top of her curly head.

"You be safe with all of us, little Nell. Now – back to your new family."

He set her down beside James and Avril, then went over to Dick Allen and grabbed a large pewter tankard. He beamed at everyone as he drank it all down in one massive swallow.

--------------------- OOOOOOOOOO --------------------

According to Avril, early March was as good a time as any to plant potatoes – or so she believed. Consequently, the next morning Gil took a small sack of them and followed what his aunt had told him. He dug a shallow trench, planted the potatoes a set distance apart, and then mounded soil above them.

Nell had arrived as breakfast had finished. She listened carefully as Ella told her what she had to do. As Ella scooped out the hole, Nell dropped a large bean into it from the supply held in a piece of old cloth. Then she did the same with a row of peas.

"When will they grow up?" she asked.

"Aunt Avril says they should start to show above the earth in two or three weeks. Then we have to put big sticks in the ground so that the new plants can climb up them."

"Is your Aunty Avril now my new mama?"

That brought Ella up with a jerk. She knew that she had to answer this very carefully.

"Your own mama died and went to Jesus when you were born. Aunt Avril cannot ever be your true mama, but she will be everything your mama would have wanted to be."

"Is she with my dada?"

"Yes, sweetheart – she will most certainly be. They be together as they had been when they were young."

"Will I see them again when I go to Jesus?"

"Aye – and they will be waiting for you to give you a big hug."

"Will you have babies?"

"That is our great wish. But if we have a little girl half as sweet as you, then I shall be the happiest mama in the whole world!"

"What do I do with these? They're very tiny."

"Oh – they are little seeds that grow into carrots. We rake the earth very fine, then scatter them gently. And then we cover them up, but not very deep."

Mary called by on her way down for her afternoon at the apothecary's shop.

"And how is our little vegetable farmer faring?" she asked.

"She is faring very well, are you not, Nell?"

"I've worked so hard!" Nell said very seriously.

"So hard that we must now wash and have our dinner," Ella said, taking one rather muddy little hand and leading Nell around the back of the small cottage to get cleaned up.

Ella and Gill returned a clean and tidy Nell back to Avril before supper. The next day, Nell would be taken up to the bakery so that she could help Evelyn make sweet pastries.

--------------------- OOOOOOOOOO --------------------

Chapter 27

Nicholas Andrews and Kit Warden eventually found their way to Brimley. They had taken one wrong turning, and it was not until they almost ran into the crossroads just to the west of Bovey that Warden had realised. They immediately turned back, certainly not wishing to run into any trouble. Consequently, it was not until nearly ten that morning that they walked through the open gates of the manor house at Brimley.

They walked up the weed-infested and overgrown drive until the large house came into view. It looked exactly what it was – neglected and run down.

"Plenty of work here, by the look of things," Nick Andrews commented.

They prudently walked around the house and, crossing the rear courtyard, approached an open door that emitted tantalising smells. Warden knocked on the door panel and peered in. Then he nearly staggered back in amazement. Sitting at a large kitchen table was Luke Farmer, a spoon transferring porridge into his mouth. Luke seemed as staggered as his long-time friend.

"By the balls of Satan!" he almost choked on his mouthful. "What are you doing here – and who may that be?"

"Looking for work – and this be Nick Andrews. We met up many days past. Meg said you might be here. I went looking for you."

"Then you have found me."

"Two more layabouts looking for work, no doubt," a stout woman in the white apron and cap of a cook bustled into the kitchen. "And probably hungry, I'll wager."

"Indeed, mistress. You be correct on both counts. We be looking for work and are indeed hungry. Nick, here is an old friend of mine."

"Then get away to the trough and wash. *Maisie!*" she ended with a bellow.

A young scullery maid poked her head around the door behind the cook.

"Get two more bowls of porridge for these fellows, then run to get Master Steward – I believe we may have two more mouths to feed for many a day!"

The three were halfway through their very late breakfast when Thomas Carpenter huffed and puffed his way into the kitchen. All three stood respectfully.

"Cook tells me that you are known to one another," he said.

"Indeed, Master Steward – but I know only one, Kit Warden. We were together serving the king and then did work at Lustleigh for the reeve there."

"And I met Nick Andrews – who was also a soldier for the king," Warden added.

"And the two of you seek work – as did this fellow who arrived yesterday. He is cleaning out the attics – and that will take him the rest of this week. You two may make a start on the outside of the house. You will have seen that it is covered in old ivy and that it all has to be removed. In the old barn, you may find a ladder. If you do, and if you hold your lives dear, do not trust it as it is surely as rotten as much else is. Pull the ivy off and cut it as close to the ground as you can. Then pile it in the far corner of the courtyard and set it afire."

"Make sure that you remove every last bit of the wretched stuff," came a voice from the doorway. "Even the smallest piece left can set itself back into the wall and turn it into a sponge to let the rain into the mortar."

"I shall inspect it all most carefully, my lady," Carpenter assured the old lady who stood there in an apron, a small broom in her hands.

"See – I work as hard as any of my servants," Lady Violette announced. "Do your work properly and diligently, and just mayhap I shall keep you on."

She turned and stalked off, shouting to someone, "Bring water and clothes. The windows are so begrimed I cannot see through them!"

Luke finished his bowl and said he would meet them again in the barn for their dinner. Warden and Andrews went to the old barn and indeed found a ladder, which promptly disintegrated the moment they picked it up. However, they also found billhooks and a couple of small hand axes. These they sharpened on a stone step and set to work on the front of the house.

Luke met them for their dinner, brought to them by an overworked young scullery maid. She gave them a broad grin, a waggle of her hips, and ran back to the kitchen.

"No places yet for outside workers to sleep in the house," Luke explained. "We shall sleep here until such time as spaces be ready for us. Lady Violette is quite remarkable for one of her station. She works as hard as any of her maids. But everyone here is in awe of her. They all say they have never worked so hard in their lives – but that she is a fair and generous mistress. We may have landed ourselves a good billet."

"Then you may go back to your Meg and say you have done as you promised. She is set on you – she told us so."

"I cannot go back until I have secured a permanent place. And then I have to ask mistress if I may bring back a wife. Life be difficult!"

"Life is always difficult for such as us," Andrews pulled a long face. "Go here, go there, fight this battle, fight that battle. Then, if you be still alive, go and find work elsewhere. 'Tis the lot of the working man!"

"That sounds to me as if you wished a turnabout in fortunes," Warden grinned. "That be radical talk, young Nick!"

"Aye – it is!" he grinned back. "But a man may dream, may he not?"

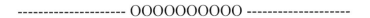

--------------------- OOOOOOOOOO --------------------

Peter Cove, the Parke estate bailiff, was a troubled man. As he sat at his desk, he drew a piece of paper to him, dipped the pen into ink, and listed his worries. Mayhap, he thought, if I write them down, some solutions may appear. Item 1, he wrote.

Parliament troops are stationed in the village. They say they are 'keeping an eye on things'.

Item 2. I know of at least three members of the king's army hereabouts. How may I keep them safe and undetected?

Item 3. My Lord Vickery will want to return to Westminster.

Item 4. I know of some men in the village who plot to attack the sergeants and their soldiers. How may I stop this? If they do attack, parliament will simply send more and will be vengeful.

He threw down his pen and glared at the paper. Item 1 he knew he could do nothing about. Item 2 – well, he knew where they were; Hob, that young rapscallion, had eyes and ears everywhere and had told him that the three were probably at Brimley. He would ride there – he had every reason to, as Lady Violette was a sub-tenant of Lord Vickery. Item 3 – well – if his Lord disappeared, his whereabouts could be kept secret! Item 4 was the immediate problem. He would send Hob messages to those he knew were potential troublemakers. He would spell out in no uncertain terms the danger they would be putting the entire village into if they persisted in their wild schemes.

He went to the front door of his house, opened it and yelled for Hob – who appeared almost immediately from the side of the house, his mouth full and the remains of a pie clutched in one grubby hand.

"Hob," he beckoned the lad close and gave quiet instructions. "Take this message to Master Wilkins, Master Hogg, Master Fletcher, and Master Goode. They are to meet with me at the tavern at seven of the clock this evening. Then go to the tavern and tell Dick Allen to keep the back parlour free for me at that time."

Hob, as was his custom, stood on one leg and whispered the message to himself until he knew it backwards. Then, stuffing the remains of the pie into his mouth, scampered off. Peter Cove went back into his office, changed his shoes for

326

riding boots, threw a cloak around his shoulders, and went to collect his horse from the estate stables. Two minutes later, he was on his way to Brimley.

-------------------- OOOOOOOOOO --------------------

Gil and Ella had risen early - not from choice, but out of a sense of duty towards their potential livelihood. They were now totally at ease with one another, in the cottage and especially in the bed chamber. They were busy planting and hoeing when Mary walked past with Nell.

"Nell be coming up to the bakery today to help make and sell pastries," Mary explained as Nell scrutinised the beds where she had planted peas, beans and seeds.

"No, Nell – no sign yet," Ella laughed.

"I'm to learn how to use the piggle and mortal," Nell announced solemnly.

Mary and Ella exchange grins at that announcement. A pestle and mortar were indispensable tools in the apothecary business.

By early dinner, All the beans and peas had been planted. Gil had made a start on the cabbages. They surveyed the long beds, and both uttered a short prayer for a successful harvest. Until they had something to sell, they were slowly eating into Gil's savings – and they would not last beyond the end of June. Neither wanted to go to their parents, cap in hand, for a loan to see them through. Both were fiercely independent.

Nell had thoroughly enjoyed her morning. She had mixed pastry dough, helped to roll it out, sprinkled raisins and honey, rolled up the pastries and watched as Evelyn put them into the oven to bake. They would cool over dinner, and then Nell would go into the shop with Mary to sell not only those but meat and fish pies as well.

As they finished the dinner, Evelyn came into the parlour with a little platter with a raisin pastry on it.

"You helped make it, Nell," she announced. "It is only right and fitting that you have the first of them to taste."

Nell picked up the still-warm pastry and took a bite.

"That is the best pastry ever!" she said, then got a fit of the giggles as Evelyn picked her up for a big hug.

That afternoon, she knelt on a high stool behind the counter and helped to sell the pies and pastries. Word soon got around the village – resulting in a steady stream of customers.

"Why – bless my soul – tis a veritable princess serving in your shop," Master Grubb said in amazement.

"Aye – she is!" Evelyn ruffled Nell's curls.

"Why does Master Grubb say I'm a princess?" Nell asked when the shop was empty. "I'm not a princess, am I?"

"Nay, sweetheart. You are not really a princess. But you look like one."

"Please, may I have another pastry?"

"You certainly may – you have done an excellent job today – and I shall tell Avril and James that you have been a treasure."

"May I come again?" she asked, somewhat coyly.

"We shall be very disappointed if you may not!" Evelyn replied. "On the morrow, you will be with James and Avril, helping them with their pills and potions. Then you will be again with Gil and Ella. And then you come here again – so that you learn all about what we do."

And that you are made a part of the village, she didn't add.

Abel and Simon could not have Nell in the smithy – it was considered far too dangerous. The same went for Grubb and his shoemaking business. However, she would be made very welcome in the dairy, learning how to milk the cows, skim the cream and churn the butter. Master Clarke also wanted to enrol her on his reading, writing and arithmetic classes. Her life would be filled every day – and that was the whole point of the exercise.

--------------------- OOOOOOOOOO --------------------

Michael Brown and Hugh Ratcliffe spent the first day in the cottage cleaning and sweeping out the dust and muck of months. They received a visitor late in the afternoon. The village reeve had heard of their arrival and came to renew his acquaintance with Brown, who he well remembered as a young lad – before Brown had gone to join the king's army.

"Master Reeve – welcome to my humble abode," Brown greeted his old friend.

Over mugs of ale, the three sat before a blazing fire, the cottage still not properly dried out.

"Do you remember old Gideon?" the reeve asked.

"Aye – miserable old sod he was!" Brown grinned. "Never the right weather – too cold to work, too hot to work, too dry to make shoots grow, too wet to grasp billhook properly!"

"He died not six months past," the reeve mentioned.

"Then may his soul find peace at last – he surely found none on this earth!"

"And he left none to carry on his work," the reeve looked at Brown and Ratcliffe meaningfully.

"What was his work, Master Reeve?" Ratcliffe asked.

"He was our hurdle maker – and none to make any now."

Hurdles were almost a vital commodity – to fence in sheep and pigs, to mark garden boundaries and a whole host of uses.

"Then 'tis as well I am a woodsman for many years past!" Ratcliffe grinned. "Show me a billhook and a splitter, and I shall make the finest hurdles in the whole of Devon – and I can teach this know-nothing fellow at the same time."

"Know-nothing, am I?" growled Brown. "I know how they are made! But will Master Bailiff agree to this?"

"Go to the coppice on the morrow and make five good hurdles – two yards by one yard – and I shall bring bailiff to see them. If you be as good as you claim, then I see no difficulties."

"Are there hazel ready for coppicing?" Ratcliffe asked.

"Aye – more than enough to keep you two busy for many a month!"

Brown and Ratcliffe celebrated with mugs of ale that evening and slept before the banked fire. Ratcliffe knew he could satisfy the most demanding of bailiffs with his craft. He had made hurdles, fences, wicket gates – nothing made of rough wood was strange to him.

--------------------- OOOOOOOOOO ---------------------

The bailiff arrived at the tavern half an hour before the others he had summoned – so that he would not be immediately associated with them should anyone be looking. He sneaked in the back way through the kitchen and was shown into the small parlour by Sal Allen – who supplied him with a mug of ale and a pie.

Cove thought long and hard about what he was going to say to the four. For all he knew, there could be many more like-minded people in the village. But those four were the most outspoken and probably the ringleaders. He would have to be careful not to inflame them more than they already were.

When they eventually arrived, Cove was pleased to note that they did not all come in at once. At least there was some semblance of caution. Then, when they were all sitting on the stools dotted about the small room, Cove made the first move.

"I've asked you here so that I can have a quiet – and a private – word. I'm aware that the four of you are not happy that we are being observed and probably reported on by those soldiers camped down by the mill."

"Aye, bailiff – we're a bit more than unhappy!" growled Jake Hogg. Hogg was a saddler and worker in leather. His shop and workshop were next to the bookshop that belonged to Hubert and Mercy Green.

"There's more than enough of us to take those ten," added Wilf Fletcher. Despite his surname, he had nothing to do with arrows or bows. He was the local ditcher, responsible for maintaining the ditches and gullies that removed rainwater, sewage and other undesirable substances.

"And what might the local parliamentary commander do if that happened?" Cove asked. "I can tell you what he would do. He would send a far larger force into the village to exact reprisals. Is this what you want? A large force bent on revenge? They could easily take hostages against your future behaviour; could hang a few as examples; rape your wives and daughters."

"We'll see them off as well!" Alf Wilkins shouted. Well-known as a loudmouthed braggart, he was probably the most dangerous of the quartet. He sometimes worked as a night soil man – when he was sober enough to do anything other than pour gallons of ale down his throat.

"Nay – listen to what Master Bailiff be saying," Ralph Goode said quietly. "He says we stay cautious – and I agree with him. It's too soon for us to go off like dry powder. I say we bide our time; we watch, and we wait."

"That is sound advice," Cove nodded.

"And when will the time be right for us to strike?" Hogg snorted. "In a year? Two years?"

"Nay – that would be stupid," Goode shook his head. "We watch, and we make a note of what they do, when they do it and where. When have seen enough, we meet secretly and make a proper plan. Until then, we do nothing daft."

"Then I agree with that," Fletcher nodded. He quite fancied himself as a master spy.

"Oh, to hell with it all," Hogg grunted. "If that be the plan, then I will abide by it."

"Ye all be like scared maids!" Wilkins sneered. "I'll have nothing to do with all this plotting and planning. What is needed is real action. And if you all be scared to do it, then I shall!" And with that, he stormed out and slammed the door behind him.

"The rest of you will do as Master Goode suggests?" Cove looked at Fletcher and Hogg.

He received assurances, and with that, he had to be satisfied. They left singly, the bailiff by the back door again. On his way back, he wondered what the hell the oaf Wilkins would do. At least Wilkins had no wife or children on whom reprisals could be visited – and the bailiff shrugged his shoulders and went to report to Lord Vickery, who had yet to decide whether to stay put or to go to Westminster..

Chapter 28

Garvey looked across at Haddock. They were on opposite sides of a midden – a steaming mass of old straw, horse manure, red soil, and whatever refuse had come from the kitchen. Each had a three-tined dung fork with a long handle. Their task for the day was to turn the steaming mass and to ensure it was mixed thoroughly, enough to satisfy the midget head gardener.

This little fellow, some forty summers in age, barely came up to Haddock's shoulder. Inevitably, he was referred to as Goliath. However, no one ever questioned his right to his position – his knowledge and expertise with the gardens and orchards were prodigious. He made sure that the Parke estate ate the freshest vegetables and the most succulent fruit; he also ensured that the inhabitants wandered through the most luxurious gardens – colour everywhere – grass regularly scythed. He was assisted by two young apprentices – and demanded from them the highest level of care and attention.

When two days earlier, Garvey and Haddock had arrived seeking work, and he had seized on them for the most thankless tasks – turning the midden, hacking down brambles, clearing patches of nettles. The two accepted it all meekly – glad for a while to stay in one place, eat regular meals, and sleep from nightfall to dawn.

Their lives were not lives of peace – they were ex-parliamentary soldiers and were working in an estate fiercely loyal to the king. They guarded their tongues, saying only that they had been displaced up in the north of the county by the fighting. So far, that story has sufficed.

"Life cannot get much worse," Garvey grinned at his co-worker.

"Oh, believe me, it can!" Haddock grinned back. "This is at least a wholesome stink. The stink of soldiers killed in battle but two days before is far worse!"

"Aye – and we've seen a few of those, have we not!"

They were interrupted by the arrival of Goliath. He trotted over to inspect the massive pile. He stood, hands on hips and inhaled deeply.

"Magnificent!" he muttered through an almost beatific smile.

After he had gone to inspect something else, the two ex-soldiers exchanged another look and burst into laughter.

-------------------- OOOOOOOOOO --------------------

Sergeant Franks walked up and down the village's main street every morning when he had finished his breakfast. He was punctilious in greeting people – with a polite 'good morning' as he passed. Most were polite back and returned the greeting. A few responded with icy correctness. A very few studiously ignored him. It was what he had expected. Most wanted nothing other than a peaceful life – and if that meant co-existing with an opponent, so be it.

One rather cold but sunny morning, he was about to pass the new cottage when he heard excited squeals coming from the plot behind it. His curiosity aroused, he walked down the little path on the right of the house and saw what had caused the excitement. A little girl was jumping up and down and clapping her hands.

"It's growed!" she squealed. "Look – it's growed!"

He recognised the young man and woman as the two who had married just a few weeks previously. The young woman was kneeling on the ground by the little girl.

"Aye, Nell – the very first sign of life in our plot. And it is one you planted – I am sure of it."

"Is it a bean?"

"Aye – and this I promise you. When it has grown all that it may, you shall have the first pickings."

"When will the funny things grow?"

"Oh – you mean the potatoes. I don't know, as we have never grown them before."

The excitement had been caused by a new green shoot with two little leaves at its tip. Franks coughed to announce his presence. The young woman looked up at him and gave him a friendly smile.

"Good morrow, sergeant. Look – our little gardener has produced a new bean."

Franks was well aware that the look the young man gave him was nowhere near as friendly as that of his young wife. However, it was not hostile, just a shade guarded. He decided to do a little probing.

"I hope your relatives returned safely to Dawlish," he ventured.

"Oh – ah – aye, they did. But 'tis Holcombe, not Dawlish."

Little did either of them know that the two in question were no more than a mile and a half from where they stood.

"And the cottage stands strong and secure?" Franks asked.

"Aye – built by our fathers and our relatives – with some loving touches by my husband," Ella grinned. "He made for me our own settle – and it is as fine a settle as I have ever seen."

Franks gave them a nod and wandered off to continue his walk, more convinced than ever that the two 'relatives' were soldiers for the king. He was loth to take matters any further – those two and the little girl were the picture of happiness and contentment. He saw little enough of that. He knew the story of the little girl and vowed that, should he ever bump into her miserable grandfather, he would make his feelings very plain.

-------------------- OOOOOOOOOO --------------------

Hubert Green sat quietly in his parlour behind the shop. He was deeply immersed in his bible – reading passages from Job. He seemed to relate to that most despondent and unfortunate of ancient characters. No matter where he looked, he found things that were distinctly not to his liking.

His wife of fifteen years sat in the shop, dusting the array of books on the bottom shelf of the small display behind the counter. Mercy Green, whilst definitely as anti-social as her husband, was nevertheless an excellent saleswoman. She was the one who bought books, renovated their binding and covers, and then re-sold them for a profit.

The stock attracted buyers from as far afield as Exeter, Crediton, Dartmouth, and Teignmouth. There were accounts of Arthur and his knights, translations of the Old Testament into English, and works by Northern European religious thinkers such as Luther and Wycliffe. Not one version of the New Testament would ever grace her shelves – they, to her mind, smacked of popery.

The two of them were ambivalent where the current state of the country was concerned. On the one hand, they were delighted that the king and his catholic wife were slowly being defeated. On the other hand, they were uncertain whether the rise of parliament would bring them what they wanted above all else – an end to the established church and its insistence on ceremony and what they saw as a continuation of Catholic idolatry.

Hubert put down his bible and sat thinking deeply for a while, listening with half an ear to his wife muttering to herself as she dusted and rearranged the display of books. The previous week, they had sold a very rare and expensive copy of a book of Arthurian legends. These were acceptable to them as they were certainly myths – and they were set in an ideal world that had never existed – and probably never would. It had fired Hubert's imagination and had almost set in concrete what he had wanted to do for years. He rose and went into the shop.

"My mind is made up," he announced. "I have prevaricated long enough. Tomorrow is the Sabbath, and I shall take my stand outside that abominable romish church. If their idolatrous reverend may preach within, then I shall preach without."

"And may the Almighty lend power to your words," Mercy nodded. "What shall be the tenor of your sermon?"

"Licentiousness, idolatry, and lewd behaviour."

"With which we are plagued daily!" Mercy nodded. "Be sure I shall pray for your success – and shall stand at your side throughout."

With that settled, Hubert closed the shop so that they might both fall to their knees and pray for guidance and strength.

Brown and Ratcliffe had certainly passed their test some days since. Their hurdles were pronounced excellent by the local bailiff. The village of Trusham now had another trade within its midst.

Daily, whatever the weather, the two would spend the morning coppicing the young hazel and ash. The afternoons were spent fashioning hurdles. Ratcliffe had even started constructing a bodger's lathe so that he could start fashioning beech into chair and cupboard legs.

Brown, not to be outdone, had gone in search of elm that he could use to fashion seats for chairs. Between the two of them, a little industry was slowly blossoming in the village.

It did not take long for the news of this new enterprise to spread to neighbouring towns and villages. The first to hear – and come to investigate – was Christow to the north of

Trusham. Their reeve was impressed. Then came Chudleigh – to the south – and then Bovey to the southwest.

So many young and not-so-young men had gone to fight for king and parliament that skilled labour was in short supply. Therefore, any new enterprise excited interest far and wide. Peter Cove was no exception. He sent one of his own men to see what all the fuss was about. The man came back and reported that the work was of a high standard and that if the Parke estate needed hurdles, that was where the best may be obtained. Cove decided to go himself to investigate.

--------------------- OOOOOOOOOO -------------------

Most of Bovey village attended church on that Sunday. The church bell summoned them to the morning service, as it had done for a hundred and more years. Previously, it had rung every day and night for the Catholic offices.

Dressed in their best clothes, the inhabitants answered the summons. Nell, holding hands between James and Avril, had a new little dress in bright red. Gil and Ella came hand in hand, followed by their parents, sister and brother. Old Master Garlick was at the porch, welcoming each family as it arrived. Each went to his or her accustomed place. There was almost no pecking order, although the front places were reserved for Lord Vickery and his bailiff and the bailiff's family. Lord John Vickery, a widower for seven years past, sat alone.

Reverend Forbes, assisted by Hob as his altar boy, celebrated the service with due solemnity. His sermon was received in good spirits as it was based on love and kindness. Not for him the fire and brimstone of some churchmen. He had seen and heard enough of that to last him a lifetime.

He positioned himself at the west door to greet each and every member of his congregation as they filed out. He had no sooner offered his hand to Master Grubb – the first to leave – when everyone was astounded to hear a voice raised aloud on the top step of the path that led to the church.

"Woe to all you sinners!" boomed Hubert Green, his wife holding her bible in her hands and eyes shut in an attitude of prayer.

"Woe to you! You emerge from your worship and go about your lives changed not one whit. You fall on your knees in that place of idolatry; you pay lip service to your prayers; you then laugh and roister as you have always done. Ale and wine will flow, and you will make merry. Not one amongst you will even dwell upon the words you have mimed like parrots!"

By then, most of the congregation had gathered to witness this highly unusual spectacle.

"Bugger off, you miserable sod and take that sour bitch with you!" came a call from somewhere in the crowd.

"Foul words come from your mouths," Hubert seized on this interruption. "Blasphemy is your currency! Licentiousness be your watchword. You hold hands and dance to wild music when you should be on your knees praying for forgiveness. Repent or be damned for all eternity! Eschew strong drink. Cast aside your fripperies and bright colours. Don the black of repentance! Pray each and every hour of every day unless you suffer eternal damnation!"

"I'll eternally damn you, you mealy-mouthed misery!" came another voice.

"Just what the bloody hell is going on here?" came a strident voice from the street.

Sergeant Lovelace, whose turn it was to supervise the patrols, stood, legs braced and hands on hips. Two of his soldiers stood just behind him, grinning at the spectacle, which they thought promised to be entertaining.

Reverend Forbes, ever the peacemaker, called out.

"Oh – merely a difference of opinion," he said. "This good man wished merely to offer advice."

"Who gave you leave to speak on my behalf?" Hubert bawled. "I give not advice – I give God's own instruction!"

"You're still a miserable bugger!" came from the back of the crowd. "Why don't you piss off and mind your own business?"

"This is *God's* business, not mine, not yours! Mine is to steer you back to the path of righteousness!"

"Path of gloom and misery, more like!" That led to guffaws of laughter, and more shouted comments.

Lovelace faced Hubert and a still praying Mercy.

"You can see that you are doing little good here," he said. "I would strongly advise that you go to your home and stay there in peace and quiet."

"That is sound advice," Bailiff Cove, who had so far kept his tongue silent, walked down to confront Hubert.

"You have not the authority to silence me!" Hubert shouted, red in the face with indignation. "Neither you, bailiff, not that idolatrous priest nor this sergeant here – no one may stop the word of God! I see evil and the hand of Satan everywhere I look in this iniquitous place. I shall speak out; I shall condemn, and no one may say me nay!"

"A good kick in the bollocks will say thee nay!" came the same voice from the back.

"That is not helping," the bailiff called out. "Batty – for I know it be you – keep silent!"

Oscar Batt, one of the Parks estate labourers, gave a broad grin but held his peace.

"Now, Master Green, Mistress Green – do as the sergeant here says and go to your home and let's have no more of this!"

"And where will all of you be going?" Hubert screeched. "Into the tavern! Out of the church and into that sinful place. What good will your brief visit to the church have done you then? You have said brief prayers and have done a minimum duty towards God! That gives you the license to return to sin for another week! Woe be to all of you. You shall stand accursed before His throne!"

Cove decided that enough was enough.

"Return to your home and cease this rant! If you do not, I shall bring you before the manor court, where you shall be fined. Now *GO!*"

He stood and glared at the pair. Hubert realised at long last that he was in a losing battle. The bailiff had the authority to do exactly as he had said.

"Come, wife. We shall have to find other means."

To a barrage of catcalls and rude noises, the two walked back down the village and locked themselves firmly into their house. Most of the rest of the village went to their homes for Sunday dinner. Some, however, went straight to the tavern and were soon downing mugs of excellent ale, laughing and making rude jokes about the two puritans.

Peter Cove gave the sergeant a smile and a shrug. He went back to his own home, leaving the sergeant and two disappointed soldiers to go on with their patrol. The two troopers had wanted to see at least a little blood spilt from a broken nose or two.

Alf Wilkins nursed his grievances for days following the meeting in the tavern's back parlour. Unusually for him, he drank moderately, knowing himself well enough to realise that any plan he made whilst in his cups was likely to come unravelled. Therefore, he drank in moderation and did his nightly job quietly and properly.

All the while, he was making and then discarding one plan after another. Eventually, after many days of unaccustomed cogitation, he settled on a plan that he believed would work. He would wait a few days when all would have calmed down again.

After much deliberation, he decided that he would go it alone. He had no trust in any of his three original conspirators. Ralph Goode, he considered to be too timid, whilst Wilf Fletcher would probably talk things over with his wife. Jake Hogg was the only one he believed to be wholeheartedly behind an act of retribution – but was probably the least skilled of all with weapons.

No - he would go it alone. He slept most mornings until noon – his night soil gathering kept him up and about until the early hours. During the afternoons, he kept watch on the two sergeants and the patrols, looking for patterns in behaviour and groupings. He had already marked out the two soldiers he considered the least conscientious. He knew for a fact that their patrols always ended with them taking a long break of half an hour or more in that old, broken-down barn.

Every third day the two would be on patrol duty during the hours after midnight until four the following morning. Wilkins adapted his plan accordingly. One night when he was trundling his barrow around the privies, he caught sight of the patrol down at the bottom of the village. Hiding his barrow behind a hedge, he sprinted in deep shadow up the field and shot across to the old barn. By the side of the gaping doorway, he hid a very sharp billhook under a pile of rotting planks. He raced back again and resumed his collection round. He was ready for the next night when his chosen duo were on patrol.

The following day, he flew caution to the wind and got noisily drunk. All he had to do was to wait.

Chapter 29

Primrose Hogg could hardly contain her excitement. She was to be that year's May Queen. She attended the first rehearsal fervently, hoping that she didn't make a complete fool of herself. The May Queen had to sit on a throne and be serene and calm. Primrose knew that normally she was anything but serene and calm. Her natural inclination was to climb trees and generally behave like a tomboy.

Her parents, Jake and Eleanor Hogg, sometimes despaired of her. Her father was a saddler, and her mother did smaller leather work – and both were quite serious-minded.

"Try to model yourself more on Mary Ramsey," her mother was always telling her. "You don't see Mary up trees, ripping her clothes and generally behaving like some hellion!"

"But mother, there is no *fun* in always working!" she would pout.

"And who is going to want you as a wife? Always scampering about – never learning how to keep a house properly?"

"Then I shall never marry!"

Contrary to what her mother said, the lads in Bovey never discriminated against Primrose. On the contrary, they sought her out as she was always up to some prank or other. It helped, of course, that Primrose was rather pretty!

Primrose presented herself at the little hall that stood just behind the church. Already there were Reverend Forbes, Master Garlick, Avril Ramsey, Nell, and Mistress Cove – the bailiff's wife. Laura Cove had been organising the May pageant for the past five years. She knew that she was going to have a few problems with the ebullient Primrose.

One of the wagons from the Parke estate was always used as the May Queen's transport. With the sides and back removed, it would be draped in gaily coloured cloths and garlanded with flowers. The 'throne' was one of the large chairs from the hall itself.

That year was to be a little different. By the side of the large 'throne' was another smaller chair for the May Princess – a totally new innovation to welcome little Nell into the Bovey community. Primrose was well aware that the presence of the little girl would take a lot of the attention from her. The May Queen was a role coveted by every girl in every town and village. For one day, she was the star attraction.

Avril was acutely aware of this and had planned to make sure that Nell had a purely supporting role. In her own home village of Harberton, Avril had been May Queen eighteen years previously. She well remembered the attention, not to mention the advances she had received from the young (and not so young) male members.

Consequently, she clambered up onto the wagon and dragged the large throne further forward and pushed the smaller one back. She then ushered Primrose and Nell into position by the church gate. Primrose had on her normal dress plus a 'train' of rough cloth. On the day, she would be dressed in yellow satin and would have a scarlet train. She had them practise walking and getting onto the wagon, Nell behind holding the train.

Having satisfied herself that all would be well, she called proceedings to a halt, praising her two girls for their performance. She took Nell's hand and walked back home. Nell immediately perched herself at the counter and insisted on giving James a blow-by-blow account.

--------------------- OOOOOOOOOO ---------------------

Alf Wilkins made sure he had finished his night soil collection well before noon on the following Wednesday. If he had calculated correctly, this would be the night when the two laziest soldiers were due to take over the night patrol. He slumped in the tavern, sitting alone on a quiet corner as he ate his way through a lamb and onion pie. He strictly limited himself to one large mug of ale. Looking around the large taproom, he was surprised to see it far more sparsely populated than normal. Dick Allen, the tavernkeeper, and his wife, Sal, were sitting at a small table just outside the kitchen, eating an early dinner. Glory, their daughter, was chatting with two young lads from the pig farm. Even Zachary, their young son, was sitting in front of the fire, whittling a piece of wood. Alf and the two farm lads were the only customers in the place.

Taking a last bite of his pie, he was pleased and annoyed to see the arrival of one of the sergeants from the small force that was 'keeping a close eye' on the village. Pleased because that meant that everything was normal – annoyed because any sight of those parliamentary soldiers made his hackles rise. He immediately swallowed his annoyance and gave himself an inner chuckle. They would soon learn that they were not welcome!

Richard Lovelace called a 'good day' to Dick and Sal and then asked for a large bowl of that excellent lamb stew. He went to a table near the fire and sat down, and he shrugged off the leather baldric that held up his broadsword and put it on the table in front of him. Tucked into his broad leather belt were a couple of pistols. He stretched out his legs, his booted feet seeking a little extra warmth from the fire.

"As if he owns the bloody place," Alf snarled to himself. "By this time tomorrow, you will know what we think of you."

Rather than stalk out in disgust, he had enough self-control to stay for another ten minutes to finish his ale. Some inner caution said, 'do not walk out immediately, or you may draw attention to yourself'.

To his great annoyance, Glory served Lovelace his large bowl of stew and a tankard of ale. She stopped to pass the time of day, smiling and chatting to the sergeant as if he was a treasured guest rather than a wretched imposition.

The tavern suddenly got busy as more customers arrived for their dinner – Sal's lamb stew was a big draw, and everyone in the village knew what day it would appear as the day's staple. Dick Allen, Glory and Zachary were immediately busy taking orders and bringing jugs of ale and mugs to tables, whilst Sal disappeared into the kitchen to chivvy her two kitchen maids into action. Alf used this sudden burst of activity to stand up and walk out slowly as if he had nothing special on his mind.

Once outside, he made his way to the lean-to behind his shed. He flung himself down on his straw palliasse and went to sleep, knowing that he would wake again when it was dark – and the later, the better. Nothing disturbed his sleep, not even a dream of action!

He was annoyed again when he awoke – to find that the world was still light, the watery sun about to disappear over the moor to the west. He knew immediately that he had at least four hours before he could make a move. What to do to pass the time, he wondered. He would not trust himself to go to the tavern as the lure of many mugs of ale would probably prove too strong to resist – and he needed his wits about him that coming night. He struck his tinder and lit a small lantern that provided just enough light for him to start sharpening his thin dagger – really more like a poniard. Long ago, he had fashioned the handle himself, with rounded grooves for his fingers and thumb. Satisfied that it was sharp and wickedly pointed, he slid it back into his thick leather sheath and clipped it to the left side of his belt.

The moon was obscured by thick clouds – a fact that almost had him thanking a God in which he had little or no belief. There was a slight breeze rustling the tall trees, enough to mask any stealthy sounds he might make. He lay down again and waited patiently until the church bell sounded midnight. And then he doused his lantern and waited until his eyes accustomed themselves to the pitch dark of the lean-to. And then he crept out and made his way across the main street, around the top bend and out of sight of all the cottages.

Once in the large field on the far side of the street, he kept to the hedge and slowly and carefully made his way to a point opposite the dilapidated barn. There he stopped and stayed as silent as the grave. After a few minutes, his face broke into a very satisfied smile – a deep rumbling snore reached his ears. The two were spending their patrol having a good rest. Alf went down on all fours and carefully crawled across to the barn. He went all the way around it to where the pile of rotting timbers still stayed where he had last seen it. He slid his hand under the pile, his fingers closing on the handle of the sharpened billhook. He silently drew it out and crawled to the gaping old doorway.

There was just enough dim light for him to see into the barn. Down at the far end was the big pile of old straw where he knew the two soldiers would be curled up asleep. He went to the right side of the barn and tiptoed down towards the straw until he could make out the two sleeping figures. He would attack the one nearest to him, bring the billhook down on the head of the soldier, and then immediately do the same to the other one. He crept a bit closer and raised the billhook for the first killing stroke.

"Good evening," came a soft voice to his left. Alf froze, prepared to flee back out through the doorway.

"Put the weapon down. Stand where you are and do not move!" came the same soft voice. Alf turned and fled. He managed only three steps. There came a loud explosion and then a hideous pain in the small of his back. His legs ceased to function, and he crumpled onto the floor of the barn, whimpering in pain.

A tall figure detached itself from the left wall of the barn and came over to loom over the stricken man.

"Yes – thought it was probably you," Sergeant Franks said. "The others seemed to take the warning seriously. I've had my eyes on you for some days now. That billhook was a clever idea – or it was until I watched you slide it under that wood pile."

Alf just laid there, unable to do anything but whimper with the awful pain. The two soldiers came over and peered down at him. It was then that Alf realised that they had been part of the trap as well – pretending to creep into the barn to have a sneaky sleep.

"Shall I whip his head off, sergeant?" one of them said, unsheathing his sword.

"No – he's not going to last much longer. We shall leave him here and muster the village to witness what happens to anyone seeking our death. It will prove an excellent deterrent!"

Franks crouched down beside Alf and started chatting in an almost friendly way.

"Did you think for one moment that we had no notion of these two and their neglect of duty? Sergeant Lovelace and I suspected something of the kind and caught them at it days ago. Then, when I saw you make your furtive preparations, all I had to do was to set up this trap, and you walked into it very obligingly."

Alf could do nothing but try to stifle the screams of agony. His legs were useless, the lower spine shattered by the lead bullet that Franks had fired from his pistol.

A large pool of blood was spreading about his lower back and buttocks. There would be no stopping it. He would very soon have bled to death, his vital organs shutting down one after another. He sensed that he was floating, his head as light as a feather. Then he was sinking; it seemed to his senses that he was slowly being drawn deep into the hard soil of the barn's floor. And then he saw and sensed - nothing.

"He seems to have left us, sergeant,"

"Aye, he does. You two stay here and guard things – let no one enter or disturb anything. I shall muster the village here in the morning and offer this as a dire warning to any others who may have the same design."

Franks left the two and went down to the mill where Lovelace was waiting. He told him what had happened, drank a small mug of ale, dropped onto his palliasse and went sound asleep.

--------------------- OOOOOOOOOO ---------------------

The village came to life much as normal the next morning. The bread was baked and delivered, the blacksmith's forge was lit, and hammering commenced;

labourers got up, dressed and went to their fields. Reverend Forbes said an early service with a small congregation. The sun did its feeble best to pierce the clouds – and failed; a light shower did enough to turn the main street into a muddy mess. It was a typical early Spring in Devon.

Lovelace walked down to the Parke estate and asked if he could use Hob to convey a message to every inhabitant he could find. Peter Cove, having no idea what was in the wind, readily agreed.

"Well, young Hob – are you ready to memorise the message?" Lovelace squatted down at Hob's level.

"Er – well, if Master Bailiff says so," Hob squinted up at the tall bailiff.

"Here is the message. Everyone is to come to the old barn in the top field at eleven of the clock. Have you got that?"

"Aye – everyone is to gather at the old barn in the top field at eleven of the clock," Hob repeated. As messages went, it was not the hardest he had ever had to convey.

"Master Bailiff – would you be as kind as to convey that to all here on the estate?"

"Aye, sergeant. I can do that."

Hob did what he usually did – sped off as if the hounds of hell were after him.

"Does that lad ever walk?" Lovelace grinned.

"Nay – he knows only one speed."

Lovelace and Franks had decided against using their soldiers to convey the message. They both considered it better that it came from a source to which the village was accustomed. If the soldiers had done it, there was a good chance that many would have ignored the summons.

--------------------- OOOOOOOOOO ---------------------

At a few minutes before eleven, Franks and Lovelace arrived at the barn. Their first job was to get five of their soldiers to pull across one of the wrecked doors and then to stand in a line in front of the remaining gap. Thus, the inside of the barn and its grisly contents were hidden from view.

The rest of the soldiers were positioned to keep the gathering villagers well away from the barn. By eleven, most of those who worked in the village – shops, mill, churchyard – plus those who were too old to work were gathered in a muttering throng. Hob had been unable in the time to get around to the outlying farms to summon the labourers. The last to arrive were the inhabitants of the Parke estate – the bailiff, steward, workers and their families. Lord Vickery was again off somewhere that his steward would not divulge.

Reverend Forbes, unusually in an old smock and breeches, stepped up to Franks and demanded to know the reason for the summons. Franks yelled for quiet.

"Your reverend has quite reasonably asked why you have all been called here. You will all remember when we first arrived here, I told you why – and that we would respond in like measure to any threat. Well, last night, we responded. One of your community decided to attempt to assassinate two of the soldiers."

"Oh, bloody hell," Ralph Goode muttered. "I'll bet it was Alf – stupid bugger!"

Franks had an exceptional hearing and nodded.

"Aye – the man Wilkins who was your night soil man. He secreted a billhook by the side of that barn and crept up here, expecting that the night patrol would take a nap. Unfortunately for him, I had seen his preparations and was waiting for such an attempt. I ordered him to stand still and to drop his weapon. Instead, the stupid man turned and ran. I fired my pistol, and he dropped to the floor. In a few minutes, he was dead – and he still lies on the floor of the barn. Now, I have no authority to order you to view his remains, but the barn will be opened fully so that any of you who wish to may see what happens to those who violently resist us."

"And I suppose you intend that he remains there to rot!" Forbes was red with anger.

"No, reverend – on the contrary. We will respect the dead as he would not have. You are at liberty to remove his body and treat it as you would any other."

360

That effectively took the wind out of the sails of many who were muttering as angrily as their rector. Franks motioned to his soldiers to clear the gaping doorway. Wilkins' erstwhile conspirators were the first to go in. Forbes followed on immediately after, with his sexton and churchwarden.

Once the way was clear, all could see the huddled shape. A few – a very few – crossed themselves in the old way. Then silently, all the others started to leave the field and return to their homes, shops and businesses. Gil and Ella simply held hands and went back to their weeding and hoeing. Abel Smith gathered his family and returned to his forge. John, Evelyn and Mary, along with James, Avril and little Nell, went down to the apothecary shop to see Nell's new bed chamber.

Some of the others met in small groups and held quiet conversations. The general feeling was that the idiot had brought it all upon himself.

Back at the barn, Forbes spoke to Sam Fewings, his sexton. He was asked to fetch his hand cart and transfer the body to the church. Jake Hogg, Will Fletcher and Ralph Goode volunteered to help. Thirty minutes later, the barn was deserted. The mortal remains of Alf Wilkins were laid out in a side chapel, awaiting the ministrations of old Mother Hall, who would wash and shroud the body.

It was a sombre little group that ended up in the parlour behind the apothecary shop. Nell, naturally, was full of questions.

"Why did that man shoot him?"

"Because he was about to kill two of the soldiers," James answered.

"Why did he want to kill them?"

"Maybe that we will never know," Avril replied. "Maybe he had a fit of madness or had drunk too much ale. But we are not here for that. Nell, my little angel, show everyone your new bedchamber."

Nell needed no second bidding. She scampered up the stairs with everyone else following behind. She opened the door to her little bed chamber and went in to stand at the far wall. Everyone clustered inside – it was indeed a tight fit. The four walls were newly rendered in limewash, the little bed was polished, and the blankets neatly spread. On the pillow was Nell's little wooden doll. The small table and little stool stood to one side, her clothes either in a small coffer or hung on pegs. But the main attraction was the ceiling. It had been boarded over, hiding the usual beams, rafters and roofing. The boards had been painted a deep blue and sprinkled with little white stars, one being bigger than the others.

Everyone – except James and Avril, who had done the work – said it was a wonderful room – a room fit for a little princess. Nell laid down on her little bed and gazed upwards.

"When the clouds hide my special star, I can talk to my dada and see the one up there," she informed everyone.

Later that afternoon, Reverend James Forbes, Alf Garlick and Sam Fewings stood in the main aisle of the church. To the left, on a couple of trestles, lay the parish coffin. In the coffin lay the body of Alf Wilkins – cleaned and shrouded.

"Many years ago, that side aisle led to the Lady Chapel," Forbes spoke quietly. "Now, all those figures have gone – swept away by the reforms of the Mighty Henry."

"'Tis not to be regretted, Reverend," Garlick muttered. "It was mere idolatry – those figures of the Virgin and the three saints. What good was praying to statues? Prayer is to be offered to Almighty God, his Son and His Spirit. No good ever came of a prayer offered to a piece of stone!"

"And now we pray in good English – and hear His words spoken to us in our own language," Sam snorted. "Have you ever heard the words spoken in that old Latin, Reverend?"

"Aye – many a time," Forbes nodded. "There are still books and bibles in the old language that only the priest and a few others – monks and friars – could understand."

"Church must have looked different then," Garlick muttered.

"All the walls and columns decorated with paintings; the rood screen decorated with gold leaf and flowers; each niche with a statue of some saint or other. Not a house of God – more like a salon or a bower. Monasteries dripping with riches – no, that were all swept away."

"What if these parliamentarians have their way?" Garlick wondered. "Many be of a puritan turn of mind. Will they take reforms even further?"

"That, Master Churchwarden, is for Almighty God to know - and us to wait upon His pleasure."

Chapter 30

Jake, Wilf and Ralph were the only three mourners who attended the funeral and burial of Alf Wilkins. He was interred in the church cemetery just before noon the next day. Everyone else in the village was far too occupied with preparations for the Easter Parade that would take place two days hence.

Hubert Green was, as usual, incensed at this excuse for merrymaking. He wrote and posted on the church gates a large notice condemning the whole proceedings. He and Mercy, his wife, spent the whole of Easter Saturday kneeling at the gates and praying aloud for the Lord to forgive the sins and excesses that would be perpetrated on the morrow.

To their annoyance, nobody took any notice of them. They went into the church to decorate it with spring flowers or walked past blithely, ignoring the two supplicants, carrying on laughing and chattering. Word had quickly spread that this was probably the best response – no response at all.

Being of a mischievous turn of mind, Abel, the huge blacksmith, deliberately told a saucy joke in a very loud voice – and that caused gales of laughter from his audience gathered around the church.

The next day, Easter Sunday smiled on Devon and the surrounding counties. It was warm and sunny with only a gentle breeze. Most of the village crammed into the church for the morning service to hail the risen Christ. And then they all trooped out to finish readying the parade. Carts and wagons drawn by horses and oxen were all decorated in fresh greenery and spring flowers. Every woman and girl wore garlands of flowers in their hair – with the exception of Mercy Green. She and Hubert were again on their knees in their home.

The procession started at the church gates, wound its way down the village street, then through the path beside the mill and the bridge, and onto the heath. Already set out were stalls of pies, cakes, sweetmeats, and drinks. Gil commandeered Nell, swung her onto his shoulders and, with Ella by his side, went straight to a stall where little sweetmeats were being sold in paper spills. Gil handed one of them upwards and was thanked by a kiss on the top of his head.

And then the visitors started to arrive. Bovey, being by far the largest village for some miles, people arrived on carts and wagons from Lustleigh, Hennock, Chudleigh Knighton, Liverton, and Brimley. One of the first to arrive was Lady Charlton in her own splendid carriage. Thomas Carpenter, her steward, arrived with some of the servants – all mounted on a large wagon. Kit Warden and Luke Farmer were a bit taken aback when they noticed the soldiers under the two sergeants.

"They will not recognise us," Luke said quietly to Kit. "After all, they have never even seen us."

The next to arrive was a group from Parke Estate. They had the least distance to travel – just over a quarter of a mile. Even so, the Brimley contingent arrived well before them. Goliath, the diminutive head gardener, made straight for a stall selling very large meat pies. He bought two and wandered off, a pie in each hand and taking alternate bites.

Garvey and Haddock wandered down the heath and stopped at the left side, looking over to where they had hidden all those weeks ago, spying on the king's troops.

"Does not look any different," Haddock muttered. "I wonder what happened to Dick and Ratty."

"Probably ended up with the general, fighting for their lives in some other god-awful place," Sam replied. "Still – here we are again, safe and sound."

They wandered back up the heath to where the river went under the main street, just by the mill and the bridge.

"I do not believe my eyes!" came a shout from the mill. "What in the name of all that is holy are you two doing here?"

A face they recognised immediately came into view.

"Satan's armpits!" gasped Haddock. "Dick Lovelace!"

"Sergeant Dick Lovelace to you!" he grinned. "But my question stays the same. What brings you here – and in the clothes of garden labourers?"

And so their story came out – how they had been separated from Lovelace and Ratcliffe to the east of Torrington; how they had been unable to break through to join their forces towards South Molton; how they had been forced south across the moor; how they had landed up at Parke, working in the gardens.

"In other words, you have deserted," Lovelace grunted.

"We did try. Honestly, we did," Haddock sniffled.

"What happened to Ratty?" Garvey asked, hoping to steer the conversation onto safer grounds.

"The last I heard was that he was hurt at Torrington – probably did what you two have done and walked away."

"Are you going to report us?" Haddock was desperate to know. Desertion was a serious offence.

Lovelace went silent for a while.

"You are working at Parke – a very well-known place for supporters of the king. I will not report you if you agree to report to me anything you hear that is harmful to parliament."

"Then we agree, don't we, Sam?"

"Aye – readily!" Garvey nodded.

"Then enjoy the day, and I shall pretend I have never seen you." Lovelace nodded at them and walked back to the mill.

The two watched as he disappeared.

"I shall fall to my knees this night and offer a prayer of thanksgiving to Saint Mungo," Haddock muttered.

"Who the hell was Saint Mungo?" Garvey stuttered.

"Oh, some ancient saint. Was something to do with Scotland," Haddock answered.

"Then why offer him a prayer?"

"Don't know. His name just popped into my head!"

"You are a complete mutton-head," Garvey thumped him on the arm. "Come on – those pies look excellent."

A few people were unable to attend the heath and its attractions. Hubert and Mercy Green stayed away deliberately as they saw any merrymaking as a dereliction of duty to their God and their need for constant repentance. Dick, Sal, Glory and Zachary Allen stayed away as they had a tavern to run – along with the kitchen maids. That tavern would be heaving come noon dinner and evening supper.

There were others who were wildly enthusiastic about attending. Ella's brother Simon, still only twelve years old, saw this as an ideal opportunity to pursue the daughter of Josiah Grubb, the shoemaker. Imelda Grubb was also twelve and was the possessor of a mass of blonde hair that flowed down to her waist, plus a pair of cornflower blue eyes that sparkled. Simon knew that he would have stiff competition. However, he had one massive advantage – he was the son of Abel Smith, the massive blacksmith (and a hugely popular character), and he was slowly assuming the size and strength of his father.

Young Hob, the bailiff's irrepressible messenger, saw it as the ideal opportunity to play as many pranks as he could get away with. Already players at the ninepins alley were perplexed at their inability to knock down two of the pins – little knowing that they had sprouted iron prongs that were firmly embedded into the ground. A shout of alarm came from a stall where a charcoal brazier had been lit to roast the last of the previous autumn's chestnuts. Clouds of foul-smelling smoke were billowing from the brazier – the stallholder rushing off to get water to douse it. Hob watched from a safe distance, clutching his sides with merriment, tears rolling down his cheeks. Just wait until the apple juice stall opened the second barrel, he chuckled. He had assiduously collected as many worms as he could over the previous few days. They were now floating in a dense cloud in the liquid.

Gil and Ella were happy to leave off work on that day. Nell had visited their plot the previous day and had run up and down the rows shouting in excitement.

"Look – they've all growed!" she said, paying particular attention to the rows of beans and peas that she had helped to plant. Indeed, these were showing well, as were the new potatoes. Carrots, parsnips and leeks were showing as well. The two burgeoning smallholders were quietly confident that they would build this into a success.

Apart from Lovelace, Garvey, Haddock, Warden and Farmer, very few paid any heed to the fact that they were merrymaking on the site of the 'battle' that had raged for a few hours on that night only three months previously. Because of the relatively few deaths that had occurred, it quickly faded from memory. Churchwarden Garlick remembered, as did Sam Fewings, the sexton. Certainly, Peter Cove, the bailiff, did. Nearly all the rest erased it from their memory – only too happy to snatch this day of joy and to leave until the morrow to worry and wonder what the future would bring now that their king was in such a sorry plight.

--------------------- OOOOOOOOOO ---------------------

On a Monday, a small army of volunteers helped to clear the mess left by the Easter celebration on the heath. Franks thought it would be a gesture of goodwill if he and four of his soldiers also pitched in. Their presence was slowly being accepted, albeit reluctantly.

Garvey and Haddock, now back at their duties on the Parke estate, remembered all too vividly their reunion with Lovelace – and took to heart his promise of silence in return for their vigilance and reports of anything untoward.

Warden and Farmer, back again at Brimley, had told Andrews where they had been and how memories of that fateful night had been brought sharply into focus. Andrews vowed that he would never set foot anywhere near Bovey Heath.

Brown and Ratcliffe in Trusham had not gone to Bovey. Instead, they had joined in a small celebration in their adopted village. The fact that they had fought on opposite sides was a thing of the past. The two were the firmest of friends and concentrated solely on their own new life and business.

Young Simon, blowing the furnace into fierce heat, reminisced on his own good fortune. Not only had he been Imelda's constant companion at the celebration ground, but he had also even managed to sneak a kiss when they were behind the large awning that protected the pie stall. Simon was a very happy young lad, given that Imelda had responded happily and eagerly. He grinned contentedly as he forced the bellows up and down.

372

Hob was thinking back with slightly different feelings. The owner of the charcoal brazier had immediately known who was responsible for lacing the charcoal with whatever noxious substance had caused the disgusting clouds. Once he had doused the brazier, he had sought out young Hob and had administered a sound thrashing on the seat of Hob's breeches. Hob wriggled as he passed the bailiff's house, not comforted by the chuckles that greeted him. However, nobody had accused him of the worms or ninepins, although suspicion was centred on him and on nobody else.

Reverend Forbes and Churchwarden Garlick sat on the steps before the rood screen. They looked back with happiness on the previous day's celebration – and started wondering if there would even be a reason to celebrate the next year. Of course, they would celebrate Easter and its meaning to them, but would they have any other reason to celebrate?

--------------------- OOOOOOOOOO --------------------

On the following Sunday, the church was just as packed as usual for the Sunday service. James Forbes gave as the text for his sermon the need for tolerance and forgiveness. And then, just before dismissing his congregation, he returned to the pulpit.

"I have an announcement to make to all of you good people," he said, not knowing how his news would be received. He certainly got their immediate attention. "I have learned that the king has escaped from the besieging of Oxford and has fled north. He has sought shelter with the Scots."

Uproar in the church as neighbour turned to a neighbour.

"Has he abandoned us?" one voice called out.

"Always was more Scottish than English!" another cried out.

Forbes raised his hands to quell the hubbub.

"I doubt that the king has abandoned us," he shook his white head. "Remember always that our king regards himself as God's anointed. How could he abandon what he regards as God's own gift? No – he has sought shelter and safety with those of his own birth. Parliament is already seeking negotiations with the Scots for his return."

"And in the meantime, we are left at the mercy of parliament!" Grubb shouted. "Where is that wretched queen- has she also fled to a Catholic haven?"

"That is not known," Forbes was forced to admit. "Rumour is rife, as usual. Some say she is still at Oxford; others say she is with the French court; still, others say she is with the king – wherever that may be."

"Wherever she is, I'll wager she is attending a Catholic mass!" one woman shouted. "Something she would have us all do under pain of death!"

That caused a wave of agreement. Bovey, like most communities in England at that time, was staunchly royalist and Anglican.

"That is the news I have for you," Forbes stated sadly. "I only wish it could be better news."

Many people gathered in groups outside the church to mull over, argue and wrangle over that information. Inevitably, doom-mongers predicted the end of life as they knew it. More sage heads thought it through and saw a continuation of the struggle. But on one thing, they all agreed. Nothing good would come out of the new situation!

Gil and Ella joined Ella's family for their Sunday dinner. It was a sombre affair until Abel started to rib his son.

"Our young Simon is smitten with Imelda – or so it would appear," he grinned.

"Oh, hush, father!" Simon turned red with embarrassment.

"'Tis nothing to be ashamed of," his mother ruffled her son's hair. "Imelda is a lovely young maid, and she would be lucky to have attracted so comely a lad!"

"Oh, hush, mother!" Simon wriggled on his stool.

Gil gave his young brother-in-law a slap on the back.

"Pursue the maid with gentleness as I did your sister. See where it got me – in such a happy state as I could never have imagined."

That earned him a glance from Ella – one that had him rejoicing yet again at his own good fortune.

They lingered over the meal, finishing off with the usual honey mead. And then Ella helped her mother clear the dishes into the kitchen. She glanced back into the parlour and saw the three males deep in conversation. She gently closed the door.

"Mother," she said quietly to Faith.

Faith Smith took one look at her daughter and caught her up in a hug.

"Are you sure?" she whispered.

"As sure as I may be, mother. My courses were due two weeks past – and nothing."

Faith said nothing but held her daughter fast, tears of joy trickling down her face.

"Have you told Gil?"

"No, mother. Not yet. I planned to tell him this evening when we are alone. But I need you now more than ever – right up to the birth of our little one."

"You shall have me through thick and thin. Now Ella, heed your mother. Take no notice of those who say you must rest all the time. 'Tis of no use and will make you weak. You will need strength. So – work at your crops and at your house, but do not make unnecessary, hard effort – that is what husbands are for! Gil will try to wrap you in soft wool – tell him to come and speak to me and to his own mother. We will set him to rights."

The two stayed where they were, close together, enjoying the bond of mother and child – and child.

All thoughts of the king, parliament, and the fate of England, faded into nothingness as they contemplated a new and precious future.

--------------------- OOOOOOOOOO --------------------

In the small house behind the church, two middle-aged men sat in front of a fire, mugs of warmed ale in their hands.

"What be your real thoughts, reverend?" churchwarden Garlick asked.

"My thoughts? I wonder what be the use of my thoughts?" Reverend Forbes stared into the fire, watching the flames above the logs dance and flicker. "But still and all, they are probably of as much use any anyone. 'Tis five years now since we were plunged into this mess – five years when we have seen favours flit from one side to the other – and now settle on the one side - seemingly set in concrete. Parliament will have its way – and our king will either be set aside for another more compliant - or emasculated to serve as a mere figurehead."

"That cannot be the natural and right order of things!" Garlick remonstrated. "'Tis true the king will not bend – when perhaps he should bend a little. But to have him set aside cannot be right!"

"It has been done many times before," Forbes reminded him. "Stephen was the first to do so. The third Edward, great a king though he was, also did it. The fourth Henry set aside the second Richard. The fourth Edward set aside the sixth Henry – who was again set aside by the seventh Henry. Bloody Mary set aside Jane – need I go on?"

"Aye – but all were set aside by another claimant. Never has a parliament set aside a king!"

"Believe me, my old friend; there is nothing new in this world!" Forbes gave a little smile. "If parliament – especially the likes of Master Pym – sees an advantage in setting the king aside, then they will certainly do so. Who is to say them nay?"

The two sat in silence, the fire crackling merrily away as the levels in the tankards were lowered. Outside, the evening slowly darkened. Forbes shook himself and got up to light a couple of lanterns. He sat down again with a sigh.

"All this – five years of shame – and more shame to come," he muttered.

Author's Note

First and foremost, this is a work of fiction. It takes place during momentous, real events in English History, and in places that exist.

Some of the characters certainly existed – Cromwell, Fairfax, Pym, James Forbes, Hopton, Wentworth, Prince Rupert. In Bovey Church you will find Forbes listed as vicar from 1628 until 1668. All other characters are of my own imagination. There was a 'manor house' in Brimley – but probably not one as I describe it.

Lord John Vickery is my invention. During the period, there were Members of Parliament representing areas in South Devon. Lord John Maynard represented Totnes; Sir John Northcote represented the area around Crediton.

Parke estate certainly exists – and did during the period of this book. I have 'allocated' it to Lord John Vickery. It certainly looked nothing like its modern appearance!

I have taken some liberties with the Battle of Bovey Heath. It certainly took place on the 9th of January 1646, but very little written record of it exists – perhaps because it was not really a significant battle. Those records that do exist tell varying tales – and that is why I feel at liberty to add my version. Torrington and, later, Launceston were of greater significance as far as loss of life was concerned. However, Bovey had its own significance – in that it confirmed that the disorganised royalist troops were no match for the professional New Model Army.

Baron Thomas Wentworth was, to quote a contemporary, 'a fine fellow and a merry one'. That did not make and never has made a competent military commander. Prince Rupert was probably from the same mould – despite his earlier successes.

Wentworth and his senior officers (including the fictitious Stephen Long) according to some records did throw coins from the tavern window to distract the parliamentary soldiers – enough for the bulk of them to make their escape. Whether or not this is true, I have included it as it is too good a story to be omitted.

Lord Hopton, from all contemporary accounts, was a far more able commander but was given an already hopeless task.

Torrington suffered a ghastly fate – the church exploding must have seemed to the inhabitants exactly like the prophets had said the last day on earth would be. Loss of life from that explosion, added to the loss of life from the hand-to-hand fighting, was truly dreadful.

Bovey and Torrington established both Cromwell and Fairfax as the masters of command and tactics.

Bovey Tracey still has its Heath – the bulk of it now known as Heathfield. In its top corner, before the Pottery Roundabout, is a small memorial stone that anyone can see to this present day. The bridge and the old mill building still stand, as does the church dedicated to Saints Peter, Paul and Thomas. Whether or not the 'mill' was used for that purpose is not clear.

Just off what used to be the square, you will find something called The Cromwell Arch – just past the pub called The Cromwell Arms.

I am following this story with a second helping – nearly three years later, the 'fateful' year of 1649!

That story is titled **A TIME OF CONFUSION.**

Ingram Content Group UK Ltd.
Milton Keynes UK
UKHW020044210623
423745UK00014B/440